CW01425581

Scrooge and the
Widow of Pewsey

Other books by Anne Moore

Topp Family Secrets
Passionate Affairs

Scrooge and the Widow of Pewsey

Anne Moore

Kingsfield

First published in 2002 by Kingsfield Publications
1 Kingsfield Close, Bradford on Avon
Wiltshire, BA15 1AW

British Library Cataloguing in Publication Data
A catalogue record for this book is available from the British Library

ISBN 1 903988 03 9

Printed and bound by Antony Rowe Ltd, Eastbourne

Part One

1

Scrooge woke up, turned over, and groaned. He felt hot and uncomfortable, and his forehead was damp with sweat.

He was aware that he had been having vivid dreams, and not at all pleasant dreams either – nightmares almost. Fortunately he couldn't remember the details. Just that he had met his old business partner again. And Marley was long since dead. Seven years dead, to be precise.

Scrooge pushed back the covers and immediately felt cooler. Then he pulled aside the heavy curtain which surrounded his bed and glanced towards the window. The window was also curtained, but he could see light around the edges. And bright light too. He must have slept late, he realised, so he had better get on. There were things to do, even if it was Christmas Day. In fact there were things to do *because* it was Christmas Day.

Scrooge padded across the cold floor to the window. Then he looked out on to the yard below, and to his delight he saw snow. Snow! A couple of inches of it. Gone was the filthy, choking, sulphurous fog of the night before – the fog which he had found so dark and depressing – and in its place was bright sunlight and blinding white crystal. Wonderful!

The view from Scrooge's window had nothing much to recommend it in normal circumstances, but today was different. He gazed out over the city rooftops with pleasure, noting the sharp blacks and whites, the grey smoke rising from the chimneys, the light flashing off the icicles and frost-encrusted gutters.

Then he noticed a movement below. It was a boy, busy making snowballs and hurling them at the gateway of the house if you please.

In other times Scrooge would have leaned out and bawled a warning, sending the boy on his way in a hurry, but today he had different business to transact. He pushed up the sash of his window and called in a gentler tone.

'Boy! Can you spare me a minute?'

The lad looked up. He was small, with a cap too big for him and a grubby, pinched face. 'Yes, sir?'

'Do you know that poulterer's in the next street but one, on the corner?'

'Yes, sir.'

'Do you know whether they've sold that prize turkey that was hanging up there yesterday? Not the little prize turkey, the big one.'

'I dunno, sir, but I can find out.'

'Good lad. I want you to go round and tell them I want it. And if they've sold that big one, I want the best of whatever they've got left. Tell them to bring it round here and I'll give them the money and instructions as to where it's to go.'

'How much?' demanded the urchin.

Scrooge sighed and pretended not to understand. 'I'll pay them the market price and no more.'

'No, I mean how much for doing the job – for you.'

A tough negotiator it seemed. All of ten years old, Scrooge estimated, and hardened by years of haggling in the streets. Still, it was Christmas. Rather to his own surprise, Scrooge felt a generous impulse rising to the surface.

'Come back with the man and I'll give you a shilling. Come back in less than five minutes and I'll give you half a crown.'

The lad was off like a bullet.

Big mistake there, young man, thought Scrooge. You should have demanded sixpence in advance.

But then he thought about what he himself had said. Had he really promised the boy a shilling? And even half a crown? What in Mammon's name had he been thinking of? Scrooge pulled the window shut and moved away, shaking his head. Must be mad, he thought. Or not properly awake.

Scrooge washed, shaved, and dressed himself, all the while with his ear cocked for the doorknocker.

Just as he was lacing his shoes he heard a series of great sonorous bangs on the front door below. It was a formidable doorknocker, that one. Marley had chosen it specially because he had begun to grow deaf in his old age.

Scrooge went down and opened up. He paid the poulterer (actually it was the poulterer's assistant, a spotty youth with a squint), gave him an envelope which bore the Cratchits' address and had a note inside; and, by dint of giving the fellow five shillings and telling him to keep the change, managed to persuade him to deliver the turkey that morning by cab.

'It's a big un,' said Squinty, stating the obvious. 'They won't have time to cook it today.'

'I know that, but I want them to have it today. They can cook it tonight and it'll feed them for a week, even though they're a big family. And make sure you give them my note.'

'Very good sir. And you did say, keep the change?'

Yes, he had said that. And he was stone cold sober too. Had he meant it? Apparently he had, for he found himself saying, 'Yes, young fellow, you may keep the change.'

For some unaccountable reason Squinty seemed as surprised as Scrooge was. 'Oh!' he said, and hopped off quick before there was a change of mind.

The urchin remained on the doorstep, looking up with an air of anticipation. 'Half a crown you said, guv.'

Scrooge frowned. 'I said half a crown if you were back in five minutes. But you were more like half an hour.'

The boy hung his head. 'I done my best. They was busy.'

Scrooge looked down at him. He was a scruffy little soul, and like most of his kind he was dressed in fourth-hand clothes. His trousers hung in rags below his knees and the jacket was too small. It also had holes in the elbows. But at least he had boots, of a sort, if not socks; Scrooge had seen many who went barefoot, even in winter.

'How old are you, son?'

'I think I'm twelve, sir.'

No birthday party for him then, or he would have remembered. 'Twelve,' repeated Scrooge.

'Yes, sir. I reckon.'

'And what's your name?'

'Billy, sir.' Emboldened by Scrooge's interest, he looked up eagerly. 'Got any more jobs, sir? I'm saving up for an overcoat.'

'No doubt you are,' said Scrooge. 'I'm not known for feeling the cold, but if I had holes in my jacket I dare say I would want an overcoat too.' He reached into his pocket and found a florin. 'Let's call it two shillings, shall we?'

Billy's eyes widened. 'Cor, thank you, guv.'

'Sir will do,' said Scrooge. 'And my name is Mr Scrooge.'

'Thank you, sir. Thank you, Mr Scrooge.' Billy rubbed the shiny silver coin on his sleeve and took in every detail of it. 'I ain't never had one of these before.... And I our new Queen Victoria. I reckon she's pretty.' With exaggerated care he stored his reward safely away.

Scrooge hesitated for a moment, and then made up his

mind. 'Come inside, Billy,' he said. 'I may have something for you.'

Scrooge led the way up the stairs to his apartment, where he went into his bedroom and poked around in the wardrobe. He emerged holding an old tweed jacket that he had not worn for some time. 'Here. Try this on.'

Billy slipped his arms into the coat and pulled it around him. It was, of course, far too big, even though Scrooge was a small man, and Billy looked ridiculous; but no more so than half the poor of London, who were dressed in some-body else's cast-offs, and the other half were wearing mere rags.

'There,' said Scrooge. 'That should do for an overcoat, Billy. For today, anyway. Later you may be able to trade it for something better.'

'You mean... I can have it?'

'Yes.'

'Cor! Thank you, guv – er, sir.'

'That's all right. I don't need it any more.'

Scrooge leaned forward and folded back the sleeves so that Billy could use his hands. Then he straightened up and hesitated once more. He looked at the uplifted face in front of him. What in the world was he doing, he wondered, inviting this lad into his apartment and giving him cloth-ing? Was he quite sane?

The boy stared at him, evidently waiting for Scrooge to say something, and finally Scrooge said: 'Had any breakfast yet?'

'No sir.'

'Come on then. I'll treat you.'

2

Scrooge made his way to Mr Montini's café, in Lime Street, where he habitually took breakfast.

As Billy followed him through the door, Mr Montini, not surprisingly, turned to shoo the boy out. This was not exactly a high-class establishment but street urchins were not encouraged, even if they had any money.

'Oy, you – hop it.'

Scrooge intervened. 'It's all right, Mr Montini. The lad is with me.'

Mr Montini raised his eyebrows. He was largely bald but had a bushy moustache to make up for it. 'Well stone me. It really is Christmas.' He evidently was not pleased by Scrooge's choice of companion, but he said no more, perhaps because the room was almost empty.

It was comfortably warm in the café, and both Scrooge and Billy took off their top layer of clothing. Then they sat down and the proprietor gave them menus. He hovered, and sighed faintly, not quite holding his nose but clearly less than happy. Scrooge ignored him.

'Can you read, Billy?' he asked.

'No, not really. I can read numbers.'

'Very well.... If I might make a suggestion, perhaps we should begin with porridge, and then a boiled egg. Followed by toast and coffee. That sound all right to you?'

'Cor! Not half!'

Mr Montini turned away, bawling out the order to Mrs Montini, who was never seen but lurked somewhere in the kitchen.

While he and Billy were waiting, Scrooge took the opportunity to examine the boy more closely. He could not remember ever before having taken any notice of someone as poor as Billy. He had seen such people in the streets often enough, of course: men, women, and children, of all ages. But he had seldom troubled to speak to any of them and certainly never taken one of them out for a meal. In fact he wasn't quite sure why he was doing it now, except that for some reason he had found it hard to send the boy away after he had bought the turkey.

Scrooge looked at Billy with some curiosity. The boy's hands and face were dirty, but then street urchins seldom washed. His brown hair seemed to have been not so much cut as hacked with a knife; it was greasy and filthy, and was probably the home of a whole colony of lice. What was more, his nose was running, and if there was one thing Scrooge could not abide it was a runny nose; he passed over his handkerchief and gave instructions for its use.

Billy used it and made to pass it back.

'No,' said Scrooge sharply. 'Keep it.'

'Cor, thanks.... Er, sir.'

'Not at all.'

The porridge arrived and consequently conversation ceased for a while.

Billy had evidently been taught how to use a spoon at some point, but his table manners were none too polished. However, Scrooge made no comment, not even when the plate was held up and licked clean. Very thoroughly clean.

'If I'm not mistaken,' said Scrooge, when he had finished with his own plate, 'you were the lad who came round to my office yesterday afternoon, singing carols. Was that you?'

'I've been singing,' said Billy. 'Yeah.'

'Make any money?'

'Some. Not much. Ha'pennies mostly.'

'I'm afraid in my case, Billy, I chased you away.'

'Yeah. I remember.' Billy grinned.

Scrooge looked down at the table. 'I'm sorry about that. But the truth is, Christmas annoys me. Always has. Well, in recent years anyway. So many people coming round with begging bowls, asking for money for this, that, and the other. I'm afraid I find it irritating.'

Billy didn't mind. 'S'all right.'

'Anyway, I think I've made up for it now.'

An even broader grin. 'Yes, sir, I should say so.'

Scrooge liked that grin. It was the grin of a boy who had not eaten a decent meal for some time, who was halfway through one now, and who had every prospect of more good grub to come. Scrooge could have survived for some time on a grin like that. And it came pretty cheap too.

Their boiled eggs arrived, and silence descended on the table once more. After that there was a good deal of munching of toast, followed by a call for further slices. Finally they sat quietly and drank their coffee.

'Tell me, Billy, have you got any family?'

'No. Ain't got no fambly.'

'Your father and mother are dead?'

'Yes.'

It was evident that this question hurt, so Scrooge didn't press for details.

'And where do you live?'

'Don't live nowhere. Of a night, if I have a penny, I sleeps at one of the lodging-houses in Kent Street. But I only go there in the winter. The rooms is packed, forty and fifty to a room, six to a bed, and I don't like the things the big boys do with you.' He gave Scrooge a careful look without raising his chin. 'Bash you up and that. The big girls too, come to that. Most nights I sneak round the back of a baker's I know, cos their ovens is nice and warm and you can curl up over the grille.'

Scrooge struggled to imagine what it must be like to be a small boy who slept through a winter's night, curled up over a metal vent at the back of some commercial building.

'I see,' he said at last, though he didn't see at all. Scrooge himself was not a man who worried overmuch about his creature comforts, but to sleep on the streets was beyond his imagination. He doubted if he would survive even one night in such conditions. 'And how long have you been living like that, Billy?'

'Three years.'

'Do you ever go to school?'

'Nah.' The idea was absurd.

'Did you ever go to school when you were younger?'

'Nah.'

Scrooge sighed. He became quiet for some minutes.

The meal over, he rose to have a word with Mr Montini at the counter. He took out his wallet and unfolded a five-pound note.

'Mr Montini, I apologise for bringing an unexpected guest, but today is, I think you will agree, a special day. And in view of that, perhaps I might give you this note and ask you to use it to treat some of your customers to a free lunch. Perhaps some of those who have, as we say, fallen upon hard times. Would that be possible do you think?'

Mr Montini gazed at the proffered note with some astonishment.

'What I have in mind,' Scrooge continued, 'is that you might feel able to provide a meal for some of those, like my young friend here, who would otherwise go hungry. Round the back, if you wish, rather than in the café itself.'

Mr Montini took the note at last. 'You sure, Mr Scrooge?'

'Oh yes. Quite sure. But I want it to be anonymous, you understand. Not a word to anyone.'

'Well, very kind of you, Mr Scrooge. Very kind indeed. And I can promise you it will all be used to good purpose. There'll be no shortage of takers.'

Scrooge turned to go.

'Um, will you be joining us yourself, sir?'

'No, I think not. I have been invited to my nephew's house.'

'Oh, so you'll be going there then.'

'Well,' said Scrooge. 'Probably.'

There, he thought, as he turned away to collect his coat, that wasn't so difficult, was it? He could not remember ever having given away five pounds in one lump before, but it had not resulted in either apoplexy or a stroke. Not yet, anyway.

3

Scrooge and Billy went out on to the street again.

Billy was clearly delighted with his new 'overcoat' and was doubly fortified by a good breakfast. 'What now?' he enquired, evidently convinced that Scrooge had something in mind.

'Well, I suppose we could go to church. It's about that time.'

Billy was not keen. He wrinkled his nose and kicked at the snow.

'It's warm,' said Scrooge encouragingly. 'Well, warmer than out here. And there's company. And you get a free dinner after it.'

That last made a significant difference. 'Oh, all right then.'

Scrooge led the way to St Andrew's, which was the church of his parish. It was close enough for the clock to be heard striking, every quarter of an hour, both from his apartment and from his office.

Their feet crunched on the still-frozen snow as they walked along the street.

'There isn't anywhere else *to* go,' said Scrooge, hoping to make Billy feel more comfortable. 'Not really. It's too early to go to my nephew's, and there's no point in going to my office, for the 'Change is shut. And it's scarcely the weather for a walk.... Have you ever been to church before, Billy?'

'Not for a long time.'

'Do you know why people go to church on Christmas

17

Day?'

Billy pondered. 'I reckon it's because it's Jesus's birthday.'

'Well, so they say. But in fact the Christians did not begin to mark it as the birthday of their saviour until about four hundred AD. So I myself am inclined to think that the celebrations at this time of year are a festival to mark the rebirth of the sun. The Romans used to feast at this time of year, long before Jesus ever appeared. And they did all the things we do – they decorated their temples with greenery and holly. They gave gifts too. It was called the festival of Saturn.'

'Saturn?'

'Yes. He was the Roman god of agriculture. You see, Billy, up until Christmas-time the days were getting shorter, and the nights longer. But from now on the reverse is true. The days will lengthen, spring will come, and then summer. And that will make the crops grow, to feed us all. And if that isn't worth celebrating I don't know what is.'

'Well, summer's better than winter, that's for sure. I can earn more in the summer.'

Scrooge picked up this cue. 'How do you earn, Billy?'

'Well, mostly I helps collect the pure.'

Scrooge didn't understand. 'The pure? What's that?'

'Dog muck....'

'Dog muck?'

Then, seeing that Scrooge had stood still for a moment because he still didn't follow, Billy continued: 'That's what they call it, Mr Scrooge. The dog muck, picked up off the street, where the dogs leave it – they calls it the pure, see.'

'Why do they call it that?'

'Because they use it to pure the leather.'

'What leather?'

'In tanneries. Where they makes leather from cows' skin.'

Scrooge could hardly believe what he was being told. 'And you collect this stuff? In the street?'

'Most days. It's good trade, Mr Scrooge, you can get a shilling a bucket.' Billy was enthusiastic now, realising that Scrooge knew nothing of this arcane commerce. 'Most of the collectors is men, see, and they don't want the likes of me stealing their muck. They kick us up the arse if they find us, and some of 'em kicks werry hard. But there's some old women as can't move as fast as what they used to, and I helps them, see. Between us we get a bucket a day, and they sells it for a shilling, sometimes more, to the tannery. Then they gives me tuppence or so, for helping.'

'I see.' Scrooge suddenly felt deeply depressed. 'And that's how you manage to live, is it? By picking up dog dirt in the street?'

'Mostly, yes. But it's a better trade in the summer than winter. Days is longer, like you say. And your feet don't get so cold.'

'Yes indeed,' said Scrooge sadly. 'I can well believe it.'

They arrived at St Andrew's just as the service was about to start. The church was fairly full, and Scrooge chose an empty pew in one of the aisles, near the back. He guided Billy in first, so that no late-arriving but otherwise respectable parishioner would have to sit next to him.

Their arrival caused a bit of a stir. The parish was home to some very wealthy and well-connected people. Most of the men held a responsible position in one of the City of London's financial institutions, which were all close by, and their womenfolk lived and dressed accordingly; they were not used to seeing the likes of Billy in their midst. Scrooge noticed people turning round to see who had arrived (they had probably been alerted by the smell); then they raised eyebrows at each other, and one woman muttered, 'Well, really!', not quite under her breath. But Scrooge didn't care. In fact it made him smile.

Once seated, Scrooge and Billy waited patiently for the service to begin. Scrooge took the opportunity to have a look round, and he was impressed by what he saw. He was by no means a regular attender at the church, but he could see that for Christmas Day an attempt had been made to put on a special show. No absurd amounts of money had been spent (Scrooge was particularly pleased to note that), but there was plenty of ivy, holly and rosemary about. Two large brass candelabra had been placed before the altar, which itself boasted a white embroidered frontal. In the chancel there were red hangings on the wall, and there were flowers on the altar screen. Throughout, the church was filled with light.

Scrooge was impressed with all this, and he could see that Billy was too: the boy's mouth hung open in astonishment. Billy also needed to use the handkerchief again, and Scrooge nudged him and mimed what had to be done.

Billy's interest in the church decorations soon lapsed, however, to the extent that he fell asleep during the sermon. To Scrooge, on the other hand, the sermon was tolerably interesting.

Scrooge knew the Vicar by sight: he was a tall, strongly built man, in his mid-thirties, and had been in office for just over a year. On the rare occasions when Scrooge had heard the Vicar preach he had found him well-meaning but dull. Today, however, what the Vicar had to say seemed to coincide with the way Scrooge's own thoughts were turning. Was that pure coincidence, Scrooge wondered, or had the

Vicar noticed that Scrooge had brought into the church a member of that social class who had seldom been seen there before?

'Christmas,' said the Vicar, 'is traditionally a time of goodwill to all men. And the new year is a time when we review our lives and make resolutions to change. We should all take stock once a year, in our lives as in our businesses. We should consider our hopes and plans for the future.'

(Hear, hear, thought Scrooge.)

'Are our plans sensible and wise? Are they appropriate to our means and station? Are we living in the best possible way? Most of us, of course, cannot be saints, but we can all help each other just a fraction more than we have in the past. Even if we do it just once a day. The beggar on the street corner, perhaps. We can spare him a penny, surely. And we can smile at those who are sick at heart. We can provide advice when asked, and keep our opinions to ourselves when we might cause offence by voicing them. Let us all resolve, therefore, to do a little more good each day than we have achieved in the past.'

For the final hymn Billy awoke and rose to his feet. He even seemed to remember some of the words, though he held the hymn book upside down. The hymn was 'God rest ye merry, gentlemen', and the large congregation, no doubt looking forward eagerly to an enormous lunch, gave it full voice.

It was during this hymn that the collection plate came round, and once again Scrooge found the bile rising in his throat. He rubbed his forehead and tried to work out why it was that requests for money angered him so much, especially in view of what the Vicar had just said. And he agreed with the man too! During the sermon he had sat there nodding his head, and yet now he was conscious of a

21

wild, irrational rage burning within him. Scrooge just couldn't understand himself at all. He had plenty of money in his pocket, and a mountain more in the bank, so why did the sight of a man with a plate in his hand produce such resentment?

Scrooge wasn't sure, but he put a sovereign in the plate anyway.

The service over, Scrooge made Billy wait until everyone else had left the church. Then they made their way out too, at the end of the line.

The Vicar and his wife were standing at the west door, bidding farewell to everyone and shaking their hand. To give them credit, neither of them so much as blinked when Scrooge pushed Billy forward in front of himself. They both shook hands with him and wished him a happy Christmas.

'Good morning, Mr Scrooge,' said the Vicar's wife courteously, when it came to Scrooge's turn.

'Er, good morning, er, ma'am.' To his chagrin, Scrooge did not know the lady's surname, and he was puzzled as to how she knew his. She was a handsome, well-built woman with striking blue eyes.

'I trust you gave most generously to the collection,' the lady continued. 'It will be used, as always at this time of year, to assist the poor of parish. And so it was, I hope, a note that you proffered, rather than coin?' And she smiled at him without a trace of artifice.

Scrooge was stunned, and for a moment he was speech-less. Had this woman asked the same question of everyone who left the church? And if not, how had she touched upon the one point which was causing him so much anguish? Was it written on his forehead?

'I, er, I...' he stammered. 'The truth is, ma'am, I was taken by surprise when the plate arrived and had no time to get at me wallet. Allow me to rectify that omission now.'

He fumbled in the breast pocket of his jacket and eventually managed to hand over yet another five-pound note.

The Vicar's wife nodded her approval and pocketed the note with a practised air. 'Very kind of you, Mr Scrooge. You should never forget that, whatever you do, good or ill, it is returned to you threefold.'

'Er, yes, quite....' Scrooge was embarrassed. 'Well.... Mustn't detain you.'

'I hope we shall see you here again before long,' said the Vicar. 'And bring your young friend with you too, if you wish.'

'Er, thank you, sir, but I'm afraid I am a most irregular attender. You will not set eyes on me often.'

The Vicar looked at his wife, and then they each smiled at the other. 'Oh,' said the wife cheerfully, 'I think our paths may cross rather sooner than you think, Mr Scrooge!'

4

Scrooge gave a small gasp of relief as the Vicar and his wife moved off. 'Phew!'

And then he thought, what in the world was he gasping about? He had anticipated this sort of thing, had he not? Had he not been to the bank specially, to equip himself for giving to charity over the Christmas period? Yes he had, and yet, when it came to the point, he still found himself not wanting to part with the cash.

He paused at the church gate and made a note of the Vicar's name on the noticeboard: The Reverend Mr H. Bannister. Hmm. Well, whatever might be said of Mr Bannister, his wife would certainly take some watching – of that Scrooge was quite sure.

'Where to now?' said Billy. He didn't actually mention the phrase 'free lunch', with which Scrooge had enticed him into the church, but his eyes were large and round.

Scrooge dragged his attention back to more mundane matters. 'We have to walk a little way,' he said thoughtfully. 'Towards Moorgate. Turn left.'

Together he and Billy resumed trudging through the snow; fortunately it was no longer as deep as when it had first fallen, because the passage of numerous feet on the pavement had trampled it down, but it was slippery, and care was needed. The sun, which had formerly been shining, had now taken to sulking behind a curtain of low grey cloud. Scrooge wondered idly if it had taken offence because not enough praise had been heaped upon it during the church service.

The streets were thronged with pedestrians, despite the fact that it was Christmas Day. Some were on their way home from church or chapel, and some were in search of last-minute supplies; happily for them, many of the shops were still open, though preparing to close.

Billy paid particular attention to the shops selling food. His nose twitched as they approached one, and he peered through the half-closed shutters at the piles of pears and apples, glowing oranges and yellow lemons, shiny black bunches of grapes and dark-brown nuts. Every so often something especially impressed him, and he nudged Scrooge with his elbow and said: 'Cor, look at that!'

They were heading north, in the general direction of the home of Scrooge's nephew Fred, and the shortest route led them up streets which housed some of the poorer members of the community. At one point they came across a small crowd outside a baker's shop.

The baker was forbidden by law from carrying out his usual trade on Christmas Day, and instead he did good business by using his ovens to cook the meals of the poor. They brought along their pie, or a goose, or whatever, and the baker did the rest.

Outside the shop, Scrooge and Billy were passed by one proud woman bearing home a steaming, freshly-roasted chicken which sat stark naked upon a plate (she had only a few doors' journey). It was as much as Billy could do to refrain from stealing a leg of it.

'Cor, did you see that, Mr Scrooge?' he enquired. 'I reckon there won't be much left of that by teatime.'

Scrooge decided that he had better issue a word of caution. 'Perhaps,' he said slowly, 'I ought not to build up your hopes too high, Billy. I did indeed mention a free lunch, and lunch of a sort there will certainly be. But I ought to warn you that although I have been invited to my nephew's house, I was confoundedly rude to him yesterday. He may not be altogether pleased to see me.' (Or you either, Billy, he thought, but didn't mention it.) 'And so I shall have to apologise to him first. And his wife. It is no more than their due, but even after I have made my apologies I may still have to make a tactical withdrawal. So we shall just have to play it by ear, my dear chap.'

Billy professed to be unconcerned. ''S all right, Mr Scrooge. We'll manage.'

'It wouldn't be the first time that I've had me Christmas dinner in a tavern,' said Scrooge. 'Often with no more than a book for company, and felt I was better off for it. But this year, somehow, I feel different.'

After a moment Billy had a thought. ''Ere – we're going to Moorgate, ain't we?'

'We are indeed.'

'Let's dive through here then. Short cut.'

Billy led the way down an alley. Halfway along it he indicated the doorway to a public lavatory.

'Gents in there,' he said.

'Thank you, but I don't need one at the moment.'

'I picks up some good business there when I'm stuck,' volunteered Billy.

He was a step or two ahead of Scrooge when he said this, and Scrooge could not see his face.

Scrooge walked five further steps before he could bring himself to speak. 'What do you mean, good business?'

Billy turned. 'Well, there's always blokes hanging around in there that want a bit of a rub. You know? Pay you to toss 'em off.'

Scrooge shuddered, despite his overcoat. He put a hand

on Billy's shoulder to bring him to a halt. Then he turned the boy to face him.

'Now, Billy,' he said. 'I'm sure you know that you should not be doing any such thing. Don't you?'

Billy looked just a little abashed. 'Well, yer. But if you're stuck for a meal, Mr Scrooge....'

Scrooge prodded Billy's shoulder with his forefinger. 'If you're stuck for a meal, Billy, you come and see me. At my office. You know where it is, don't you?'

'Yes, sir.'

'Good. So now you know what to do in the future.'

'Yes, sir. Thank you, sir.'

'That's all right,' Scrooge managed to say. 'Carry on now.'

Billy turned and continued up the alley. It was narrow, and there was insufficient space for them to walk side by side, which was just as well, for Scrooge would not have cared to have Billy to see his stricken face just at that moment. Nor would have cared to have been caught wiping a tear from his cheek. It was, of course, just the cutting wind in the alley, swirling up the drifted snow, which had made his eye water.

They emerged from the far end of the alley and to Scrooge's relief were then able to resume their walk in a more open street.

Now they were back in a more prosperous area, and they attracted a few curious glances from passers-by. Scrooge was self-evidently a gentleman, while Billy had obviously never held any post in a gentleman's household, not even the most menial. Scrooge ignored all the enquiring glances, except of course to raise his hat at those who stared longest and wish them a cheery 'Happy Christmas!' Not all such good wishes were returned.

As they neared Fred's house, Scrooge suddenly caught sight of two familiar figures walking towards him. At first his spirits sank, for the two men approaching were people he would have preferred not to meet again, especially on Christmas morning. They were the two portly and smartly-dressed gentlemen who had called on him the previous afternoon, at his office.

On that occasion they had been out collecting funds for the poor, but in Scrooge's premises they had met with a pronounced lack of success: he had sent them away without so much as a penny. Now, when they noticed Scrooge walking towards them, the two gentlemen naturally regarded him with something less than wholehearted joy.

Initially, Scrooge was inclined to cross the street to avoid them, but after a moment's reflection he realised that this fortuitous meeting gave him an opportunity to retrieve the situation.

The two gentlemen might well have walked past him without even a glance, but Scrooge stopped them with a hand on the arm of one.

'Gentlemen,' he said. 'There are many people in this world to whom I owe an apology, and you two are perhaps foremost among them.'

The portly gentlemen looked at each other, but neither made any attempt to deny this.

'On the morning of Christmas Eve I drew out a largish sum from the bank, for I knew in my heart that this year I should make a particular effort to contribute to worthy causes. And yet, when you called at my office yesterday afternoon, with a most reasonable request, I refused to help you. I was not only unhelpful but rude, and I can only say that you caught me at a bad moment. That is no excuse, of course, and I was quite wrong to treat you the way I did.'

'Well, Mr Scrooge,' said the shorter and bolder of the two men, 'you do have some reputation for being careful with your money.'

'No doubt. But I am conscious that those of us who have the good fortune to be in good health and possessed of adequate means must do something to relieve the plight of those who are less fortunate. Particularly at this time of year. Perhaps, even at this late stage, you might allow me to make some amends?'

The gentlemen looked at each other with some astonishment, while Scrooge groped for his wallet yet again. Eventually he located two more five-pound notes, which he pressed into the palm of the man nearest him.

'There,' he said. 'And perhaps, if you would like to call on me a second time, at your convenience, I think I can promise that I shall be more forthcoming than on the first occasion.'

'Well, thank you very much, sir,' said the first of the two to find his tongue.

'Yes, indeed, sir. Thank you,' said the other.

'Please do remember to call on me,' Scrooge emphasised.

'We will, sir, we will!' responded the taller man. 'We shall be veritable bulldogs in our persistence.'

'That's the stuff!' said Scrooge. After which, with much doffing of hats, both parties went on their way.

As he and Billy resumed their progress down the street, Scrooge examined his feelings. He discovered, contrary to his expectations, that he felt quite jaunty.

'There, that wasn't so bad, either, was it?' he remarked to Billy. 'I've handed over... oh, at least twenty pounds this morning, and me ears haven't dropped off, have they, Billy? No, nor me nose either.'

Billy giggled. Then he said, 'Twenty quid, did you say?

Cor!'

'Oh, I have plenty more,' said Scrooge. 'Plenty more. Tell me I can afford it, Billy.'

'You can afford it, Mr Scrooge!' said Billy. And they both laughed.

5

Scrooge's steps began to slow as they turned into the street where his nephew Fred resided. Billy noticed, and turned to see what was troubling him.

'Can't say I'm looking forward to this, Billy. My face may not fit, you see. I was unforgivably rude to my nephew yesterday.'

Billy had got past the stage of being shy about offering an opinion. 'Look,' he said, 'what's the worst he can do? Tell you to piss off, right?'

'Mmm, something along those lines,' Scrooge agreed glumly.

'Well then, sticks and stones. You go in and see him, Mr Scrooge. You say you're sorry, if you think you have to, and see what he says to that.'

Billy was right, of course, and Scrooge decided that he would have to take the plunge. 'Sound thinking, Billy. But if you don't mind, I'd like you to wait outside. Just for a minute.'

Billy shrugged, and Scrooge could tell that he hadn't really believed that his luck would last all day. Now, evidently, it had run out. Billy fully expected to be left outside until eventually, tired of waiting, he went elsewhere.

Scrooge mounted the steps of Fred's house and rang the bell. The street was a terrace, constructed about forty years earlier. The houses were not enormous, but they were pleasantly spacious, with a strong Georgian flavour to them.

After a moment the front door was opened by a young maid whom Scrooge had not seen before. She was about sixteen, by the look of her, dressed in an apron and cap to identify her status, and with an anxious air about her. Perhaps today would be her first serious experience of receiving guests.

'Is your master at home?'

'Yes, sir, he's in the dining-room with the mistress, checking the arrangements. I'll show you upstairs if you please.'

'Thank you, but your master knows me. I'll just have a quick word with him first.'

Scrooge stepped inside and turned towards the dining-room. The maid did not like this at all. She was supposed to show guests into the drawing-room, upstairs, and here was one popping into somewhere quite different without even taking his coat off.

Scrooge noticed the girl's almost tearful distress and smiled at her reassuringly. 'It's all right. I'm his uncle.'

He turned the handle of the dining-room and stepped inside.

As he entered the room, Fred and his wife Deborah turned to face him. And at once, to Scrooge's relief, Fred's features revealed genuine pleasure.

'Why, Uncle,' he said, coming forward with his hand outstretched. 'How marvellous to see you.'

Scrooge shook his nephew's hand, noticing as he did so that Deborah, for her part, was not quite so pleased to see him.

'Fred.... My dear chap.' Then he shook Deborah's hand equally warmly, and she managed a smile.

Scrooge knew perfectly well that Deborah was not one of

his admirers. She thought him a hard, bad-tempered and selfish old man. And why should she not? That was the side of him that she had always seen.

Scrooge twisted his hat in his hands like some nervous schoolboy. 'I do have to say,' he said, 'before I utter another word, that I owe you both a most humble apology. When you called upon me yesterday afternoon, Fred, with the most civil and kind invitation to join you here today, I regret to say that I treated you quite abominably.'

'Nonsense!' Fred looked to his wife to join in the denial, but she simply smiled politely and waited for Scrooge to continue.

'No, it is true. I was in poor spirits and I snapped at you and was ungracious. Deeply so. As soon as you had gone I regretted it, and I can only add, as a small measure of my regret, that I immediately went out and ordered a crate of champagne to be delivered to you, as a gift from me.'

'It's arrived already!' Fred assured him. 'And most impressed we were too.'

'Indeed we were,' Deborah confirmed. 'It is a generous gift, and we thank you most warmly.'

'Well.... In the circumstances it was the least I could do.'

'And you will stay to lunch I hope?' This from Fred.

Scrooge hesitated. 'But in view of my churlishness you will no doubt have made other arrangements.'

Deborah moved to the table. 'Not at all. We did hope you would come, for it is Christmas when all is said and done. And to prove it – look.'

She pointed to the table, where Scrooge saw that a card had been put out to show each guest where to sit. And there was one with his own name on it. He was quite touched.

Deborah came forward and took his hand. 'And since you have evidently recovered your normal spirits, and have offered an apology which of course we accept, then I hope – we both hope – that you will join us and our guests for the rest of the day.'

Scrooge shuffled his feet. He had not felt so ill at ease for some time. His eyes roamed over the table, which shone with reflected light from the silver and glass, from the bright white of the snow outside and the yellow flickering flame of the fire piled up into the hearth. The table was a big one, but it seemed to have been laid for some twenty guests or so, and they would all have to sit with their elbows well tucked in. And yet despite that, Fred and his wife had still left a place for him.

'Thank you,' he muttered. 'Thank you very much. Oh – and I'm afraid there is one other thing.'

Fred raised his eyebrows enquiringly.

'Er.... This may not be quite so easy for you to accommodate.' Scrooge moved towards the window and motioned the others to join him. 'But earlier this morning I persuaded a young lad to run an errand for me. There he is, out there.'

They looked out and saw Billy waiting patiently at the foot of the steps. He was watching a cab roll by, the snow flicking out backwards from under its wheels.

'To tell you the truth I didn't have the heart to just tip him and send him away. He is homeless and friendless of course, has no family like so many of them, and I'm afraid I went so far as to offer him a free lunch. I did wonder, perhaps, if he might be made useful in the kitchen and so earn a bite to eat? If not,' he added hurriedly, 'I will simply give him a shilling and send him on his way.'

At that moment, Billy turned towards the house, saw the three of them peering out of the dining-room window, and gave them a grubby-faced grin. Then, somewhat shocked by his own impertinence, he hastily turned away again. But he had already earned his lunch.

'Why, Uncle Scrooge,' said Deborah. 'If I had not seen it with my own eyes I would not have believed it. That you of all people...' She stopped, before she said too much, and Fred chuckled nervously at what she had said so far. But Scrooge wasn't offended.

'Yes,' he admitted. 'I surprise myself sometimes.'

Deborah declared that since Fred had invited every bachelor and widower in the office to join them for lunch, one more lame duck would make no difference. Billy was therefore brought in, introduced to Mrs Weatherby, a motherly woman who was the household's cook, and deposited out of sight in the kitchens. He would, Mrs Weatherby declared, be able to make himself useful by washing up knives and forks, for he could hardly break those and there were scarcely enough to go round as it was.

Cassie, the maid, was mightily relieved to find that she was not at fault for allowing Mr Scrooge to march straight into the dining-room.

And Scrooge himself was impressed to note the style in which young Fred was living these days. A cook *and* a maid indeed. That meant he must be earning at least five hundred a year. Probably more, since Fred had always tended to be on the cautious side where expenditure was concerned (a family trait, Scrooge liked to think). It was Scrooge who had obtained for his nephew that important first position on the Stock Exchange, some years earlier. The boy had a wonderful head for figures, of course, but it was one thing to have the mathematical talent and quite another to put it to effective use. So Scrooge was delighted to find that his protégé was doing well.

Not all the guests had yet arrived, but Scrooge was taken

upstairs and introduced to those who were there.

As Deborah had told him, there were several young bachelors and two older men, all colleagues of Fred's who might otherwise have spent Christmas Day in some dreary lodging-house. To assist the balance of the sexes, both Deborah's sisters were on hand, serving coffee and chattering happily to put the nervous young fellows at their ease.

Caroline, aged about twenty, was the plump sister with the lace tucker – Scrooge always needed some identifying characteristic to help him remember names – and she also had particularly long and dazzling eyelashes. It was clear even to an old bachelor like Scrooge that much thought had gone into her choice of dress. Care had been needed to select something which showed off her figure to advantage while not emphasising that there was quite a lot of it. And the young lady had succeeded admirably. Melanie, Deborah's other sister, was a couple of years younger, and definitely slimmer than either of her kin.

A little later two familiar faces were admitted: the Reverend Mr Bannister and his wife. It turned out that Mrs Bannister was aunt to Deborah (and the two other sisters). They had also brought with them another aunt of Deborah's, Mrs Bannister's widowed sister, a Mrs Kincaid. She was visiting London from the country, Scrooge understood; she normally lived somewhere in the Vale of Pewsey, in the county of Wiltshire.

'So you see I was right,' Mrs Bannister told Scrooge triumphantly. 'I said we would meet again.'

'Most impressive,' said Scrooge. 'But if you had told me we were related by marriage I might have predicted it myself.'

The party was completed by the arrival of an old school

friend of Fred's, Topper by name, and by a scattering of neighbours.

If you had asked him a week earlier, Scrooge would have said that he despised such gatherings. Wearisome, tedious, noisy, hot, stuffy, and boring, were the words which might have tripped off his lips. And yet somehow he had not wished to be alone this Christmas. In the past, yes. But this year, no.

Left to his own devices, however, Scrooge might have chosen a smaller group for company. It was therefore something of a surprise, as the day wore on, for him to realise that not only was he enjoying himself, but he was experiencing no great desire for the proceedings to end. Not once did he draw out his watch, grope around in the recesses of his memory until he came up with a halfway convincing reason for early departure, and then announce that he really must be going before long.

(Scrooge's watch, incidentally, was a perfectly good old hunter which he had had for thirty years and which still kept perfect time. Always provided, of course, that you remembered to advance it by five minutes first thing in the morning, when the church clock struck seven. Scrooge was convinced that there was a lot of life in that watch yet.)

Coffee, on guests' arrival, gave way to sherry for those who wished it, and lunch began at a civilised hour for Christmas Day, which was to say two p.m. Whether this was planned or the result of some last-minute hitch in the kitchen no one enquired and no one cared, for it was an excellent meal when it started.

At the table, Scrooge found himself squeezed between the plump sister with the lace tucker on the one side, and, on his other side, the widow of Pewsey, who was also quite well upholstered. This situation caused Scrooge no pain at all, for he had always preferred ladies who were generously proportioned.

Vegetable soup, with fresh hot rolls and butter, gave way to a huge turkey which had been many hours a-cooking, Scrooge had no doubt. There were seven kinds of vegetables that Scrooge could see (possibly more, out of his range of vision), gravy, bread sauce, and cranberry sauce. There were rolls of bacon, sausages, and a garnish of watercress. Beer sufficed as an accompaniment for some, but others were pleased to partake of a few bottles of first-class claret.

Despite this formidable main course, those assembled then had a choice of dessert: either a bowl of fruit salad, with a jug of cream beside it, or a traditional, vast plum pudding, bathed in enough rum to threaten the security of all present when it was lit. The pudding was accompanied by brandy butter and custard.

With this third course disposed of, Scrooge and his immediate neighbours had had more than enough to eat, but a large cheeseboard was brought in for those still able to contemplate more. Syllabubs were also available. To conclude the meal, port and brandy were on offer, with coffee as an alternative. A large box of chocolates, provided by Topper, was passed from hand to hand.

Fred presided genially over all this feast, with his wife at the other end of the table, nearest the door. Fred was in good form. He was wearing a new suit, or at any rate one which Scrooge had not seen before, and Scrooge was pleased to note that, although the lapels were cut in the latest style, they were not so extravagantly cut that the owner would be obliged to abandon the suit before it was properly worn out. This was an instruction which Scrooge had always given to his own tailor, and he was pleased to see that Fred was following his example.

Deborah was less able to relax than Fred, of course, for as hostess she was continually on edge lest something dreadful should go wrong. Perhaps the roast potatoes might turn out to be tooth-breakers, or the cream be past its best. But nothing did prove amiss, and, towards the end, something of the tension was removed from her pleasing features.

After lunch, the younger members of the group were ordered out for a brief walk. It was by then almost dark, but perhaps half an hour's light remained, and the expedition was led by Fred. His wife, visibly relieved that all the culinary arrangements had gone so well, disappeared down the stairs both to congratulate the troops on their performance so far and to check on plans for the rest of the day.

Scrooge excused himself from the walk and, by mutual agreement with another gentleman of about his own age, snoozed happily in front of the drawing-room fire.

When the party was reunited, Scrooge found himself chatting to Mrs Bannister, the Vicar's wife. He asked how she was finding the parish, now that she and her husband had completed their first year.

'Oh, we like it well enough,' said Mrs Bannister. 'But there is much to be done, of course. And I shall be looking to you for help, Mr Scrooge.'

It was, Scrooge reflected, one of the hazards of such occasions that, in a careless moment, one might find oneself inveigled into agreeing to something which one might later regret.

'Oh,' he said casually, 'I'm afraid I am not a regular churchgoer.'

'That's no guarantee of anything,' said Mrs Bannister briskly. 'Some of the biggest sinners are regular communicants, and the reverse is also true. No, I have high hopes of you, Mr Scrooge, and I shall be calling upon you soon, never fear.'

Well, forewarned is forearmed, thought Scrooge, and changed the subject.

Soon, tea and mince pies were served, while those who had ventured out told of a snowball fight (in which they had allegedly been victorious) against a similar party from number ninety-three. And then, as the evening drew on, various members of the company were induced, invited, or just plain bullied into providing some entertainment.

Deborah, the hostess, broke the ice by playing the harp, which she did exceedingly well and to much applause. It was, so the widow of Pewsey assured Scrooge, a most difficult instrument to play.

Afterwards, Deborah looked well pleased with herself, as she had every right to be, and she glowed not only with satisfaction but with that inner beauty which made Scrooge positively envy his nephew. When he saw a special smile pass between Fred and his wife, Scrooge felt a pang of memory.

Once, years ago, he had exchanged a similar smile with an equally beautiful young lady – and she too had had a very kissable mouth. But the years had passed, they had never married, and now, of course, it was far too late. As for the young woman – she had long since married someone else, and been all the happier for it, Scrooge had no doubt.

Topper, the handsome bachelor with a mass of curly brown hair which would keep falling down over his eyes, was next on stage. He sang a series of familiar (but rather serious) songs in a strong bass voice, accompanied on the piano by the plump sister with the lace tucker. Scrooge really did hope that they had been properly chaperoned during the lengthy rehearsals which had no doubt been necessary for this performance, because otherwise – well, who could say what improprieties they might not otherwise have been tempted to?

The widow of Pewsey also sang, rather to Scrooge's astonishment. She had a good clear voice, with no pretensions whatever to formal polish, and she sang a series of traditional songs such as 'I saw three ships', 'Deck the halls', and 'The twelve days of Christmas'.

To Scrooge, the widow was at least as interesting to look at as to hear. She was, he guessed, not far off forty, but she was a good-looking woman to whom the years had been kind, and the soft lighting flattered her skin. Like her sister, Mrs Bannister, she had fair hair and blue eyes, and although she was smartly dressed she was clearly not over-fussed about her appearance. She wore a brooch, and a modest necklace, since this was a festive occasion, but unlike one or two of the other ladies she was no advertisement for the local jeweller. To Scrooge, however, her most remarkable feature was that she had an air of authority and confidence about her, as if she were one of nature's aristocrats. He remarked as such to her sister.

'Ah yes,' said the Vicar's wife. 'She has the mark upon her all right.'

Whatever that meant.

Later Scrooge spoke to the Vicar about his sister-in-law. He learnt that she had been a widow for five years, and was regularly pursued by suitors, in whom she was showing no interest whatever. She was also a skilled herbalist, and spent all her time treating the ailments of the villagers for miles around her home.

'She has healing hands, Mr Scrooge,' said the Vicar, which Scrooge thought was a most odd thing for him to say. 'She has worked wonders for my headaches, so if you yourself have any infirmities, you should give her a try.'

'Thank you,' said Scrooge, feeling somewhat bemused. 'I'll bear it in mind.'

The musical interlude was followed by parlour games, mostly of a sober and restrained variety, as befitted an adult gathering, but at Fred's insistence there were several rounds of blind man's buff. Topper was elected as the first blind man, and after being blindfolded he caused a good deal of squealing among the younger ladies as he groped his way around the room.

To Scrooge, however, the whole thing was an obvious fraud. Why, he had not seen such a transparent conjuring trick for forty years. Topper, it was clear, was determined to catch nobody but Fred's plump sister-in-law (the one with the lace tucker). And Fred, it was clear to Scrooge, was giving him directions. One cough meant turn left, two coughs meant turn right. Such is the chicanery which several years at the same boarding school produces in fellows who might in all other respects pass as gentlemen. Scrooge was quite shocked.

The result of this conspiracy was that Topper was able to catch the plump sister behind the curtains, and not just once, either, but twice, to the great joy of the assembled watchers. The young lady complained bitterly that this was grossly unfair, but no one was convinced.

Finally, the cheeseboard was brought back in, the hostess having complained that not enough had been eaten at lunch, and Fred declaring that he really didn't wish to live off it for the rest of the week. Several bottles of Scrooge's champagne were opened, and some of the company began to look at the clock and declare, with justification, that they really must be going, for they were due at the office again the following morning.

Scrooge seized this opportunity to rise to his feet and knock on a table to call for silence.

'Ladies and gentlemen,' he said, when the voices had been stilled. 'I think I am perhaps the oldest here, and I am certainly the one who deserves least the splendid hospitality which has been offered to us today. My nephew Fred and his wife Deborah have set a new standard for us all, both in the food and drink which they have provided, and in the warmth of their welcome. I for one will try to learn from their example. May I therefore, on behalf of the good folk assembled here, offer our must humble and heartfelt thanks to our host and hostess.' He raised his glass. 'A toast – to our host and hostess.'

'Our host, and hostess.'

6

Scrooge waited until all the others had gone – their departure occupying some minutes – before he ventured downstairs. Then, at last, he pulled on his coat and took possession of his hat.

Finally he said: 'One other thing – I do believe I had a boy with me when I came.'

'Oh!' Deborah had genuinely forgotten, though Fred hadn't.

Deborah led the way to the kitchen in the basement, and Scrooge followed. Down there he found a sight which would have daunted even the boldest employee. Most of the plates, pans and dishes from lunchtime had been washed up and put away, but there was still a mountain of crockery from tea and supper. And there was, of course, a whole sideboard full of leftover food, for Fred and his wife had concluded that there could be no worse sin than running short.

Mrs Weatherby, the cook, and Cassie, the maid, both looked exhausted, and were attempting to revive their energy with a cup of tea.

'No, no, please don't stand up,' Scrooge insisted, though neither took any notice. 'I have just come to collect my young companion.'

'He's over here, sir,' said Mrs Weatherby, though at first the light was too dim for Scrooge to make out where she was indicating. But after a moment he caught sight of Billy, curled up on an old wooden bench, fast asleep. Scrooge couldn't have got comfortable on that bench for an instant, but Billy had had years of practice.

'He's been as good as gold, sir,' said Mrs Weatherby. 'Did what he was told, never complained, never dropped nothing, and never stopped talking and asking questions. Not till he fell asleep, anyhow.'

'Did he eat well?' enquired Scrooge.

Mrs Weatherby laughed. 'Oh yes, sir, I think I could say so. We three down here ate after the rest of you, of course. But he enjoyed the soup – had two bowls, as I recall. Then the turkey, of course. Reckoned he'd never had any before, but he picked clean the bones of what we give him and no mistake. And then he had the fruit salad and the cream. Quite a lot of cream he had, but as the mistress says, it'll only go off if it's left. Very partial to cream he is. Oh, and then he had a bit of plum pudding as well.'

'And then he was sick,' said Cassie.

'Well, yes, that's true,' acknowledged Mrs Weatherby, who would no doubt advise Cassie later that she might have left that last remark unsaid. 'But at least he did it in the sink, and he got the benefit of most of what he'd had, that much I'm sure of.'

Scrooge nodded with satisfaction. 'Thank you very much, Mrs Weatherby,' he said, and he passed her a sovereign, with half that amount going to Cassie, who was so overcome that she curtsied.

'God bless you, sir,' cried the cook, when she had glanced at the coin. 'I'm sure I'll never hear another hard word said against you.'

Scrooge pretended not to notice the implication that hard words had been said against him in the past, and simply murmured, 'I hope you'll never have to.'

He woke up Billy, and the two of them walked home

together.

More snow was falling, but the gas lights showed them the way without difficulty. Scrooge avoided the short cut through the alley, and Billy didn't mention it.

As they walked, Scrooge explained to Billy that he could sleep in a spare room for the night, and Billy was too tired to do more than say, 'Thank you, sir.'

They arrived at Scrooge's house and he led the way up the huge, wide staircase to his apartment above. Once there, he lit some candles and showed Billy the bed in what was mostly used as a lumber-room.

'Here you are, Billy. You can sleep here tonight, with these blankets to keep you warm.'

Billy clambered on to the bed, boots and all, and Scrooge realised that this was the way he was used to retiring for the night.

'That's right,' he said. 'Sleep in your clothes tonight, Billy, and tomorrow we'll get you some new ones.'

'What, new clothes?'

'Yes.'

'You mean, a new pair of trousis?'

'Yes, Billy. New everything.... Settle down now.'

Billy manoeuvred himself under the blanket. But just as Scrooge turned to go he said, 'Mr Scrooge....'

'Yes, Billy?'

'Do you want me to do anything for you?'

Scrooge wasn't quite sure what that guarded question meant, but he had a pretty strong suspicion. If Billy ever had been shown any kindness in the past, it was odds on that it came from men who *did* want him to do something for them.

'No, thank you, Billy,' he said firmly. 'I don't want you to do anything for me. And you'll never have to do that sort of thing again. I promise.... Now – settle down and go to sleep, do you hear?'

'Yes, sir,' said Billy in a very faint, weary voice.

And then, just as Scrooge entered his own room, he heard two final words: 'Goodnight, sir.'

'Goodnight son,' said Scrooge.

Part Two

7

In Scrooge's time, there were only three public holidays in the entire year: Christmas Day, Shrove Tuesday, and Good Friday. The following morning was therefore a normal working day, and Scrooge was up at his usual time: six o'clock. Much of the rest of working London rose at the same hour.

The snow was still on the ground, but no more of it had fallen. Scrooge had a suspicion, based on little but the feeling in his bones, that it would soon start to melt.

When he was dressed and ready, he bustled into the old lumber-room and roused Billy. And rouse him he had to, for the boy was sound asleep. However, mention of the word 'breakfast' soon had Billy swinging his feet off the bed.

Outside, the street was not yet slushy. The air was crisp, and their breath harsh in the throat.

A short, brisk walk in the cold sharpened their appetite, and on arrival at Scrooge's usual café they demolished two considerable portions of Mr Montini's kedgeree.

Scrooge was slightly suspicious of this dish, reckoning that the bulk of it was almost certainly leftovers from yesterday, given a good warming and flavoured with a few extras. But it tasted well enough. And besides, he asked himself, what in the world had got into him that he should think of criticising a man for allowing nothing to go to waste?

Mr Montini, choosing a moment when the other

customers were busily engaged, bent low and whispered in Scrooge's ear that his generosity of the previous day had been much appreciated.

'If God's blessings are of any use to you, Mr Scrooge,' he said, 'you should have many of them. Your ears should have burning something rotten.'

'I must confess,' said Scrooge, 'that I did feel a slight tingling from time to time. And I trust you had enough cash to cover your expenses?'

'Ample,' Mr Montini assured him. 'And what little was left I shall use for more of the same, when I see a deserving cause.'

Scrooge nodded. 'A sensible solution, sir.'

When Scrooge and Billy returned to the apartment they found it a whirl of brushes and dustpans. Scrooge's housekeeper, Mrs Molloy, was hard at work.

Mrs Molloy was a thin, grey-haired, wiry little woman. Her husband had been an Irishman, but she was now widowed. The lady was well over sixty, Scrooge knew that for a fact. She could describe events which had occurred well before he was born, so he could roughly guess her age.

These days Mrs Molloy was just a little bowed in the back from her many years of hard work, but she was still quite spry and alert. Her chief characteristic was that she found almost everything inexplicably amusing, and went around with a constant smile on her face, as if she were party to some secret joke which was unknown to the rest of the world.

Normally, Scrooge was gone for the day, once he was out of the house, and so Mrs Molloy was surprised to see him. Some cleaning ladies of Scrooge's acquaintance would have turned him away at his own door, and told him to come back when they were finished. Mrs Molloy, however, merely tittered with amusement when he entered, and asked him if business was so bad at the 'Change that he was ruined already.

'No, Mrs Molloy,' said Scrooge equably, he being well used to having the lady question his financial acumen. 'No, I am not quite bankrupt, not as yet, though if the nation insists on continuing to waste perfectly good working time with frivolity and foolishness, as it did yesterday, I dare say I soon shall be. No, madam, the reason for returning this morning is to introduce you to Master Billy here.' Scrooge turned to find Billy, who had come over unaccountably shy. 'Here, boy, shake Mrs Molloy's hand.'

Billy did so, and Mrs Molloy found that as much a source of hilarity as she habitually did almost everything else. 'Hee hee hee hee hee!' she said. And Billy, not knowing quite what to make of that, retreated once again behind Scrooge.

'I intend to give Billy a job,' announced Scrooge. 'As an errand boy, at the office.'

Mrs Molloy's smile grew broader still. 'Do you indeed?' she asked. 'Hee hee hee hee hee!' Clearly, her employer's follies were an endless source of pleasure to her, and Scrooge had the uneasy feeling that she entertained whole streets with her accounts of his eccentric ways.

'Yes,' he asserted with a frown. 'I do. But first, I want you to take him out, Mrs Molloy, and buy him new sets of clothes. Two of everything, from the skin up. Nothing too fancy, mind.'

'Oh no.'

'But new – not second-hand. And not your cheap and nasty, either.'

'Oh no.' Mrs Molloy beamed at the very idea.

'Then you are to bring him home, give him a good bath, and burn what he's got on.'

'I should think so,' said Mrs Molloy, forgetting herself to the point where she actually ceased to smile. 'Smells somethink awful, he does. I could tell you'd had a visitor, soon as I come in the door. And that bed what he slept in has still got a stink about it. Mind you, at least he didn't wet it. And I note you had the decency to give him a separate bed, Mr Scrooge.'

'Well,' said Scrooge, 'I certainly should hope so.'

Mrs Molloy nodded. 'I've heard many a bad thing said about you, Mr Scrooge, but never that you was interested in little boys.'

Scrooge sighed. He was becoming just the tiniest bit weary of hearing that people had been making criticisms of him behind his back. Once upon a time he would have thought nothing of it – been proud, in fact, to hear that he had incurred the displeasure of some remarkably soft-hearted and overly sentimental souls. But now, somehow, the fun had gone out of it.

'Be that as it may, Mrs Molloy,' said Scrooge. 'Young Billy has not had our good fortune, and you and I would smell just as bad had we fallen upon similarly unfortunate circumstances.'

He opened his wallet, took out yet another five-pound note, and handed it over to the housekeeper. 'Now, do you think that will suffice for what I have described?'

Mrs Molloy examined the note and found it the funniest thing she had seen for some time. 'Hee hee hee hee hee!' she said. 'Yes, I shouldn't wonder if it will suffice, Mr Scrooge. If suffice is the word. Might run to a saucer of hot eels too, if we're careful.' She smiled at Billy with genuine affection, and he managed to grin back. Evidently Mrs

Molloy was not as fearsome as she looked, once you got used to her.

Scrooge coughed tactfully as he looked down upon the top of Billy's head. 'And, er, while you're about it, a good close haircut and a little delousing powder might not go amiss. No offence, Billy.'

'None taken, Mr Scrooge.' Billy ran an exploratory hand through his hair. 'Things do get a bit scratchy from time to time.'

'Off you go then, Billy,' said Scrooge. 'You go along with Mrs Molloy and do whatever she says. No need to be nervous of her.'

'Hee hee hee hee hee,' said Mrs Molloy.

'She won't bite,' said Scrooge. Not got the teeth for it, he almost added, but that would have been unkind.

Scrooge's office was in St Michael's Alley, just off Cornhill. It lay conveniently close to his principal place of business, the Royal Exchange, and nearby were other major financial institutions such as the Bank of England, the Stock Exchange, and Lloyd's. All of these, Scrooge was fond of pointing out, were located within comfortable walking distance of the Tower of London, where, in the past, many a malefactor had been imprisoned and beheaded.

The building in which Scrooge rented office space housed a number of other businesses, and the man whose job it was to act as caretaker for them had laid a fire both in the inner room, which was Scrooge's precinct, and in the outer office, his clerk's domain. But these 'fires' were currently small, smoky little piles of reluctant coal, and even Scrooge felt chilled. He poked both of them restlessly while he thought about how to allocate his time for the day.

He looked at the clock: Cratchit was late, dammit.

Cratchit was Scrooge's clerk, and each year he and Scrooge acted out a little charade, in which Cratchit promised faithfully to be in the office bang on time on the day after his Christmas holiday, and each year he was late. Scrooge didn't really mind, not to the extent of reprimanding the fellow, but it did irritate him. It was part of the general irritation of Christmas – all that nauseating goodwill and cheeriness. Enough to make a chap sick. Most years. But this year, Scrooge was forced to admit, he had quite enjoyed himself.

While he was waiting, Scrooge had a think about Cratchit.

The truth was, he and Cratchit got on well together, which was more than could be said for some clerks he had had. Several had lasted only a few weeks before finding another berth, and one only three days. Cratchit, however, seemed to catch on pretty quick that Scrooge was not quite as nasty and mean as he sounded. He understood very well that Scrooge did not have a heart of gold – but that, underneath his cold, stony exterior, there was at least a touch of irony, some little awareness of the grim humour of life as it was lived in nineteenth-century London.

And then there was the money. Cratchit's pay. Fifteen shillings a week, no less. Cratchit might be able to do better – in fact he could do better, for a man who was known to have satisfied Scrooge's exacting standards would have no difficulty in getting a job elsewhere. But Cratchit evidently liked it well where he was. He was his own master, more or less. When Scrooge wandered over to the Royal Exchange, Cratchit could relax – perhaps nip out and do a bit of shopping. Scrooge had come in many a time and seen the bags, tucked away half out of sight under Cratchit's feet. Nevertheless, the time had come – yes it had, there was no denying it – the time had come when Scrooge might have to think about giving Cratchit a little bit more. It seemed an odd thing to do, given that the chap showed no sign of leaving, but nevertheless Scrooge thought that it was his due.

Through the open door of the inner office Scrooge saw the street door open. Cratchit at last came in, his long scarf trailing, his breath white on the air. Probably he had run part of the way to warm himself, and now he stamped his feet on the mat to get rid of the excess snow.

'Cratchit!' bawled Scrooge. 'You're late.'

Cratchit glanced anxiously in Scrooge's direction as he unwound his scarf. No doubt he hoped that his employer might have had a lie-in just for once. But no such luck.

'Yes, sir, very sorry, sir,' gasped Cratchit. 'But it is only once a year, and we were up rather late last night.'

Scrooge growled unintelligibly, expressing his general dissatisfaction that this feeble comment should be offered as an excuse. He stood with his back to the struggling little fire, warming his bottom.

'Come in here,' he called. 'I want to talk to you.'

After a moment the clerk appeared, pad and pencil in hand.

Cratchit was a man just short of forty, and of average height and build. His clothes were somewhat shabby if you looked closely, but since he was the father of a growing family he preferred not to pay fancy tailor's bills; he worked on his father's principle that if you had a clean collar and clean shoes you could get away with quite a lot in between.

Bob Cratchit was the son of a London shopkeeper who had had four children: the elder son inherited the shop (but was doing badly with it); the two daughters married; and his father had seen to it that young Bob was educated to the point where he could be sure of a clerking job for life.

Cratchit was a quiet man, not one of nature's leaders, but he was meticulous in his work and prided himself on never being a penny out in his accounts; these were virtues much appreciated by his current employer.

Normally, on such a morning, Scrooge would not have wasted a second in talking about Christmas. In former years he would have taken the view that Christmas was now over, thank God, and he would have jumped straight into the business of the day. But this year, rather to his own surprise, he found himself making small talk.

'I trust, Mr Cratchit,' he said, 'that you and your family had an enjoyable day yesterday?'

Cratchit's eyes opened wide, as if he did not entirely trust his own ears. 'Oh yes, sir, thank you. Very enjoyable indeed. Oh – and thank you very much for sending the turkey, sir. It was most unexpected.'

'Unexpected?' growled Scrooge, as if taking offence.

Cratchit became rather breathless with nerves and sought to retrieve his mistake. 'Well, sir, it was a most pleasant surprise, one which we had not anticipated, let me put it that way. Mrs Cratchit said I must make sure to thank you most warmly. In fact – ' He groped in his pocket and brought out an envelope. 'She wrote you a little note, sir. Just a personal word from her.'

'Oh.' Scrooge took the offered note and placed it on his desk. 'How kind.... Well, I had the idea that a big bird would come in useful. You have a fair number of young mouths to feed, I believe. Six, isn't it?'

'Yes, sir.'

'I did a bit of celebrating myself, if it comes to that. Went to me nephew's.'

Cratchit seemed both astonished and pleased. 'Oh,

really, sir? I had so hoped you would. Young Mr Watson is a most kind and thoughtful gentleman, sir, it would have been a shame not to take advantage of his offer.'

'Hmm, yes, quite,' grumbled Scrooge. 'Anyway, I have to make a little thank you myself, on account of that. I want you to order a crate of decent claret and send it round to Mrs Watson with my compliments.'

'Claret, sir? A crate, did you say?'

Scrooge stared him in the eye. 'I did. Anything unusual about that?'

'Oh no, sir, no,' said Cratchit hastily. 'Nothing unusual at all. Just wanted to make sure that I'd heard you aright, sir.' He scribbled a note on his pad.

'Yes,' Scrooge repeated thoughtfully. 'A crate of the stuff. We had some excellent claret at lunch, so young Fred's cellar will no doubt need replenishing. I can afford it, can't I?'

'Oh yes, sir. Comfortably.'

'Hmm,' Scrooge growled again. 'Not excessive, is it? To send a crate? Not absurdly over-generous?'

'No sir, I would not say so.'

'Just a bit unusual for me, you seem to imply.'

'Well, sir....' Cratchit coughed discreetly.

'Why is it so hard for me to spend money, Cratchit?' The question was actually one which Scrooge was asking himself, though as he had tagged his clerk's name on the end Cratchit felt obliged to comment.

'I couldn't say, sir, I'm sure.'

'Neither can I,' said Scrooge with a sigh. 'But it is hard, you will grant me that.'

Cratchit chose his words with care. 'You are undoubtedly a thrifty gentleman, sir. No question of that.'

'The wine merchants – I believe there's quite a good one

on Gracechurch Street – they will send us a bill no doubt?'

'Oh yes, sir. Your credit is good.'

'Always take credit where you can get it, Cratchit.'

'Indeed, sir, I make it a golden rule.'

Well, that was enough small talk for one day. Quite enough.

'Have a seat, Cratchit,' said Scrooge. ' I want to talk to you.'

And he himself sat down too.

'I've been doing a bit of thinking,' said Scrooge, when they were settled.

Cratchit raised an eyebrow. A slightly apprehensive eyebrow, Scrooge noticed.

'Yes.... Fact is, you see, I'm not getting any younger. I'm fifty now, and I've been working on 'Change for twenty-five years. Quite a long time. First I was in partnership with Marley, and then I traded on me own account. Well, I can't go on for another twenty-five years. Won't be able to.'

'Perhaps not. But you're still a fit man, sir.'

'Oh yes. And there's no need to be alarmed, Bob. I'm not packing up just yet, so your job is as safe as houses. In fact, I might be able to do a bit better for you in the next year or two than I have in the past.'

'Thank you, sir,' said Cratchit, in the tones of a man who has no expectation of a pious hope becoming a reality.

'Make a note on your pad, Cratchit. Ten per cent increase in your salary, with effect from the first of January.'

Cratchit's eyes bulged. 'Ten per cent, sir? Increase?'

Scrooge growled at him. 'Isn't it enough?'

'Oh yes, sir, ample, sir. Thank you very much, sir.'

'Not at all. Worth every penny, I'm sure. No, the thing is,

you see, I've been doing a bit of thinking. Been wondering whether I should go on doing the same old thing until I drop – or whether I should take a slightly different direction.... I don't know whether you're familiar with Aristotle's *Nicomachean Ethics*, Cratchit?'

'No, sir. Can't say that I am.'

'No, well, I dare say you can manage your life perfectly well without having read it. But that book deals, in short, with the question of how a man should live his life – and hence how he should die.'

Scrooge paused and turned to look into the fire.

'If I have a fault, Cratchit, it is that I read too much. Costs me a fortune in fuel, for I like a good light to read by. Always have. It was a habit that began when I was a boy. My father and I fell out when I was thirteen, and I was obliged to remain at school during the holidays, when all the other fellows had gone home. And there is nothing in this world, Cratchit, quite so desolate as a boys' boarding school during the holidays, when all those noisy brats have departed. All save one, in my case, and he had nothing to do but read. But my reading recently has disturbed me. It's made me think – think about my past, present and future. And it's disturbed my sleep too. So I know that I shan't be settled in my own mind until I've sorted myself out.'

Scrooge stood up.

'The first thing to do is to find out how much I'm worth. I have a fair idea, of course, but I could be out by ten or twenty per cent. So the first thing to do this morning is for both of us, you and me, to add up the value of my holdings.'

He picked up a ledger.

'You take the Marley money, and I'll take the rest. That should be a fair division of labour. And by the end of today I want to have a pretty good idea of my net worth.'

Cratchit rose to his feet. 'Very good, sir.' He turned to go.

'Oh, and Cratchit?'

'Yes, sir?'

'For goodness' sake see if you can get these fires to burn up bright. It's positively arctic in here.'

8

Scrooge spent the remainder of the morning checking through his bank accounts and share-holdings. He wanted to know how rich a man he was, but at the same time he wished to keep the calculation as simple as possible; he therefore listed the value of each item to the nearest pound, writing the figures on a sheet of ledger paper.

The fire in the hearth had by now responded well to Cratchit's chidings, and it was backed up high in the chimney, its warmth making Scrooge positively cheerful for once.

At some point after mid-morning he pulled out a number of old boxes which had been piled up behind his desk for several years. They had been there for rather longer than he had realised, apparently, for many of the contents came as a great surprise to him.

In one box there was a considerable sum in Swiss currency, taken in part settlement of a scheme which had gone badly awry. When Scrooge came to look at the associated paperwork he could well understand why he had put the matter out of his mind, for his error of judgement had cost him dear. Now he just pursed his lips and hissed with disapproval at his youthful folly.

Another box contained a selection of gold watches and some jewellery. A third revealed some share certificates for a Peruvian mining company. Now where on earth had they come from, and were they as worthless as they looked? To Scrooge's experienced eye they appeared to have 'fraudulent and worse' engraved all over them. But once, perhaps, he had bought them with the wholehearted conviction that he was getting in on the ground floor of, quite literally, a gold-mine.

All these items were briefly listed and a value for each was not just pencilled in but inked in. Scrooge was determined to resist the temptation to make detailed enquiries as to the true and present value of these strange accumulations. Perfect accuracy was not the object of the exercise. Close enough would do.

Towards lunchtime Mrs Molloy turned up with a scrubbed and polished young Billy. He was hardly recognisable with a clean (pale) face, new clothes, shiny boots, hair so short that the pate was almost polished, and – above all – a proper overcoat. In herring-bone tweed, no less. What was more Mrs Molloy had gone the whole hog and bought scarf and gloves.

Introductions were made, Cratchit declared himself quite speechless with amazement at Scrooge's unprecedented liberality, and Billy made several revolutions in front of the admiring audience to show off his new outfit. He seemed quite bemused by the situation; from the look on his face he appeared to be not quite sure whether he was awake and fully conscious, or simply dreaming it all as he lay curled up above a baker's oven.

'Well, well, well!' said Scrooge. 'That will do nicely, Mrs Molloy. That's a good piece of worsted, that suit is, of the highest quality, one can see at a glance. And I pride myself that having been involved in the cloth trade as a young man, I do know my worsted. I am very grateful to you, Mrs Molloy. Of course,' he told Billy, 'it will all feel very stiff and new for a while. Whenever I have a new suit – and I had one as recently as three summers ago – I find it needs whacking against the bedroom wall a few times before it quite conforms to me shape. And even then it takes a while.'

'Hee hee hee hee hee,' giggled Mrs Molloy, probably picturing Scrooge in action as a wall-basher. Billy turned his cap round and round in his hand, his face quite rosy from all the attention he was getting.

'I dare say this would have cost a fair bit?' remarked Scrooge.

'Four pounds, seven shillings and threepence three-farthings,' said Mrs Molloy. 'On account of I demanded a two per cent discount from Mr Isaacs in Fenchurch Street. He being one of your tenants, Mr Scrooge.'

'So he is,' said Scrooge. 'So he is. And how is the old villain?'

'Passing well, Mr Scrooge, passing well. He sends you his compliments.'

Scrooge scratched his head. 'Yes, it's extraordinary how one overlooks things, you know. Until you mentioned it I had forgotten that property in Fenchurch Street. I took it from another tailor, one who fell upon hard times through an excess of drink, I fear. It's managed for me by agents and the rent is dealt with by Mr Cratchit here, so I am inclined to forget it. It would be cheaper of course to manage the whole thing oneself, but there is never the time, is there?'

He looked for agreement from his colleagues, and all present shook their head as if to say, no, there was never enough time for that sort of thing. Ever tactful in the presence of a rich man, they did their best to appear familiar with the difficulties of managing properties which they barely remembered owning.

'Well now,' Scrooge continued, 'your expenditure to date, Mrs Molloy, leaves a sum of twelve shillings and eight pence one farthing.'

'I have it here,' declared Mrs Molloy, reaching for the bag which she invariably carried with her.

'No, no, I was not asking for it back,' said Scrooge. 'In fact, I think you had better keep it for your trouble, Mrs Molloy.'

A sudden silence fell. Even the fire stopped hissing.

'You mean, hold on to it because the lad will need to be bought more stuff?'

'No, I mean keep it for yourself. If I might make so bold, Mrs Molloy, a new bonnet might not be out of order. You have worn that black one both indoors and out for at least a year.'

'Two,' said Mrs Molloy. 'Give to me by the late Mrs Chadwick it was, and we buried her on new year's day, two winters since.'

'Well then.' Scrooge rested his case.

'What's wrong with this bonnet?' demanded Mrs Molloy, for once in her life failing to find the situation amusing.

'Nothing, nothing. I merely make the point that it might be allowed a rest from time to time. A new bonnet would allow for some variation in wear, as perhaps, between weekdays and Sundays.'

Mrs Molloy rose to her feet, her face serious in expression. 'I think I shall go, Mr Scrooge, afore you falls down with the apoplexy, for you cannot be yourself. You are my witness, Mr Cratchit,' she added, waving a finger under that gentleman's nose. (Although Cratchit's eyes were bulging nearly as far out as her own.) 'Mr Scrooge's sudden fit of madness was none of my doing. He brought it upon himself.'

And with that, she departed.

*

Scrooge decided that it was time for lunch.

They all three took lunch together, in a nearby tavern. Without pressing the matter too hard, Scrooge volunteered that he had just wondered, Mr Cratchit, whether it might not be possible to make use of young Billy about the office. After all, there were numerous occasions when an extra pair of hands, not to mention a pair of feet, might be useful about the place. There were always messages to be delivered, newspapers to be fetched, odd bits of shopping and tidying and so forth to be done. Was that not so?

Cratchit agreed that it was. But could Master Billy read and write?

Not much, as yet, Scrooge acknowledged. But that could be attended to.

The matter was settled. Billy would work for Mr Scrooge, taking orders from either him or Mr Cratchit. Wage: a penny an hour, plus his keep. And in due course, arrangements would be made to teach him to read and write.

After lunch, Cratchit soon found work for Billy. Cratchit was, after all, busy working out the value of the late Mr Marley's estate, which involved consulting numerous files, which had to be fetched and put back. And where a job could be done quicker himself than by asking Billy to do it, Cratchit was adept at inventing something else for the boy to do. For Cratchit was, after all, the father of three sons. He knew all about preventing the rapid onset of boredom in the young.

At four o'clock Cratchit announced to Scrooge that he had completed his task. Not, he gave Mr Scrooge to understand, as accurately as he would have wished, had they been obliged to account to shareholders, but good enough, he thought, for Mr Scrooge's purposes.

By that time, Scrooge reckoned that he too had a

satisfactory picture of the overall state of affairs in that aspect of the business which he was dealing with. 'Come along in then,' he said, 'and we'll go through it together.'

Cratchit coughed. 'Ahem. What about the lad, sir?'

'Oh, bring him in too. We will use him as an adviser. For we do need advice, Cratchit.'

'Do we, sir?'

'Indeed we do. There are important decisions to be made, Cratchit.'

'Oh,' said Cratchit, who looked alarmed.

'So we will use young Billy as a consultant. He is, after all, a representative of those less well off than ourselves.'

Cratchit clearly couldn't make much sense of that, but Scrooge said no more for the present.

The two men and Billy assembled in Scrooge's office and seated themselves around a table. It was a table which had been used for meetings and discussions of one sort and another in the days when Scrooge had bothered to have discussions and meetings in the office. These days he did all his business in the Royal Exchange, sealed it with a handshake, and dealt with the paperwork in the office afterwards.

Outside it was beginning to grow dark, so Scrooge brought up a lamp and placed it in the centre of the table so that they could see what they were doing. He also reached into his pocket and brought out the spectacles which he now used for reading by artificial light. Scrooge had resisted the use of reading-glasses for a long time, until one day he found that he had misread a 3 for an 8, and had written a cheque for five pounds too much.

'Now then,' Scrooge began. 'Our object today was to work out, in round figures, how much money I have available to me, in one form or another. Of course, not all that I own is in cash, or even in a form which could quickly be converted to cash. Mr Isaacs's shop in Fenchurch Street, to give but one example, has a value, but it is not a value that we can do more than make an educated guess at, and it would take a while to sell the premises, even if selling was what we chose to do. Nevertheless, Cratchit, we have both of us formed a view of the value of things, based on our many years of experience, and I dare say we shall not be far out. On the conservative side, if anything, I surmise.'

'Indeed, sir. Where an exact value is not known, I have pitched it a little low.'

Scrooge nodded. 'Good. Well, you first, I think. The value of the Marley estate.'

'Yes, sir. Well, sir, Mr Marley has been dead these seven years, as you well recall, and although it took a while to tidy up his affairs, they have long since been settled. The partnership between the two of you was dissolved, and under the terms of his will, since he had no wife or children, he left all his worldly wealth to you.'

Scrooge sighed and rubbed his chin thoughtfully. He addressed the boy to his right.

'Mr Marley, Billy, was a solitary man. He lived alone in that big old barn where I now live, and which you have seen from the inside. He owned the building, of course, though in his day he rented out no other part of it. Preferred to be all on his own in that huge great space. Well, now I do things differently. The cellars are let to a wine merchant, Mrs Molloy lives in a set of rooms at the back, and the rest, other than my quarters, is let as offices. I always found it odd that Marley, who was always interested in turning a penny, should have wasted his resources so, but there it is.'

Cratchit waited until he was quite sure that Scrooge had finished before continuing.

'Well, sir, since round figures are the order of the day, I can say that Mr Marley left a quarter of a million pounds in Consols and various other Funds. And, in broad terms, he had as much again in property. You've done nothing with most of that, sir. Just let it lie, and ploughed the income back. So the capital's been accumulating at three per cent compound ever since. Some of it's at five per cent. Once or twice we've sold off a bit of land or a building – the railway companies has bought some, and a factory was bought by the firm that rented it. But mostly the property's just been sitting there, appreciating. Rents have been put into Consols. Result, total value something over six hundred and fifty thousand pounds.'

'Hmm.' Scrooge was thoughtful. 'Yes, you are quite right, Cratchit. I have done nothing with Marley's estate. Taken nothing out, and put nothing in.' He turned to Billy. 'I was Marley's sole legatee, you see, Billy. Which means that he left me all his money. And the truth is, I didn't know what to do with it. Still don't if it comes to that. Anyway, we'll think about that in a moment.'

Scrooge stood up, went to his desk, and returned with the folder containing the figures which he himself had prepared.

'Now, Mr Cratchit, my side of the house. This is a little harder to estimate, because my money is put out to work, and therefore much depends on the outcome of various business enterprises which I have agreed to support. By definition, both the individual entrepreneurs and myself are convinced that each scheme which I invest in is sound, otherwise we would not be spending our time and money on it. However, experience tells us that not every enterprise will prosper. And perhaps all will fail. But what I have done, Cratchit, is to take liquid funds in hand at face value, regard loans due to fall in this year as certain, longer-term loans as less certain, and allow a measure for complete failure. That done, the sum total amounts to just under four hundred thousand pounds.'

'My word!' Cratchit leaned back and turned a trifle pale. 'As much as that.'

'Indeed,' echoed Scrooge. 'Total, over one million pounds.' He might have added: 'What do you think of that, Billy?' But he didn't, because he knew full well that the boy could have no concept of what a million pounds meant. Billy had probably never even handled a one-pound coin.

Cratchit looked quite stunned. 'This is not an exercise that we have ever done before, sir, and it has taken me quite by surprise.'

'Me too,' murmured Scrooge. 'One forgets, you see.... Well, I was miles out in my own estimate. If you had asked me at breakfast this morning I would have guessed no more than a quarter of a million on my own account, and perhaps the same for Marley.'

Scrooge rose to his feet and began to pace about.

'Truth is, you see, I was embarrassed that Marley left me what he had. We were partners, yes, but barely friends. He was a cold man, not given to confidences. He told me that I was to be the executor of his will, but not that I was to be a beneficiary.'

'He had no one else to leave it to, sir. And certainly no thought of charity.'

'You're right, Cratchit, you're right.' Scrooge sighed. 'And today has proved one thing to me – I don't want to die like Marley. He is dead these seven years, and it is as if he never lived. Not a soul mentions his name or his memory. There is nothing left of him, barring a gravestone, which is out of sight in a cemetery, for no one could stand the man.

No one came to his funeral.'

'He was not much liked, sir,' Cratchit admitted.

'Liked! Huh! He was feared and despised, that's the truth of it.'

Scrooge sat down again. He slapped the table with his hand.

'Well! Our figures prove one thing! They prove I am not a miser. If I was a miser I would have known how much I had, to the penny. I would keep it in gold, stored under me bed, and I would gloat over it nightly. But I am not a miser. Am I, Cratchit?'

'Certainly not, sir,' said Cratchit stoutly.

'I've been known to rub me hands with satisfaction at a deal well done. But I take no unseemly pleasure at the hardships of others. Do I?'

'No, sir.... Well, just the occasional cackle, perhaps.'

'Cackle?'

'Well, sir, when Messrs Carter and Ratchett was hammered you did have a little laugh, sir.'

'Ah, yes, but they were crooks, Cratchit, crooks. I think every honest man can allow himself a small celebration when villains meet a timely end.... No, I don't think my worst enemy could say that I am as hard a man as Marley.'

Scrooge placed his elbows on the table and adopted a brisk manner.

'Now then, Cratchit – and you, young Billy. We've added up all the money, more or less. And the thing is this. What are we going to do with it? Eh?' He glanced from face to face and saw nothing but gapes and puzzlement. 'Eh? What, what? Hmm?'

Silence prevailed for some moments, so Scrooge did some prompting.

'Well, let me put it this way, fellows. I have a million

pounds at my disposal, and I can't take it with me when I die, can I? Even if I was going anywhere but the church-yard, which I don't believe. And it's not much use to anyone, just sitting there accumulating at three per cent compound, is it? So what am I going to do with it? Eh?'

'Well, sir,' said Billy in a quiet treble. 'If you've really got a lot of money, I reckon as how you should spend it.'

Scrooge turned and stared at the boy. 'Spend it?' he croaked.

'Yes, sir. Well, that's what money's for, isn't it?'

9

That evening, as Scrooge and Billy walked home from the office, Billy explained that, after buying his new clothes, Mrs Molloy had had a talk with him about his living accommodation. She had decided, Billy said, that it would be wrong for him to continue sleeping in Scrooge's spare bedroom, and that it would be better for all concerned if he were to have his sleeping quarters in her apartment. In fact, she had already shown Billy where he would be sleeping from now on, and had made up a bed for him.

Well, Scrooge could certainly see the sense of all this, and so, after he and Billy had had a meal together, he delivered the boy to Mrs Molloy's front door. Her apartment was on the ground floor of the building in which he had his own rooms, the entrance being tucked away round the back.

After taking young Billy inside, Mrs Molloy gave Scrooge an explanation for her decision. 'Thing is, you see, I am used to little boys, on account of having had four of me own. Whereas you, Mr Scrooge, are not.'

Scrooge realised that this was a polite way of telling him that the novelty of Billy's company might very soon wear off. And no doubt there was some risk of that; Scrooge had, after all, led a solitary life for many years, and the introduction of a small boy into his routine, particularly on a twenty-four hour basis, might be more than he could cope with. Whereas, if Billy had Mrs Molloy's apartment to retire to, relations between him and the boy might continue on an even keel for longer than would otherwise be the case.

In the circumstances, therefore, Scrooge bowed to Mrs Molloy's better judgement. But he would, he said, see Billy for breakfast the following morning.

The next day, after he and Billy had paid their usual visit to Mr Montini's, Scrooge announced that later in the morning he would be going to see his doctor.

'Oh,' said Billy. 'Are you feeling ill?'

'No, fit as a fiddle. But I haven't had a chat with my doctor for quite some time, and there are things I want to ask.'

Shortly after nine o'clock, which Scrooge considered a civilised hour for calling on a professional man, he set off for the doctor's surgery, taking Billy with him.

The snow was beginning to melt now, and the pavements were wet with slush and mud. The two elements mixed together to form a kind of filthy slurry which Scrooge hated.

As they turned into Brandon Street, Billy paused in his tracks and then said, ''Ere – what's this doctor's name then?'

'Doctor Medway.'

Billy was triumphant. 'I fort it was. I recognise this street. I've heard of him! They say if you're really poor, and you go round the back of his house, he'll give you medicine and that for nothing.'

'Do they indeed?' said Scrooge. 'Well, it wouldn't surprise me, but the good doctor has kept his charitable activities mighty quiet, that's all I can say. He has never,' Scrooge added grimly, 'neglected to send a bill to me.'

After five minutes in the waiting-room, Dr Medway opened the door of his surgery and invited Scrooge to come in. Scrooge rose, and when Billy remained seated Scrooge took him by the arm.

'Come along, Billy,' he said. 'You too.'

Dr Medway's expression betrayed no emotion when he saw that Scrooge had a young companion with him. No doubt, Scrooge reflected, he saw stranger things three and four times a day. The doctor certainly didn't ask who the boy was, and at first Scrooge didn't explain.

Medway was a man in his forties, with a balding head, and brown, thoughtful eyes. He was well dressed, but in a practical style: his jacket cuffs were heavily buttoned to permit them to be folded back when dealing with blood and other bodily fluids.

'Please take a seat, Mr Scrooge,' he said. And then, when they were all three seated: 'Well now, what can I do for you today?'

'You're the doctor,' Scrooge responded. 'What's your diagnosis?'

If Dr Medway felt any irritation at this, he hid it well. He just narrowed his eyes, pursed his lips, and gave Scrooge a careful scrutiny. 'Well, you look a little older than when I last saw you. And a bit more cheerful than your usual self. Can't see any obvious problems. I do hope you're not wasting my time, Mr Scrooge. Unless you're really ill I don't think I want to bother with you.'

'Now, now,' said Scrooge. 'I expect a little more interest than that for my half-guinea.'

'It's a whole guinea. At least.'

Scrooge waved a hand in dismissal of mere money. 'Two guineas, three guineas, charge me what you like…. Truth is, you see, I've been thinking things over, doctor. Contemplating a few changes in my life. And what I want to know is, am I a fit man? How long can I reasonably expect to live?

76

That sort of thing.'

Dr Medway gave Scrooge a strange look, but evidently decided to humour him. 'Take off your jacket then, and roll up your shirt-sleeve.'

For the next twenty minutes or so, Dr Medway conducted a number of tests. He took Scrooge's pulse; looked at his tongue; asked for a detailed account of his diet and drinking habits; rubbed his finger and thumb together behind Scrooge's ears and asked him what he could hear; invited him to describe in detail the clothes worn by a man on the other side of the street, and then to read from a text which was printed in a fiendishly small font (Scrooge failed this test without his glasses); and, finally, the doctor posed a number of embarrassingly intimate questions about bowel movements and the workings of Scrooge's bladder. When it was all over he instructed Scrooge to put his jacket back on and he himself sat down and wrote extensive notes.

'How old are you?' the doctor asked while scribbling.

'Fifty.'

More notes. Then he said: 'Well, for a man of fifty you're in good shape. Lots of chaps don't get that far. Your teeth are sound, and your digestion seems able to cope with anything you shovel into it. You're too thin, of course, but by your own account you're a healthy eater, so that's just the way you are. You tell me you've seldom been ill in your life, apart from the occasional cold, and I've not seen much of you in my surgery, so my guess is that you'll manage the biblical threescore years and ten.'

'Hmm,' sniffed Scrooge. 'And is that it? Is that all I get for my money?'

Dr Medway was unmoved. 'It'll probably be five guineas, in the circumstances – the rich must subsidise the poor. And, yes, that is it. It's the best estimate I can give you, and what's more there are no guarantees.'

Scrooge sighed. 'Ah well, I suppose that's helpful.... Now then, I would also like you to take a look at my young friend here. Do much the same for him as you have for me. Sound him out, count his teeth or whatever it is, and tell me if there's anything needs doing for him.'

Dr Medway gave Scrooge another hard look. 'Very well, but I want you to wait outside while I do it.'

Scrooge was surprised, but agreed. He went out into the waiting-room.

Half an hour passed. Fortunately no other patients appeared, so Scrooge did not feel that he was inconveniencing anyone.

Eventually Dr Medway opened the surgery door, ushered Billy out, and called Scrooge back in.

Scrooge sat down in front of the doctor's desk.

'Now then, Scrooge.' No 'Mr' Scrooge noticed. 'What's your connection with this boy?'

'No connection, but he ran an errand for me on Christmas Day. When I spoke to him it turned out that he is homeless. Has no family. Or fambly, as he calls it. So I decided to give him a job. I bought him some new clothes, my housekeeper is prepared to have him as a lodger, and he will work for me at the office, running errands and so forth.'

Dr Medway looked down at his interlocked hands on the desk. 'I see. And your purpose in asking me to examine him?'

Scrooge hesitated. 'Well, he has lived very rough. Had a hard time of it. He certainly had lice. And I did wonder if he might have picked up something worse, which we could do something about.'

Dr Medway grunted. 'Well, I will take you at your word, Scrooge, about employing the boy. Though in some cases I would have had harsh things to say to you. I have had some men bring boys in here, to check that they were healthy, because they wished to make use of them for less respectable purposes.' The Doctor leaned back in his chair. 'However, although I have sometimes heard your name mentioned with something close to a curse, I have never heard you accused of that.'

Scrooge winced and found himself at a loss for words. 'I am greatly relieved to hear,' he finally managed to say, 'that I am given the benefit of the doubt in this matter.' Though he still could not meet the doctor's eye.

'Well, having got that out of the way, let me tell you that I have had a very good look at young Billy, right down to the skin. He is severely under-nourished. Says he's twelve, and he may be, but he's mighty small for that age.... You'll be pleased to hear that there are no obvious diseases, either hereditary or acquired. No syphilis, for example.'

Scrooge was quite shocked even to hear the word. 'Good, good,' he muttered.

'In the past, Mr Scrooge, but not the recent past, this boy has been subjected to physical abuse. Do you wish me to go into details?'

'No, no,' whispered Scrooge, lowering his head. 'Please don't.'

'But no long-term damage has been done. He seems to have intestinal worms, but that is very common among people of his background, and I've given him something for it. And he suffers from catarrh, but that should clear up with a decent diet and some warmer weather.'

'Yes, yes, I see,' said Scrooge softly. He was suddenly filled with an urge to get up and leave the surgery as soon as he could. But he forced himself to ask one further question.

'And you think that, given decent food, and clothing, and living conditions, young Billy might grow up to manhood and live to a reasonable age?'

'A reasonable age?'

'Yes.'

'What is a reasonable age, Mr Scrooge? Twenty? Thirty? Or your three score years and ten?'

Dr Medway rose to his feet and moved towards the window.

'If I seem short with you, it is because I have been up half the night with a patient. He was a healthy chap, until he fell ill. Twenty-eight years old. Climbed mountains when he went on holiday. He was married, with one young child. Three days ago he caught pneumonia, and last night, at three a.m., he died. Now, is that reasonable, Mr Scrooge? And in a world where that can happen, is it reasonable of you to expect me to predict the future?'

As they walked back to the office, Billy asked Scrooge what the doctor had said about him.

'Oh, he said that you're in pretty good fettle, Billy, but you need feeding up.'

Billy chuckled. 'So do you, I reckon.'

'Very possibly, very possibly. We must both tuck in, Billy.'

They walked a little further in silence. Then Billy said: 'I ain't never been to a doctor before.'

'Well, let's hope you never have to again. I have seldom been to one myself.'

Another silence.

'Mr Scrooge....'

'Yes, Billy?'

'I've been thinking over what you said yesterday. About what to do with your money.'

'Ah. Yes. Any ideas?'

'Well, there's lots of poor people.'

Scrooge sighed. 'Yes, indeed there are.'

Billy stopped walking and nodded towards the other side of the street. 'Like her, fr'instance.'

Scrooge stopped too, and noticed that on the opposite side of the street a badly dressed woman sat curled up in a doorway. Every item of her clothing was dark in colour, mostly black, and the hem of her skirt was darker still, wet from the slush. In her arms the woman was holding a baby.

Scrooge had seen this woman before. Seen her on Christmas Eve, to be precise, in the court below his apartment, but he had taken little notice. She was pre-sumably young, or she would not have had a young child, but Scrooge could tell that she was prematurely old. Even from a distance he could see that she had the deep-set eyes of one who is half-starved. She wasn't exactly begging – perhaps she was too proud, or too scared to be overt about it – but as each passer-by approached she looked at him hopefully, as if expecting to meet, one day, someone who would surely save her life.

'You can spare her a bit, Mr Scrooge,' said Billy. 'Can't you?'

Scrooge suddenly felt as if he had been struck across the face. It was as much as he could do not to cry out. He had to reach for the wall behind him for support. His chest became constricted, and he gasped for breath. But he knew he had to reply.

'Yes, yes, you are quite right, Billy,' he managed to stutter. 'I can spare her something.' He unbuttoned his overcoat, and produced a sovereign from his jacket pocket. 'Here – nip across the road and give her this.'

'Cor, thanks!' said Billy. His eyes opened wide in response to the high value of the coin, and in an instant he had seized it and run over to the woman. Scrooge saw him hand over the money and then point back to indicate its source.

The woman staggered to her feet and raised a hand to him. A bare hand it was, spare, thin as paper, blue from the snow and the cold.

'God bless you, sir!' she called. 'God bless you.'

Scrooge walked on. Well, not so much walked as stumbled, his eyes blurred, head down, just able to see that he did not fall over his own feet.

Billy soon caught up with him, breathless and delighted. 'There, see, that was a good thing to do with your money. And you can afford it, Mr Scrooge, can't you?'

Scrooge could barely speak, hardly breathe. 'Yes, yes,' he gasped. The word came out as he exhaled, for he was struggling to find the strength.

After another half a street he had regained some of his composure, and he was able to glance down at Billy, who was trotting along beside him.

'The trouble is, Billy,' he said, 'there are a lot of poor people in London. And a lot more in the industrial north. Believe me, I have seen them. And for that matter there is grinding poverty in the countryside too. If I gave a pound to each and every one of those people, my money would soon be gone, but none of them would be all that much better off. So while I do not begrudge that poor woman my money, Billy, I'm not sure that's the answer.'

10

When Scrooge arrived back at his office he was told that a letter had been delivered by hand. A young woman had brought it, Cratchit said.

Scrooge opened the envelope and discovered that it contained a note from Mrs Bannister, the local Vicar's wife. Would he care to call on her for coffee, at about ten-thirty a.m.? Today.

Well, normally Scrooge would have despatched such a note to the waste-paper basket in short order. 'Humbug!' he would have said. Social frippery and time-wasting! Ignore it. Get back to work! Why should a man of business take coffee with a lady, when he should be marching ever onward, earning ever more and more pounds – pounds to be spent on.... Well, spent on what?

Yes, that was the problem. The old Scrooge would have had no truck with such an invitation. But the new Scrooge was a somewhat different man. He sighed when he read the note, and sat down heavily at his desk.

He remembered Mrs Bannister very well from their meeting on Christmas Day. He remembered her sister too, the widow of Pewsey. Both of them were well-rounded, good-looking women, and Scrooge was not immune to the charms of such ladies. If truth were told, he was rather fond of their company. It was just that, in the past, there had been more pressing matters to attend to than taking coffee with them of a morning. There was always money to be made if a man was on the spot, in the 'Change, ears pricked

83

and eyes wary.

Although tempted, the new Scrooge was still cautious about accepting this invitation. To begin with, there was the question of what the lady wanted. For she would assuredly want something: she was not inviting him round to her house just because she liked the cut of his jib. Dear me no. Respectable ladies who were married to vicars did not indulge in dalliance. Especially not with elderly and not very prepossessing bachelors, even if they were well heeled. So if he accepted a cup or two of Mrs Bannister's coffee he would undoubtedly be stung for some good cause or other.

Scrooge sighed again, and hesitated. But then he thought, well, dammit, why not? I can afford it.

He put his hat and coat back on and moved into the outer office.

'Going out,' he called to Cratchit and Billy. 'Won't be long.'

The Reverend Mr Bannister's vicarage was a modest town-house. It was part of a terrace located quite close to the church, and it was no different on the outside from a score of other houses in the street.

Scrooge rang the doorbell and was admitted by a maid. Pretty girl. Called him by his name too, so she had evidently been briefed to expect him. Sure of herself, this Mrs Bannister.

The maid led the way down the short hall and showed Scrooge into one of the front rooms.

Mrs Bannister was there already. She rose to greet him and they exchanged the usual pleasantries.

While Scrooge was following his hostess's suggestion that he should make himself comfortable, he made a quick and discreet survey of his surroundings.

This was a lady's room, by the look of it – the female equivalent of a man's study. There were bits of sewing scattered here and there; a table which evidently functioned as a desk, with correspondence upon it; and a good warm fire. The chairs were well cushioned, and the two windows were tall and wide, with almost dazzling light reflected up from the street outside.

'Just the pair of us, then?' enquired Scrooge, when he was seated.

Mrs Bannister smiled. 'Just us two, Mr Scrooge. Do you feel the need of a chaperone?'

Scrooge smiled back. 'I think our reputations will survive intact without one.'

Mrs Bannister came straight to the point. 'Mr Scrooge, I understand from Mr Redmayne that when he called on you yesterday afternoon, you gave him a most generous cheque in support of his charitable work.'

Ah yes. Redmayne. The plump fellow.

'Yes, I believe I did,' said Scrooge. 'It made me hand tremble something shocking, but I managed to sign the cheque in the end. After my clerk had assured me I could afford it. Several times. I was rude to Redmayne on Christmas Eve, do you see. He called on me then with a friend, another portly fellow, and I'm afraid I was less than polite. So when I saw him later, in the street, I apologised and said I would make good my omission. Which I did.'

'Good. Splendid.'

'I suppose the word has now got around that Scrooge has gone soft in his old age and is an easy touch.'

'No, no,' said Mrs Bannister slowly. 'No, I would not say that. In fact, the word is that you are seldom a generous donor.'

'Correct.'

'But why not? You are a Christian.'

'I wouldn't call myself a Christian.'

'You came to church.'

'True. But then I've walked into a stable from time to time, and that doesn't make me a horse.'

Immediately Scrooge regretted his sharp tone.

'I'm sorry,' he said. 'I apologise for that uncalled-for remark.'

Mrs Bannister laughed good-humouredly. 'Never fear, Mr Scrooge. Your reputation for plain speaking has preceded you.'

'In any case,' Scrooge continued, 'what I say is true. I was brought up in the Church of England, as you would expect, but when I was a youth I began to have doubts about religion, and nowadays I believe scarcely a word of it.'

Mrs Bannister smiled again, which took Scrooge somewhat by surprise. 'Perhaps it is just that you have not yet found the right religion,' she suggested.

Before Scrooge could reply to that, there was a knock on the door and the maid came in to serve them coffee.

There was a pause in the conversation while the maid carried out her duties. She was a girl of about sixteen, fair-haired with blue eyes, and it was Scrooge's impression that she looked at him very directly, as if anxious to discern what sort of a man it was who was taking refreshment with her mistress. Could he be entirely trusted? Was he a suitable sort of companion? Was her mistress safe with him? Those seemed to be the questions she was asking herself, and her eyes were frank and faintly alarming.

Scrooge distracted himself by taking a closer look at his hostess.

Mrs Bannister was in her mid-thirties, he estimated.

Well dressed, but without ostentation. She had no airs and graces, and indeed had the look of a woman who was quite willing to undertake domestic chores from time to time. On a table beside her was some sewing work in progress, and Scrooge sensed that, had she not thought it discourteous, she would have carried on with her sewing while talking to him.

When the maid had left the room, Scrooge decided to take a direct approach himself. 'Tell me, Mrs Bannister, why have you invited me to see you? The church roof, is it? Or is there some other scheme which requires support?'

Mrs Bannister evidently took no offence at the suggestion that she had an ulterior motive. 'I have no immediate request to make of you, Mr Scrooge. But on Christmas Day, when we spent some time together at your nephew's house, I formed the impression that you were in need of someone to talk to.'

Scrooge was astonished.

'Talk to?'

'Yes.'

'What about?'

'Mr Scrooge, one can see at a glance that you are a troubled man. A man who is dissatisfied with his life, and is thinking of change.'

Scrooge gave a nervous laugh. 'How on earth can you tell that?'

'I was born on Halloween, and therefore have the second sight. Well known for it. Besides, reading people's minds from their faces is a gift that runs in my family. My sister, who is a witch, is even better at it than I. We can see things which others are blind to.'

Scrooge assumed that all this was a joke, and he chuckled politely. But Mrs Bannister was serious.

'Come now. Is it or is it not the case that you are wrestling with a problem? Something which perturbs you. Which causes you to sigh and frown so severely, and disturbs your sleep.'

This was so perceptive an analysis of his situation that Scrooge found himself quite unable to dissemble.

'Well, yes,' he mumbled. 'Yes, since you put it to me so plainly, I have to agree, that is pretty much my position.'

At first he was disinclined to say more, to be as taciturn and surly as usual. But then he thought, well dammit, in for a penny, in for a pound. If he did not talk to this lady he would soon feel the need to talk to someone else.

'It is true,' he began haltingly, 'that in these past few months I have come to understand that I don't want to go on as I am. I am not really very good at putting my feelings into words, ma'am, but I have been thinking about my future for some time. Since my fiftieth birthday, in fact. And it has made me bad-tempered – more than usually bad-tempered – and I have found myself dreaming peculiar dreams. At Christmas-time the whole thing seemed to come to a head. All that goodwill to all men stuff – I can't tell you how irritating I found it. And then I remembered Marley, my old business partner, for he died on Christmas Eve, do you see, seven years ago. And I knew for sure that I did not want to die as Marley did. He was a very rich man, yet he died alone. And miserable. He was known to all as foul-tempered, stingy, and mean. In his last year or two he found no satisfaction in anything, not even his work. And there was not a friend at his funeral, save me.'

'A nasty fate,' agreed Mrs Bannister. 'So you are unhappy, Mr Scrooge.'

Scrooge couldn't quite accept that. 'Not *un*happy, I would say, as such. But not happy, either. For many years my work was sufficient to fill my day, and to give me a sense of purpose. But now.... Now the work no longer seems enough.'

Mrs Bannister poured him another cup of coffee.

'Tell me about your work.'

The old Scrooge would have snarled back. Without even trying to be polite he would have told the lady to mind her own business. But today he paused, gathered his thoughts, and sought to summarise his activities in as brief a form as he could.

'These days,' he said, 'I deal almost entirely in money. In former years, when Marley and I first started together, we bought and sold goods. Had a warehouse to store them in. But as the years passed, and certainly since Marley died, I have got rid of all that, and today I simply buy and sell money.'

'You will have to be a little more precise. For we vicars' wives know little of the world of commerce.'

Scrooge was beginning to doubt that, but he willingly explained.

'The way it works is like this. For part of each working day, I sit in the Royal Exchange, and men of business come and talk to me, much as I am talking to you now. They seek support for a business – either an existing business or a new one which they intend to start. They tell me a story, show me papers and plans. And they ask me to lend them money to create or extend that business. I either say yes, or no. If I say yes, we discuss terms. How much money do they want, and how long for? And at what rate of interest, for there must be interest – that is society's decision, not mine. Other cultures do not permit usury, but ours does. And what security can they offer for the loan? For there must be security – again, that is society's decision, not mine alone.

It is a custom and practice of the world of business as a whole.'

'And is it your own money that you lend?'

'Some of it is, but not all, by any means. Over the years I have acquired some reputation as a man of good judgement. So there are certain individuals and certain institutions which have authorised me to act on their behalf. From them I can borrow money at a lower rate than it would be available to others. And I therefore have a high responsibility to those lenders, for they in turn look after the interests of some vulnerable members of society – the widows and orphans.'

'And if you approve the business plans that are put to you, what then?'

Scrooge moved rapidly on. He was at ease now, dealing with matters which were second nature to him.

'Well, when all the details are settled, the loan is made and business commences. And that is the basis on which our national welfare rests, of course. It rests on the efforts of businessmen and manufacturers, buying and selling and creating wealth. So in my darkest hours I remind myself that the work which I do is worthwhile work. A serious and thoughtful man might call it moral and noble work, though to hear some speak you would think it was a form of robbery.'

'These loans that you make – are they long-term or short-term?'

Interesting question from a woman, thought Scrooge. But then, the more he spoke to her, the more unusual and the better-informed this lady appeared.

'I never lend for more than three years, and often for less. And with luck, and much hard work and effort, each business that I support will prosper, the loan will be repaid, and the cycle begins again.'

Mrs Bannister thought for a moment. 'And what if the business does not prosper?'

'Why then I must call in the security that was offered.'

'And it is this, I suppose – this calling-in of security as you describe it – which has created your reputation as a hard man of business, Mr Scrooge.'

Once again, Scrooge was taken aback to find that a vicar's wife should appear to know so much of his reputation. Judging by her comment, she had heard him spoken of in less than complimentary terms. But he struggled to give a reasoned reply.

'Yes, indeed,' he admitted. 'If I have, as you say, as reputation as a hard man – and I would like to think that I have a reputation as a *fair* man – then that is its source. But I make no apology for it. I have to be able to function. When repayments are due, I demand repayment. If I advance the capital for a venture, and the venture fails, despite my hopes and the best efforts of the entrepreneur, then I need that capital back to finance other and better schemes. That is in society's interest as well as my own.'

'And for that some call you hard.'

'So be it. But I am no harder than life. This morning, for example, my doctor told me about a young man who had died unexpectedly. Now that is a bitter blow for his wife and family. It is unforeseen, unexpected. But my blows, if blows they be, are seen far off. They arise from arrangements freely made and willingly entered into. A man who borrows from me or through me knows what to expect. He knows my reputation or he would not come to me. I may, as you say, have a reputation as a hard man, but I am also known as a good judge of a business proposition. If I refuse a plan, the applicant knows that his proposal is flawed. It gives him reason to rethink his ideas. And that advice comes free.'

'I see. So much for what you do, Mr Scrooge, and have been doing for many years. But what is it about this situation that troubles you?'

'Ah. Well now.' Scrooge leaned back in his chair. 'What troubles me is that the work has ceased to be interesting. Ceased to be rewarding, in and of itself. For many years it was a satisfaction and a pleasure to use my wits in the world of business – to pick winners and reject losers. I revelled in my work, Mrs Bannister, revelled in it. Weekends were a tedious interruption – holidays unthinkable. And the profit and loss account provided a handy measure of how well or how badly I was doing. It was a measure of how far I was fulfilling my ambition. And, please note, the account was a measure not of personal greed, but of how far I was able to help others and benefit the community. But now – well, somehow, the work has lost its relish. Now, it seems to be just the same old thing, day after day.'

'But what else can you do with your time?'

'Exactly. You are very percipient. For the truth is, I have no other interests. What is more, I have built up a considerable sum in capital – my own money, and the money which was left to me by Marley – and if I do not continue to operate as a money broker then I have to ask myself what is to be done with it.'

'So we are back to charity and philanthropy, are we?'

Scrooge sighed yet again and immediately asked forgiveness for doing so.

'I apologise for seeming impatient. The question is a fair one, a proper one, and I should not appear to be irritated by it. Yes, indeed, we are back to the possibility of charity, and philanthropy. But it is against my instincts just to hand

92

over money without much thought of how it is to be used. As I have explained to you, my whole life has been involved in investing, and that, I think, is what I wish to continue to do, but in a different way. For instance, within the last few days I have made the acquaintance of a young boy.'

'Billy.'

'Yes, Billy.' At this stage in the conversation he was not remotely surprised that she knew the name. 'When I came across him, Billy was homeless and jobless, and without help he would probably have come to a bad end. But with the assistance of my housekeeper and clerk I have picked this boy off the streets. I have bathed him, clothed him, had him checked over by a doctor, and have given him a modest job at a modest wage. That is an investment, Mrs Bannister. An investment, if you will, in human capital. And I think I could be persuaded to do more of the same.'

Mrs Bannister nodded and seemed very thoughtful. 'It is as I suspected, Mr Scrooge. You have acted in respect of the boy in much the same way as I have acted in regard to some girls. And like all investments, some succeed better than others. But is it true to say that, subject to certain qualifications, you are no longer a man in search of good businesses, but a man in search of good works which require financial support?'

Scrooge thought about it. 'Subject to qualifications – yes.'

Mrs Bannister nodded. 'Good....'

She picked up a little bell and tinkled it to call for the maid.

'Well, this has been a most productive morning, Mr Scrooge. I will speak to my husband, and ask him to show you a number of good causes which are close to his heart, and which are in dire need of assistance. You are under no obligation, of course, but at least it will demonstrate to you the range of possibilities.'

Scrooge prepared to leave, but as he stood up Mrs Bannister put her hand on his arm.

'Pay close attention to my maid, Mr Scrooge. Her name is Sasha, and I have a number of plans for her future.' She gave him one of her puzzling smiles. 'Some of them involve you.'

11

The following Monday, after breakfast, Scrooge informed Billy that he was going to look round a school. Would Billy like to come along too?

'What sort of a school is it?'

'It's a school for poor boys.'

'Is that where you're going to send me?'

'Not unless you want to go there....'

Scrooge paused, for he could see that his announcement had made Billy cautious and suspicious.

'Look here, Billy, I give you my word that you will go nowhere unless you are comfortable with it. But I'd like you see to see this place – I'd like to hear your opinion of it.'

Billy frowned darkly. 'Hm, well, all right then.'

The snow had disappeared over the weekend, though some filthy dark slush remained. Scrooge and Billy had to pick their way carefully as they walked round to the Reverend Mr Bannister's home. There the three of them hailed a cab and climbed in, and immediately Billy cheered up.

'I ain't never been in a cab before,' he told them, and was clearly impressed by the quality of the fittings and the padded seat.

Scrooge was pleased that the boy could derive pleasure from something so simple, but he made a mental note to give Billy some instruction about avoiding double negatives.

The Vicar, meanwhile, began to brief Scrooge about their

destination.

'This school, Mr Scrooge, scarcely merits the title in the sense that you and I would understand it. It consists of three rooms in a rotting old house which is in urgent need of repair. In one room girls are taught, and in the other two, boys.'

'Ages?'

'From five until as long as they will stay, which isn't much past ten. At that age there is paid work which they or their parents can find, and the temptation of taking it in preference to school becomes too strong. Neither would I wish to give you the impression that attendance at the school is regular. The pupils come and they go, much like migrant birds.'

'And the teaching is done by whom?' asked Scrooge.

'It is done by volunteers. The headmaster, or the person in charge would perhaps be a better title, is an Oxford friend of mine. His name is John Kemble. He is ordained but does not wear clerical dress or hold office. Happily he has both private means and a strong social conscience. And in running his school he is aided by a number of parish ladies, several of them taking turn and turn about.'

After about fifteen minutes, heading north, the cab moved from the main thoroughfare on which it had been travelling into a dark and dingy side-street. There the way was narrow, the air full of smoke and strange smells, and the inhabitants, such as could be seen from the cab, were shabbily dressed. It was a place of marked poverty, and although such a scene was far from unfamiliar to Scrooge, he did not enjoy being reacquainted with it.

The cab stopped outside a tall building with broken and missing railings which had originally been designed to prevent passers-by from falling into the basement; but the temptation to sell the metal had evidently been too strong for someone.

As he stepped down from the cab, Scrooge could hear the sound of children's voices chanting the multiplication tables in unison.

'Two twos are four, three twos are six, four twos are eight....'

By the sound of it, perhaps twenty or thirty children were involved.

A group of local residents surrounded the visitors as soon as they closed the cab door behind them. The arrival of a couple of toffs who might well be persuaded to part with the loose change in their pockets was a welcome development. But, despite several entreaties, both Scrooge and the Vicar went into the building without appearing to hear the requests for alms.

Billy followed the two men, to the jeers of a few boys of his own age.

The Vicar led the way to the back of the building, where he pushed open a door into one of the 'schoolrooms'. In reality this was no more than a modest-sized space, once the back parlour of a family home perhaps, when both the street in general and this house in particular had enjoyed better days.

On the floor were five benches with five or six children seated on each. And a curious assortment of children they were too. Ages, Scrooge guessed, from five to eight. Clothing, various rags and hand-me-downs. Expressions, wide-eyed and seemingly eager to please.

No source of heating met Scrooge's eye, and because of the cold outside the two windows were both closed. The smell of the unwashed poor was strong in the air, but the atmosphere was chilly despite the tightly packed presence of so many bodies.

Neither could Scrooge see evidence of any form of lighting, and the room was both gloomy and drab. Damp stains were visible in each corner of the ceiling, and in places the plaster was falling down. If there were no rats visible, it was only because there was scarcely room for them among the feet under the benches.

The master in charge, who was no doubt Mr Bannister's Oxford friend, smiled a greeting at them as they entered but went on leading the chant.

'We will go as far as the five times table,' he announced over the last of the four times table, 'and then pause. 'Now, one five is five....'

His obedient flock took up the cry. 'One five is five, two fives are ten, three fives are fifteen...'

When it was over, the teacher set the children some work on their slates. Scrooge noticed that the school could not provide a slate for each child. Not even one between two. But the children formed little clusters around such facilities as were available and got on with the task as best they could.

The teacher was then introduced to Scrooge and Billy.

John Kemble was about thirty-five, Scrooge guessed, taller than average, and burly with it. This was a circumstance which no doubt stood him in good stead when it came to dealing with trouble-makers, and Scrooge had no doubt that there would be a fair number in this district. He had fierce eyes, a dark beard, and a full head of dark, thick hair. His clothes were respectable, but he was obviously unconcerned about his personal appearance.

Mr Kemble gave his visitors a quick tour of the whole house, which involved calling on the two other schoolrooms on the floor above. He could not, he explained, be away from his own class for too long. They had a pronounced tendency to drift away if left unattended.

At midday, said Mr Kemble, there would be a break, with soup and bread provided for the children. This, he well knew, was often the chief motive for their presence in the first place. That plus the fact that a child in school was a child who did not need the care of a parent.

Mr Kemble was a patently good-hearted man, doing his best to improve the lot of the poor, and Scrooge took to him. More than that, Scrooge admired the fellow for sticking at a task which he himself could not have stomached for one morning.

In answer to Scrooge's question, Mr Kemble declared that he had been running the school for three years. But he seemed oddly shy with a stranger, and did not volunteer much more.

Scrooge asked how an injection of money might be used. Better equipment was the immediate answer. And uniforms for the children. This latter suggestion struck Scrooge as a hideous idea. He could just picture the ranks of identical little bodies lined up on the benches. True fodder for the factories of the industrial revolution. But he made no comment. Presumably Mr Kemble had made his suggestion about uniforms for a good reason.

The smell of food – no doubt the soup referred to earlier – was now percolating into the schoolroom and causing a certain amount of noisy speculation among the class. Although he had not been there long, Scrooge realised that his presence was a distraction, and so without further ado he took out bank-book, borrowed the teacher's pen and ink, and wrote a cheque for £100.

The Reverend Mr Bannister smiled warmly as he looked over Scrooge's shoulder, but Mr Kemble was visibly shaken when he saw the size of Scrooge's gift.

'Why, my dear sir,' he said, in a voice made gruff with emotion. 'How very generous.' He shook Scrooge's hand with almost painful violence. 'I cannot tell you how useful this will be.'

Scrooge waved a hand. 'I can see for myself that you will put it to good use. And now, Mr Kemble, we must remove ourselves from your presence and allow your work to continue.'

Scrooge, Mr Bannister, and Billy made their way back to the main thoroughfare at the end of the street. Their passage was not without difficulty, because word of a toff with money seemed to have spread. Only a handout of coins from Scrooge plus a few stern words from the Vicar enabled them to complete the short journey without having the clothes almost torn from their backs.

They were assisted too by the fact that the Vicar carried a silver-handled stick. Scrooge had thought of it as the man's sole concession to fashion and vanity, but he realised now that from time to time it might have a more practical use.

At last they found themselves seated in a cab, taking them back to the relative safety of St Michael's Alley and St Andrew's church.

Scrooge leaned back as the cab jolted along. He closed his eyes. He was no longer at all sure that it was a good idea to have accepted the Vicar's invitation to show him some worthy causes. But his wasn't the only opinion to be considered, of course.

'Well, Billy,' he said. 'What did you think of the school?'

Billy literally shuddered. 'Horrible,' he muttered. 'Horrible! The children was all younger than me, too. I can't go there.'

'No, you can't,' Scrooge agreed. He also agreed with Billy's description of the place as horrible, but he didn't want to upset the Vicar by voicing it.

He turned to his guide.

'I may well be able to help in providing some financial support for places like that,' he said. 'But I can't say that I liked the atmosphere. It seemed very regimented.'

Mr Bannister nodded. 'I take your point. But I would ask you to accept that my friend John Kemble may well have started out with very different ideas. Indeed I know that he did. But he is a man who for three years has had to wrestle with the practicalities of the situation. And what you have seen today is a demonstration of what he has found, by trial and error, to be both possible and useful. John is a wonderful man, but he is no good at raising cash because he is too impatient to be tactful and never prepared to flatter. And if you are going to practise philanthropy, Mr Scrooge, you are going to have to learn to distinguish between the charlatan, the fake, and the man who genuinely deserves support. John Kemble is one of the latter.'

'I don't doubt it,' said Scrooge. 'And I admire him for it. If he is ever desperate for funds in the future you may approach me again, and your word alone will be enough. But I believe that tomorrow you have something different to show me?'

Mr Bannister nodded. 'Different, and yet, in a way, the same.'

12

The following morning found the same three companions – Scrooge, Billy, and the Reverend Mr Bannister seated side by side in another cab. This time they were heading east.

They travelled as far as the cab-driver was able to take them, which is to say to the point at which a narrow side-street became blocked by rubbish and rubble. As they stepped down from the cab they realised that there had been a fire in this neighbourhood, probably within the last few days. A strong smell of smoke was still in the air.

On the left of the narrow roadway – which was more like an alley – the bare bones of a brick-built house reached upwards into a lowering, dirty-grey sky. Blackened, useless wood clung to the doorway and the window-frames of this house. Any timber worth stealing had long since gone, but no one had bothered to clear up the aftermath of the fire. There were piles of smelly, scorched material which had once, perhaps, been clothes, curtains and carpets; and a mixture of broken tiles and smashed glass littered the pavement.

With a brief glance at the devastation caused by the fire, the two men and Billy set off to complete their journey on foot.

They were now in territory through which Billy moved with more confidence than either of the two men. He led the way, picking the safest path through the debris, his eyes ever alert to danger.

At one point, someone lurking behind a half-closed door hurled a lump of brick at them. But Billy spotted it coming and pushed Scrooge aside. The missile hit a wall and scattered into fragments at their feet.

They hurried along as best they could, conscious of the enquiring eyes of those who leaned idly against walls or peered out from dirty windows. The watchers evidently wondered, and some of them enquired out loud, what business it was that well-dressed fellows like these had in a place like this.

The answer was, they were in search of a hostel: a house of refuge, which was run by another friend of Mr Bannister's. The hostel was a place where those who were too poor to rent a room in even the dingiest hovel might find shelter from the winter night.

As they walked along, for they still had a way to go, Mr Bannister enlarged on the explanation which he had given to Scrooge before they set out.

'As you can see, Mr Scrooge, this is as deprived an area as we are likely to find, even in the east end of London. There is nothing here but ignorance, starvation and crime.'

'So I see,' said Scrooge grimly.

The Vicar, he noticed, held his stick halfway along its length, so as to be able to use it as a club in short order, if the need arose.

'And it is precisely for those reasons,' Mr Bannister continued, 'that my friend has selected it as the location for his hostel for homeless men.'

'This friend of yours,' said Scrooge, 'is he another Oxford man?'

Mr Bannister smiled. 'No. A former companion from my schooldays.'

At length they turned a corner and came upon a

courtyard with what had once been an impressive doorway at the end of it. Now, however, the entrance to the formerly handsome mansion was much dilapidated. The steps were cracked and crumbling, the lintel was tipped sideways at a crazy angle, and the paint was peeling off the door. Still fixed to the door was a heavy lion's-head knocker. It had been protected from theft, Scrooge suspected, only by the fact that it was black with age and looked worthless.

In the court below this doorway stood two men: one a uniformed police constable, and the other a slightly-built, pale-faced fellow in a dark suit. The latter was clearly a gentleman of sorts, his general bearing quite different from that of the average citizen of this quarter.

As Mr Bannister's party approached, the suited man turned to look at them, and then gave a cry of recognition.

'Henry!' he declared. 'What a pleasure it is to see you!'

He advanced to shake Mr Bannister's hand, but then, almost at once, he had to excuse himself to complete his business with the constable. That done, the policeman departed and introductions were made.

The name of Mr Bannister's friend was Peter Carrow, and he immediately asked forgiveness for not having been able to give them his attention sooner.

'But there was, I regret to say, an incident overnight which has of necessity involved the police.'

'May I ask what kind of incident?' Scrooge enquired.

Mr Carrow sighed, but answered openly. 'That is a very proper and natural question, sir. But the fact is, this house contains some thirty to forty men of a night, and there are often squabbles between them. On this occasion – ' He sighed again. 'On this occasion I regret to say that a knife was drawn. One man was killed, and his attacker fled into the night.'

Scrooge was astonished. 'A murder,' he said. 'If I may state the obvious.'

'Yes indeed,' said Mr Carrow sadly. 'A murder. Not an everyday event, even here, but far from uncommon. News of it will not appear in *The Times*, or in any other paper for that matter, for it lacks the sensational aspects required to fascinate the masses. But it has deprived all of us of much sleep and has greatly disturbed my men.'

With that, Mr Carrow made a determined attempt to lighten the mood. He banged his hands together, as if to signify the end of that discussion.

'Well,' he said brightly, 'you have not come here to be shocked with tales of the desperate doings of some villain. You have come, have you not, to have a look round our modest premises and to hear of the work which we try to do.'

'We have indeed,' said Scrooge.

Mr Carrow led the way on a tour of the house. He was a man in his early thirties, and he was suffering, Scrooge noticed, from a heavy cold, which appeared to make him somewhat deaf. He made frequent use of a handkerchief.

The building turned out to be more spacious on the inside than it appeared from the outside. It had been built, Scrooge estimated, about a hundred and fifty years earlier, possibly for a rich merchant, for it lay near to some docks.

Mr Carrow explained that, under his direction, the present purpose of the house was to provide free overnight accommodation for men (and only men) who would otherwise be obliged to sleep rough, in the street. At seven a.m. in the mornings, bread and tea were made available, at no charge; thereafter the men were obliged to leave the building and try to find work. The whole enterprise was financed by charity, and no man was allowed to stay for more than seven nights in succession.

Downstairs, a front room had been set aside as a reception and waiting area. Another room, much smaller, provided an office for Mr Carrow. At the rear of the premises was a communal eating-room, with a substantial kitchen adjoining.

Upstairs, the principal rooms had been converted to dormitories, with some ten to twelve beds in each, tightly crammed together. In one room, a bed was occupied by a man too sick even to raise his head. Mr Carrow had a quiet word with him and promised to send someone with some soup before long.

'And are you fully occupied each night?' asked Scrooge.

Mr Carrow laughed shortly. 'More than fully. And there are those who would wish to stay for a month, if they could. For the more pathetic of them I sometimes bend the rules, but if I do so it causes disputes. And any man who owns even a decent pair of boots is likely to have them stolen unless he is careful. That, I understand, was the cause of last night's death.'

After the tour Scrooge gladly accepted the offer of a cup of tea in the kitchen at the rear of the house.

As he sat and listened to Mr Bannister and his friend talking over the problems of running the hostel, Scrooge groaned inwardly and tried not to feel depressed. But how could he not be depressed by circumstances such as these?

He was sitting in a dark, decaying mansion, full of the ghosts of a no doubt glamorous and glittering past. But now, in this kitchen where once there had been a blazing hearth, the air was freezing cold, the walls were cracked and peeling, and much of the woodwork was scarred and rotted.

106

Through the window, the sky was dark blue with the threat of rain or worse. Beyond, in the street, he could hear the cries of young boys bickering over some pathetic trophy, an apple core or a slice of bread perhaps. And across the table from him was an earnest, dedicated young man who had apparently decided to devote his life to helping those who had fallen to the very bottom of the pit of poverty.

Scrooge yearned to be gone, and he signified his wish, silently, by taking out his cheque book. This was a process which, he had noticed, usually secured the attention of others present in a room, and so it proved in this case. Mr Carrow stopped talking to the Vicar, and asked whether there was anything else which Scrooge wished to know, or to see.

'No,' said Scrooge. 'Nothing else. I salute you, Mr Carrow, for your nobility in undertaking this work. It is work which I could never do in a thousand years. I can assist you in no way other than by providing money, and that I gladly do. I can, after all, afford it. Can't I, Billy?'

'You can, sir,' grinned Billy. 'You can afford it definite.'

A pen and ink were hastily provided, and Scrooge wrote his second cheque for £100 in two days. Effusive thanks were offered.

In the cab, on the way home, Scrooge was quiet again, but eventually he asked Mr Bannister to tell him something more about Mr Carrow's background.

'He is somewhat younger than myself, Mr Scrooge. He was junior to me at school but I knew him slightly. In his twenties he took up missionary work in Africa, but his health broke down and he was forced to return home. When he recovered, he decided to take up the work which you have seen.'

107

'How long did you say he had been at it?'

'About five years.'

'And how long will he be able to continue, do you think?'

The Vicar pursed his lips. 'Not for ever, certainly. It is work which drains the energy from a man's soul. But your money will help, Mr Scrooge. Your money will help.'

The day of Scrooge's visit to the men's hostel was in fact New Year's Eve, and that evening Scrooge took his house-keeper, Mrs Molloy, and Billy out to dinner. He chose a tavern which provided excellent fare and clean linen, but which was not so sophisticated that his guests would feel ill at ease.

Scrooge liked a good wine with his meal, but Mrs Molloy, with her inevitable giggle, reminded him that she had signed the pledge years ago.

'Though I likes to go in pubs,' she said. 'I likes the chat, do you see, and I tells fortunes with the cards, for a penny.'

'Will you tell mine?' asked Scrooge.

'Oh yes.' Mrs Molloy fairly cackled.

'I'll give you sixpence.'

'Oh, it won't cost you anything, sir. I done yours already, Mr Scrooge. I does yours fairly reg'lar, so as to be sure I'm still in a job.' This last remark caused her so much mirth that she almost doubled up.

'And what does my future hold?'

'Ah.' Mrs Molloy tapped the side of her nose with a finger, a most mysterious gesture. 'That would be telling.'

'Well, I can tell you what I've been doing in the recent past,' said Scrooge, and he described to her the visits he had made in the last two days.

'Why,' said Mrs Molloy, 'if you are seeking to help the

poor and needy, Mr Scrooge, you will spend your whole life at it and never reach the end. If the poor was to form a line it would stretch all around the world.'

Scrooge nodded sadly. 'That is rather the conclusion I have reached myself,' he said.

After their meal the three of them went out into the streets. The occasion being what it was, the pavements were full of revellers, many of them none too sober. Lamps shone in the windows of every house, and streetlights powered by gas flared brightly at intervals along the pavements.

In a square near the Bank of England they found a substantial crowd gathered; many of those present were eminently respectable residents of the high-class property nearby, but there were numbers of serving-girls and apprentices mixed among them, together with tradesmen, housewives, and no doubt pickpockets and knaves as well.

To serve all these new-year celebrants there were food stalls and sideshows set up, just for the occasion. There were jugglers and men on stilts; girls with trays of matches; costermongers selling fruit even at this hour; and the baked-potato men offered cheap hot grub on a cold frosty night.

Three separate groups of street musicians paraded up and down, and people sang along to the tunes they played. Some of them, Scrooge noticed, were regrettably vulgar versions of well-known songs, but Mrs Molloy and Billy seemed to know them all, rude words included, and joined in heartily.

In past years, on this very night, Scrooge would have been in bed long since. 'Humbug!' he would have replied, to those who suggested that he might be out with friends. 'Why should I celebrate?' he would have snarled. 'It is just the end of yet another perfectly ordinary day.'

But now he found himself wandering the streets with two very odd companions – the one a mere boy who found everything a source of wonder and excitement, and the other an elderly lady who smiled constantly. He wondered, just now and then, how and why it was that he found himself in such company. But would he rather be anywhere else? No, he decided, he would not.

When midnight struck there were cheers on all sides. The church bells rang and complete strangers shook each other by the hand. Goodwill filled the air, and much to his surprise Scrooge found himself cheerful again, after a tiring day.

'A happy new year to you, Mrs Molloy,' he cried. And by golly he meant it.

'And to you,' chortled Mrs Molloy in reply. 'And I do reckon, you know, as how the new year is going to bring a good few changes in your life, Mr Scrooge. It's in the cards, my dear. In the cards.' And she laughed and laughed and laughed.

Now what, Scrooge thought, did she mean by that?

13

On the first of January, despite having been up late the night before, Scrooge was in his office at the usual time (for in those days New Year's Day was not a public holiday).

He had been at his desk for just over an hour when the Vicar knocked on his door and asked politely whether he had forgotten that they had arranged to go on another visit.

Scrooge leaned back in his chair and looked at the clock.

'No,' he said with a sigh, 'I had not forgotten. But I did mistake the time, Mr Bannister, and my apologies for that....'

He rose to his feet and came round to the front of his desk.

'The truth is, you see, I have not been looking forward to this third outing of ours. I must confess that what I have seen so far has left me feeling mighty depressed.'

The Vicar was quite unperturbed. 'Well, there is no compulsion on your part, of course. If you would rather we cancelled it...'

'No,' said Scrooge slowly. 'No, it is not so much a question of cancelling. I shall be quite happy to write you a cheque, and if me hand hesitates I am sure that Cratchit and Billy will remind me that I can afford it. But I am not sure that I have the heart to make yet another close acquaintance with grinding poverty and deprivation. What was it you had in mind to show me today?'

Mr Bannister smiled. 'Well, I think you will find it relatively painless. I have a friend who sings in my church

111

choir. He is a doctor, and holds a senior post in a children's hospital.'

'A doctor?'

'Yes.'

'In a hospital.'

'Yes.'

'And it is for children, you say?'

'That is correct, Mr Scrooge.'

Scrooge hesitated. 'Well,' he said, 'I am beginning to understand that there is no end to the good causes which you could take me to view, Mr Bannister. But perhaps, since children are involved, perhaps I ought to force myself to make yet one more visit. But this one will be the last, I think.'

'I understand,' said the Vicar.

Leaving Billy in the care of Cratchit this time, Scrooge and the Vicar set off as on the previous two days.

Within twenty minutes they had arrived at a large building in a more prosperous area than the ones they had ventured into in the past. The hospital was a tall, imposing edifice at one end of a square. In the centre of the square was a garden for the residents, and although the trees were black and wet at this time of year, they looked as if they would provide a pleasant refuge in summer.

Unlike the buildings to which the Vicar had taken Scrooge earlier, this one was in good repair, and as they went up the steps Scrooge noticed the name of it: Campbell Street Hospital for Sick Children.

Inside there were nurses, and one or two male staff, who wore uniforms and had a professional air about them. The corridors were decorated in pale colours, the floors were polished, and it was possible to breathe the air without being tempted to hold one's noise. Scrooge was impressed.

In due course, Scrooge was introduced to this third friend of the Vicar's, by name a Dr Benjamin Dearing. He was an amiable, friendly fellow, wearing a pair of rounded spectacles which gave him an owlish air. He beamed cheerfully at Scrooge, pumped his hand, and bade him welcome.

No doubt, Scrooge thought, Dr Dearing had been told that if he played his cards right the hospital might benefit from a handsome donation; but he would, Scrooge suspected, have been a friendly and outgoing man even without that happy prospect in front of him.

After the briefest of preliminaries the three men embarked on a rapid tour of the premises. They started at the top of the hospital and worked down, calling in on a number of wards on the way. Each ward was staffed by at least one nurse, and although Scrooge had expected to witness harrowing sights of dreadfully sick children, he found that a fair number of the young patients were evidently well on the way to recovery. The noise level was often high, little hands sometimes grasped his trouser leg, and round eyes stared up at him as piping voices demanded to know who he was.

'There are few experiences in this life which are worse than being the parent of a young child, and then to have that child taken away by illness and death,' Dr Dearing reminded Scrooge. 'But we do our best here to ensure that death and disease are defeated whenever possible.'

Scrooge could see that the doctor and his colleagues were very often succeeding in their objective. The building was warm, well lit, comfortable, and clean. In one room, the nurses had even organised a choir of small patients, grouped around a piano.

No doubt, from time to time, some of the patients were lost; but Scrooge could see for himself that a great number would survive their illness and be sent home before long to their rejoicing parents.

At the end of his tour, Scrooge congratulated his guide on being associated with such a splendid institution.

'It has never been my good fortune,' he said, 'to be the father of a child of my own. I was once engaged to be married, years ago, but it came to naught. However, if I were a father, and if my child fell ill, I can think of nowhere better to send him than here. Nowhere which could do a better job of saving his life, if it were at risk. And your hospital is, I take it, supported very largely by voluntary contributions?'

'Very largely,' agreed Dr Dearing.

'Allow me then,' said Scrooge, 'to give you a small donation.'

He wrote out a cheque for the same amount that he had given to the other two causes to which the Vicar had introduced him. He did think about making it a larger sum, but he decided that might be unfair.

On the way out, he came across a child, very young, sitting in a perambulator near the front door. The nurse in charge was talking to a colleague nearby.

On an impulse Scrooge leaned down and tickled the child under the chin. To be honest, he didn't know whether it was a girl or a boy, for the woollen bonnet and coloured blanket gave no real clue.

Scrooge's reward for a moment's cootchy-cootchy-cooing was a loud chuckle and a smile, revealing only two teeth.

Scrooge was so astonished that he laughed out loud.

'My word,' he said to the Vicar. 'It has been a long time

114

since a child smiled at me like that. Worth every penny of my cheque!'

As they rode home in a cab, Scrooge felt greatly relieved that he had seen sights which lessened, rather than deepened, his depression. And he was also cheered when the Vicar told him that he had no further visits in mind.

'I have shown you a selection of activities which are in real need of philanthropy, Mr Scrooge, and you have been kind enough to bear with me and to assist them with their funding. For that I am very grateful. But now that you have seen a cross-section of charitable bodies, so to speak, you are going to have to sit down and reflect upon the situation. If I understand our discussions correctly, you have a large amount of money at your disposal, and you are thinking of putting it to some use other than investment in commerce and industry. So you will have to ponder upon what you have seen, and come to some conclusion. In the meantime, if I can be of any further assistance, please don't hesitate to ask.'

Scrooge nodded but did not reply.

The Vicar was quite right, of course. He was going to have to think hard about what to do with his money.

14

Two days later, Scrooge was brought a second summons from Mrs Bannister, the Vicar's wife. Could he, she asked, see his way clear to calling upon her at three p.m. that afternoon?

Scrooge could, and did. But as he made his way to the vicarage he found himself wondering, with some trepidation, what it was that the lady had in mind to ask him this time.

A few minutes later, Scrooge was comfortably settled in Mrs Bannister's front room, in the same chair that he had occupied a week earlier.

When they were both seated, his hostess resumed her sewing and commenced to make small talk – or, to be precise, her own peculiar version of small talk.

'Tell me, Mr Scrooge,' she began, closely examining her stitches, 'have you kicked any good dogs lately?'

An earlier Scrooge might have been taken aback, but he was wise to the lady now. He had long since realised that she was seriously unorthodox in her manner, and he batted this ball straight back.

'Oh no,' he said equably. 'No, the dogs all slink off when they see me coming.'

'Indeed.' Mrs Bannister seemed unsurprised. 'And you have, I understand, seen something of the less fortunate side of life in the early part of this week?'

Scrooge acknowledged that this was correct, and they discussed the visits which he had made in the company of

Mr Bannister. And while that discussion was proceeding, the young maid, Sasha, came in with a trolley and served them cups of tea and fruit cake.

'As far as I can see,' said Scrooge, 'there is a sort of deep mine-shaft of suffering and poverty, into which one could pour the entire nation's resources and still not achieve a reasonable level of provision overall.'

Mrs Bannister thought for a moment. 'Yes, I think you are broadly right. But that is no reason or excuse for doing nothing. What we have to do, I would argue, is work away at the edges of the problem. Do one thing at a time. And improve the circumstances of one person at a time. Take your young lad Billy, for instance. I think you will agree that he has made much progress since you first set eyes on him. He is better in health, better dressed, and better mannered. He is better housed and fed.'

Scrooge nodded. 'Yes, true.'

Mrs Bannister remained silent for a few moments, while Sasha completed her duties. But when Sasha had left the room, Mrs Bannister put down her cup and turned to the matter which had caused her to invite Scrooge to meet her for a second time.

'You will remember, Mr Scrooge, that on the first occasion when you came here, I suggested that you might take note of my maid, young Sasha.'

'I do remember,' said Scrooge in a neutral tone.

'Well now, I have been making some enquiries about your circumstances, Mr Scrooge, and it seems to me that you are a single gentleman, possessed of a good fortune, and in pressing need of a maid of your own.'

'Am I?' Scrooge was genuinely surprised to be told this.

'Oh yes.'

'But I have a housekeeper, Mrs Molloy, who does all that

sort of thing for me. She does all my domestic work. And very well too.'

'Yes, you have Mrs Molloy, and she is a hard worker,' agreed Mrs Bannister. 'I know her well, and she and I have discussed the matter. But the fact is, Mr Scrooge, that the building you live in, and which you expect Mrs Molloy to keep clean and tidy all on her own, is far too big for one person to manage. And besides, Mrs Molloy is no longer as young as she was. The lady naturally gives you first priority, since you are her employer, but I think you will acknowledge that your tenants complain regularly that she is not able to give them the service which they expect.'

'Oh well,' said Scrooge, 'tenants always complain. It is in their nature.'

'No doubt. But the fact remains, Mrs Molloy would dearly love to have a young assistant. And, as it so happens, Sasha has been with me quite long enough now, and it is time she went to another household, to put into practice the skills that I have taught her.'

Mrs Bannister gave him a beaming smile, and Scrooge knew that he was doomed. If Mrs Bannister and Mrs Molloy had been colluding behind his back, then there was no chance whatever that he would be able to undo such arrangements as they had jointly agreed.

'So,' Mrs Bannister continued, 'Mrs Molloy and I have decided that young Sasha will come and work for you with effect from five p.m. this evening.'

'Will she indeed.'

'Indeed she will. And at the usual wages, of course.'

Scrooge didn't care to ask what 'the usual wages' might be. He had an uncomfortable feeling that he would regard the figure as an outrageous recompense for a young slip of a thing who was doing no more than a bit of dusting. It was probably best if he never knew the figure, and left it to Cratchit to pay her, as he already did with Mrs Molloy.

'Now, naturally,' said Mrs Bannister, 'you would not wish to take on a new member of staff without seeking appropriate references from a previous employer.'

'Certainly not,' said Scrooge stoutly, thinking that this suggestion might provide a tiny opening into which he might drive a wedge of objection.

'But in this case, as there are no previous employers except me, you can't.'

Scrooge was puzzled. 'No previous employers,' he said slowly. 'How old is the girl?'

'Sixteen.'

'And she has been with you how long?'

'Three months.'

'So what on earth was she doing before that?'

'She was a prostitute,' said Mrs Bannister. 'A street girl. She earned her living by going with men, for money.'

Scrooge was left tongue-tied. He more embarrassed than he could remember for a long time, and he shrank back in his chair.

He had never, in his entire life, discussed the question of prostitution with a respectable married lady, and he was not at all sure how he had got sucked into doing so now. He made a mental resolve to think much more carefully before he asked questions in future.

'So there are no references,' Mrs Bannister continued. 'Except mine, of course, and I recommend the girl highly. But you are entitled to know something about Sasha, of course – it would not be fair to you otherwise – so let me tell you a little of the background....'

The Vicar's wife glanced up at Scrooge to make sure that he was listening. Which he certainly was.

119

'From time to time I make it my business to visit one of the women's prisons. While I am there I do what I can to help those who are prepared to be helped – and in particular I look for those who have the mark upon them.'

There was that phrase again. Mrs Bannister had used it before, Scrooge recalled. In relation to her sister, the widow of Pewsey, if he remembered aright.

'The mark upon her,' he repeated.

'Yes. And by that I mean a sign that a girl is capable of being something different and better. An indication that she has some innate qualities of goodness and kindness about her – a sort of natural nobility which may be buried temporarily under layers of grime and filth, but which could be brought out and exercised, given proper care and attention.'

'And young Sasha was in prison for prostitution?' asked Scrooge.

'No, she was in prison for theft. She stole some meat, with the object of getting caught, and thus being able to escape from associates who would not gladly release her.'

Scrooge was genuinely intrigued. 'And how did you find this out? Why did she confide in you? And how did you come to see this mark upon her?'

'Through experience, Mr Scrooge. All of those things came about through experience.... If I possibly can, I call at the prison when the women are out in the yard, taking exercise, if one can call it that. All it amounts to is a few minutes in the open air, walking around an enclosed yard, in a big circle. But I make it my business, as I say, to call at the prison at that time, and, if the authorities will allow me, I go to the centre of the circle and I watch the reaction of the women to my presence among them.'

Scrooge tried to envisage the scene. It seemed to him

that such an action as Mrs Bannister had described would require a good deal of self-possession. Courage was perhaps not too strong a word.

'And what sort of reaction do you get?' he asked.

'Mixed. Contempt, very often. Jeering. Insults. But some girls, you see, they will look at me with a sense of longing. The more perceptive of them can tell that I am capable of helping them if they want to be helped. And in Sasha's case I could perceive it at once. It was as if she had called out to me loudly, in words.'

'So what did you do?'

'I interviewed her, alone. And when I was close to her I could see that the true Sasha was beautiful, both in body and soul. She had been crushed, beaten, battered, and despised. She had been driven into a life not of sin, as some would call it, but a life of desperation. She had been driven into it out of a need to survive – out of recognition that if she could only survive she might one day find a way to live a better life. To have a home, and a loving husband, and a family.'

Ah yes, thought Scrooge. A home. And a family. Or fambly, as Billy would say. Both Scrooge, the bachelor businessman, and Mrs Bannister, the childless wife, could see the attraction of that.

'What are we to make of this name,' Scrooge wondered aloud. 'Sasha – is that not a foreign name?'

Mrs Bannister smiled her gentle smile again. 'In Russia I believe it is a diminutive of Alexander, or Alexandra. But it is my belief that our Sasha was christened Sarah, and that Sasha is a name given to her by a younger child, who tried to pronounce her real name and failed. It is the only remnant of a once-happy family life, which ended in tragedy some years ago and about which Sasha will tell us nothing. As yet it is too painful a memory, too sharp a loss for her to be willing to speak about it. But the time will come, when she is happy and secure, when she will tell us these things of her own volition.'

'I see.'

Scrooge stirred in his chair. He realised now that any thoughts he might have had of wriggling out of Mrs Bannister's proposed arrangements were unworthy of him. What he was being asked to do was good work, and would cost him very little.

'For your peace of mind, Mr Scrooge, let me tell you that the girl is perfectly clean. She has no disease. No syphilis or gonorrhoea. Nothing that need cause you to hesitate.'

Scrooge tried to meet Mrs Bannister's eye, and failed. He nodded dumbly.

'Mrs Molloy and I have arranged it all between us. Nothing is required of you except to treat the girl well, and I have no doubt that you will.'

'I give you my word on that,' said Scrooge hoarsely. 'And is Sasha herself content with her proposed employment?'

'She is.'

'You could find her more congenial surroundings, I think.'

Mrs Bannister smiled again. 'Not yet, I couldn't.'

She set aside her sewing, at which she had continued to work throughout their conversation, and rose to her feet.

'There, you see, Mr Scrooge. You understand now what I mean about working at the edges of the problem, taking one part of it at a time, and helping one person at a time? In Billy and Sasha you and I have found two lost souls – but between us we have got them off the streets and into useful employment. Now that is progress, Mr Scrooge! Progress!'

15

When Scrooge returned to his apartment, Sasha was there to greet him. As he came through the front door she emerged from his sitting-room and bade him good evening.

'Good evening,' said Scrooge, trying hard to disguise his uneasiness. The fact was, he had never even had a manservant in his apartment before, much less a maid. He had employed ladies who came in to clean, yes, but they had mostly been middle-aged and married. Sasha was young and single, and the fact was, Scrooge didn't know how to deal with her.

He took his coat off and Sasha hung it up for him. Also his hat. Then he stood for a moment, uncertain what to do next.

'Mrs Molloy and I have prepared my room,' said Sasha solemnly.

'Oh yes?' Room, thought Scrooge – what room?

'Yes,' repeated Sasha. 'We have. Come and see.'

She turned and led the way towards the spare bedroom, where Billy had spent a night some nine days earlier.

Scrooge followed her and as he did so he experienced a slight sense of dizziness. It felt as if he were losing control of his balance in the same way as – it appeared – he was losing control of his own domestic arrangements. Up to this moment he had assumed that Sasha would simply work for him during the day, and would otherwise lodge with Mrs Molloy, like Billy. But no – it seemed that she was to be resident here, in his own apartment.

The two of them went into the bedroom, which was lit by a paraffin lamp on a bedside table – a *new* bedside table, Scrooge noticed, with a *new* lamp – and he saw at once that the bed had been made up with clean sheets and a brightly coloured counterpane, turned down at the top. No doubt the sheets and the counterpane were new too, and charged to his account. But for once he hardly cared. He felt somewhat dazed by the progress of events.

Sasha allowed him a moment to absorb the scene, and Scrooge gradually became aware that in some mysterious way this part of his apartment had been transformed into a young woman's room. A lot of old lumber had been removed – Scrooge wondered briefly where it had gone – and already the space had a young girl's stamp upon it. It even smelt different, perhaps because it had been cleaned more thoroughly than for some time.

Eventually Sasha said: 'I am very grateful to you for taking me on as your maid, Mr Scrooge, and I promise that I will serve you to the best of my ability.'

Scrooge found himself strangely moved by the young girl's calmness and simplicity of manner. Her demeanour affected him in some way which he could not quite have explained, even to himself. Perhaps this is why I have always avoided company, he thought – because it disturbs me so.

'I'm sure that you will give every satisfaction,' he finally managed to say. And he smiled.

Then he turned to move out of the room, but he remembered something.

'Have you had an evening meal, Sasha?'

'Yes, sir, I have, thank you, sir. I had a meal with Mrs Molloy.'

Scrooge nodded. 'Good.'

*

Sasha's master – or was it the other way round? – made his way to the sitting-room, where he seated himself in his favourite chair by the fire.

Scrooge's evenings were mostly devoted to reading, and he had a pile of books, periodicals, and newspapers on the floor beside him. Now, still feeling slightly bewildered, he began to work his way through them, as usual.

To his surprise, Sasha seated herself in a chair on the other side of the hearth and began to do some sewing. She seemed to have acquired a complete sewing-basket from somewhere – probably, Scrooge suspected, it was another item which had been charged to his account – and she was definitely darning one of his socks: Scrooge recognised the pattern.

After a moment, Sasha said, 'I have received very detailed instructions from Mrs Bannister, sir, as to how I am to conduct myself. Very detailed indeed. And I shall certainly do as she told me. But if at any time what I do is not satisfactory to you, then you have only to say and I shall change my ways.'

Scrooge looked at her over his newspaper. 'Did Mrs Bannister tell you to sit with me in the evenings?'

'Yes, sir. She was very insistent on that. Would you rather I didn't?'

'Oh no, no,' said Scrooge hastily. 'No, I am glad of the company.'

He hid himself behind the newspaper again.

Glad of the company? Had he really said that? What was he talking about? A week or two ago the idea of sharing his apartment with anyone would have been anathema to him. But now – well, now the idea did not seem so dreadful. In fact, he thought he might very well come to like it.

125

Every so often, Scrooge stole a glance at Sasha, without letting her see that he was doing it. On his visits to the vicarage, Mrs Bannister had twice told him to take careful note of the girl, but the fact was that he had seldom done more than register her presence; as ever, he had been too preoccupied with his own affairs. Now, however, he realised that Mrs Bannister was right: Sasha was a beautiful young woman. She was sixteen, reportedly, but she looked a little more mature than that. And certainly the last few months, with a decent diet, regular hours and a comfortable bed to sleep in, would have done much to fill out her figure.

The girl sat very patiently, concentrating hard on her darning. Her dress was black, of course – that seemed to be the accepted uniform for female domestic servants, no doubt to hide the stains and the dirt – and she wore a white apron over it. But no cap, unlike some maids of Scrooge's acquaintance. The lamp over her right shoulder illuminated her blonde hair, which was drawn back and gathered together by a ribbon at the base of her neck. Her eyes were blue, large and shining in the lamplight.

Once, when she caught him looking at her, Sasha asked him if he was warm enough.

'Oh yes, yes, thank you. But don't hesitate to put another coal on if you feel the cold yourself. The wind outside is particularly bitter tonight.'

Where did she come from, Scrooge wondered. What had happened to her parents? And brothers and sisters, if she had any. How had she come to be working on the streets? And what scars had it left upon her soul?

Ten o'clock came, and Sasha had evidently been advised that this was bedtime, for as the St Andrew's church clock struck the hour she gathered together her sewing equipment and put it away. Then she asked Scrooge if he would like her to bring him a glass of brandy.

'Why yes,' said Scrooge, wondering how she knew that brandy was his usual night-time tipple. 'That would be very agreeable.'

Sasha crossed to the sideboard, poured him a glass and brought it over.

Scrooge took the drink but felt obliged to advise her that half the size would have been adequate.

'But Mrs Bannister told me that I have to give you a big one – especially on the first night.'

'Ah,' said Scrooge. 'Well in that case I will dispose of it manfully.' Which he did over the next few minutes, while Sasha disappeared into the bathroom and then to her own room.

Scrooge considered it safest to stay where he was until all movement had ceased, because the idea of bumping into Sasha in her nightdress left him feeling somewhat alarmed. Indeed he was beginning to wonder how this arrangement was going to work at all. However, as he sat sipping his brandy he decided that he would see how things went for a day or two and then consider the matter again.

In due course Scrooge went around the apartment, making his invariable night-time checks to see that everything was secure. Then he too prepared for bed, and just before he climbed into his spacious four-poster, he called out: 'Goodnight, Sasha.'

There was no answer, and he thought perhaps she was already asleep.

But Scrooge had no sooner put his feet under the covers, and was about to draw the heavy curtains closed about his bed, when Sasha suddenly appeared in the candlelight beside him.

Scrooge was, to say the least, taken aback.

He said nothing, but merely stared at her, goggle-eyed.

Sasha was wearing a long white gown, which covered her from throat to feet. Her hair had been loosened and hung down over her shoulders. Her eyes seemed to be larger and brighter than before.

'Mrs Bannister says that I am to sleep with you,' she announced.

'What?' croaked Scrooge.

'Yes, sir. Mrs Bannister says that I am to sleep with you.'

Scrooge babbled. Yes, indeed he did. He would not, two minutes earlier, have considered himself even a potential babbler. He was, he would have assured you, far too self-assured a fellow to disgrace himself by being at a loss for words, no matter how unusual or peculiar the circumstances. But, when he came to think about this conversation afterwards, Scrooge was forced to admit to himself that he had, at this point, babbled. Foolishly.

'Oh but I, no but I, I am sure that you, Mrs Bannister would not have, she didn't, I am absolutely certain that... Misunderstanding, can't have meant, wouldn't have... I mean, ridiculous, absurd, preposterous...'

Eventually he stopped babbling and looked at Sasha, hoping that what he had said, however incoherent, would result in her immediate departure from his bedroom.

But no. She remained at his side.

'Move over,' she said. 'Please. And let me in. Mrs Bannister would be most upset if I failed to follow her instructions.'

'Instructions?'

'She said that I was to sleep with you, Mr Scrooge. Definite. Like I said.'

Scrooge heaved the top sheet up around his chin, like some old maid protecting herself against the mere thought of a burglar.

'Sasha,' he managed to say, 'I am sure that Mrs Bannister said no such thing.'

Well. That tore it. Sasha frowned, placed her hands on her hips, and thrust her face aggressively forward into his.

'Are you calling me a liar?' she demanded.

Had he been in a position to, Scrooge would have stepped back three paces. As it was, all he could do was lean backwards against the headboard.

'Well, no,' he said lamely. 'No, I am certainly not calling you a liar, Sasha. But I am sure that Mrs Bannister cannot have meant – '

'She did!' said Sasha firmly. 'Don't argue!'

This was a new Sasha now, not the slightly hesitant young lady of earlier in the evening. This was a Sasha who knew what she had been told to do, by the lady who had helped her to a new life, and by golly she was going to do what she had been told, whether Scrooge liked it or not. Sasha's first loyalty was to Mrs Bannister, and if Scrooge did not like it he would clearly have to lump it.

Sasha took the top sheet from Scrooge's suddenly nerveless hands, flicked it back, and climbed into the bed beside him.

It was a large bed, with plenty of room for two, and as Scrooge was sitting in the middle there was certainly enough space for his new maid to establish a claim on her territory.

Scrooge made a fresh attempt to clarify the position. He babbled again. 'Mrs Bannister... well, she said... she recommended... she told you that you must spend the night with me?'

129

'She did.'

Scrooge could have believed many things about the unusual Mrs Bannister, but he was still having trouble believing this.

'But perhaps you are taking her too literally, Sarah. Sleep in the same apartment, yes, but surely she did not say that you were to share my bed?'

'Yes, she bloody did! And what's more, she said I was to make sure that you made love to me. At least once.'

'What?!'

'You're to make love to me, at least once,' Sasha told him. 'Mrs Bannister's words exactly. You tell him that from me, she said. And if his knob's as stiff as his manner, Sasha, she said, you'll be on to a damn good thing.'

16

During the night, Scrooge woke up and had a good chuckle. He chuckled because he remembered this dream he'd had.

Quite a saucy dream it was. He'd dreamed that he had gone to bed with young Sasha, Mrs Bannister's maid. And a fine old time they'd had of it! Ho ho ho, chuckled Scrooge. What a hoot that dream was! The very idea.

Then he turned over in the bed and found that lying beside him was a long, warm body, the very size and shape of...

Scrooge groaned, held his head, and wondered how on earth it was that he had got himself into this situation.

In the morning, Sasha rose early and busied herself with household chores. Scrooge was mightily grateful that she did, for he had no idea how to behave in her presence.

When he was dressed and ready for breakfast, he found that she had left the apartment altogether, presumably to take her own breakfast with Mrs Molloy.

Scrooge went as usual to Mr Montini's café, sat alone with a newspaper, and grunted bad-temperedly when asked anything. Mr Montini seemed quite relieved that Scrooge was his old self again.

After breakfast, Scrooge plucked up his courage and went round to call on Mrs Molloy. Her apartment was at the rear of his building, on the ground floor, and when she opened the door Mrs Molloy giggled happily when she saw who the caller was. But then she always giggled.

'Are you alone, Mrs Molloy?' asked Scrooge.

'I am, sir,' said Mrs Molloy, fairly hugging herself with amusement. 'Them others has gone shopping for me. And what can I do for you this fine morning?'

As the temperature was at that moment hovering around freezing-point, with a brisk breeze to match, Scrooge was not sure where she got the 'fine morning' from, but he didn't quibble.

'I need to talk to you,' he said, and stepped inside.

Once the door was closed, Scrooge revealed the nature of his difficulty. He explained that he was wholly unconvinced that it was right and proper for young Sasha to have a room in his apartment. A girl that age, living under the same roof as a man of his age – well, people might talk.

'I should very much hope they *would* talk,' said Mrs Molloy, who was quite unmoved by Scrooge's dilemma. 'If they wasn't to talk there would be something wrong with the world. And with a bit of luck we will have your reputation transformed, Mr Scrooge. If I put the word around often enough, folks will have you halfway human before the month's out.'

This was not what Scrooge had intended at all, and he had to fight hard to control his exasperation.

'But don't you think it would be more appropriate for a young girl like Sasha to have rooms with you, Mrs Molloy?'

'Oh no. Definitely not.' For once, Mrs Molloy did not laugh. 'She's to stay with you, Mr Scrooge. Mrs Bannister was most definite on that.'

The absence of even a smile from Mrs Molloy's features was certain proof, if Scrooge needed any, that Mrs Bannister's dictates were not to be trifled with. However, he persevered.

'But I can think of no reason,' he said plaintively, 'why Mrs Bannister should be permitted to make all my domestic arrangements.'

'And why not, pray? She's better at it than what you are.' And Mrs Molloy tittered again. 'Hee hee hee hee hee!'

At this point, many a man would have recognised a hopeless cause, but Scrooge persevered in the face of the evidence.

'But people will think the worst,' he argued. 'They will believe I am taking advantage of the girl.'

'Well I should hope you are, Mr Scrooge. Hee hee hee hee hee! And from what I hear, there's life in the old dog yet.'

No, it was no good. The battle was lost.

Scrooge groaned and placed a hand across his forehead. That it should come to this, he thought. That I, Ebenezer Scrooge, whose name inspires terror among failing businessmen and debtors, that I should be successfully conspired against – and not even by men, at that, but by a colloquy of women!

That night, Sasha ran a bath for him.

Somewhere in the basement of Scrooge's building there was a boiler which had been installed some years earlier in order to supply hot water to every floor. The system had never worked properly – which was another cause of complaint among Scrooge's wearied tenants – but Sasha had somehow got to the bottom of it and had waved a magic wand.

Scrooge didn't ask how it had been done. He suspected that the full, hot bath had been achieved through the purchase of large amounts of fuel and the time of a labourer to stoke the boiler.

Cratchit had probably been drawn into the conspiracy and would be paying the labourer from some secret fund which he had siphoned off from Scrooge's books. Thus does corruption creep in, thought Scrooge, through harmless little schemes for the production of something as innocent as hot water. And as he looked at the bath it seemed to Scrooge that a sign had been painted along the side – a sign which only he could read. It said: 'I am the most expensive bath in London.'

But Scrooge was past complaining.

When Sasha told him to take off his clothes and climb in, he did as he was told.

Her expression did not so much as flicker when he was naked; and for his part he pretended that being naked in the presence of a beautiful girl was something that he was quite used to and of no remark whatever.

He sat in the bath, gazed steadfastly at his feet, and allowed all parts of himself to be soaped and rinsed. All parts. To allow access to some of them he had to kneel up, but he never said a word. Didn't dare.

When he was thoroughly done he was instructed to step out and to be careful to place his feet on the mat. It was a new mat, of course; and Scrooge didn't recognise the big fluffy towels, either.

With Scrooge dealt with, Sasha said that it seemed a pity to waste the water, and she would just take a quick dip after him. Which she did. She slipped out of her clothes and stepped into the bath.

Scrooge was well nigh dry at that point, and he wrapped the towel around him and sat down on the bathroom stool to watch.

He had to sit down, because the beauty of Sasha naked made him feel weak.

Her skin glowed in the light from the one lamp in the room (another new item). Outside, the night was undoubtedly bitter, but within the bathroom the atmosphere was hot and steamy. And Sasha's skin glowed in the golden illumination. She lay back in the bath and her eyes met his, and she smiled.

Scrooge knelt down and kissed her. Her mouth was softer than he would have dreamed possible, and her lips met his willingly. And perhaps, Scrooge hoped, perhaps she was allowing him to kiss her not just out of a sense of duty. It was possible, he hoped – just remotely possible – that she might feel a touch of affection for him. He had done nothing to deserve it, of course. In fact he could not imagine what a man would have to do to deserve the privilege of kissing such a mouth. But given the opportunity of stealing a kiss from it he was not about to let scruples stand in his way. And kissing Sasha proved to be like diving into a pool of warm honey.

After a few moments he leaned back, in order to be able to admire her fully, and she smiled at him again.

'You got a regular girl, Mr Scrooge?'

'No,' said Scrooge softly.

'I thought you might have some little piece tucked away somewhere.'

'No. I'm afraid not.'

'St John's Wood, they say, is a favourite place for city men's girls.'

'So I understand. But I have no little favourite, Sasha. Though my father kept a mistress, when he was a widower, and if I'd followed his example I would have one too.'

Scrooge thought about the lady in question – his father's mistress. Susanna she had been called. He had not thought of her in years.

'As a matter of fact,' he said, 'she was the first woman I ever went with. And very nearly the last. Complained that I spent too quick, and left me feeling foolish.'

Sasha chuckled. 'That's a common enough failing with younger men. But when you're older you learn to take your time....'

'The relationship was not very satisfactory for either of us,' Scrooge admitted.

'So what do you do then, if you haven't got a special girl – go to a house?'

Scrooge hesitated. But Sasha was entitled to an answer, of course.

'I do occasionally go to a house, yes. When I find myself distracted from my work. Which isn't very often, mercifully. I am an old man, after all.'

'You're not really old,' Sasha assured him. 'Your hair's going grey, but you still got your own teeth. And you stride around pretty quick. You're still vigrus.'

Yes, indeed, Scrooge thought. He was still 'vigrus'. He had a distinct memory of being vigrus more than once last night, and he had every intention of being vigrus again before he went to sleep. Admittedly, such an action was probably immoral and wicked and sinful, but he would worry about that later. At least he would do his best to see that the pleasure was not all one-sided.

He lowered his head and kissed Sasha's lips once more, then her breasts, licked her nipples.

She laughed and pushed him away. 'Not yet, sir. Not yet.'

She sat up in the bath and set about washing herself properly.

'Mrs Molloy used to work in a house,' she told him.

Scrooge wasn't sure that he had heard her correctly. 'Mrs Molloy what? Worked in a house, did you say?'

'Oh yes. Told me she enjoyed it on the whole. A lot better than working on the streets, she said. Might have been in the place still, only one of the customers fell in love with her and took her away. An Irish gentleman, so she told me.'

Scrooge returned to the stool and pondered.

How long had he known Mrs Molloy? Seven years, was it? She had come with the house, from Marley. Seven years. And yet he had had no idea that she had once been a prostitute.

Of course he had no idea about any other aspect of her life, either. He didn't know where she had been born, how many children she had, whether her husband was alive or dead. These were not matters he had ever troubled to ask about, and since he was renowned for being uninterested in anything except making money, they were matters which had never been confided to him. Scrooge was forced to acknowledge that, even if he had been told any of these things, he would probably have forgotten them. Except the bit about working in a house, of course. He would have remembered that.

Eventually, the water cooled, and Sasha stepped out of the bath into the open towel offered by her master.

As she dried herself she looked at him from time to time, with that half-amused expression which Scrooge was beginning to realise was her natural look when she was at ease.

'You're to spend again tonight,' she told him.

'Am I?' said Scrooge dreamily.

'Oh yes. Mrs Bannister said so, definite. He'll try to get out of it, she said. He'll say he's too old, too tired, too busy. But you make sure he does it reg'lar. A man should spend all he has, she reckons – and then make more.'

Hm, well, possibly. Doing it reg'lar with a girl like Sasha

seemed very irreg'lar to Scrooge. Very irreg'lar indeed. But if that was what Mrs Bannister thought best, he asked himself, who was he to gainsay the lady?

When Sasha climbed into his bed for the second night in succession, he welcomed her with open arms, and kissed her again.

Part Three

17

There was no doubt that the arrival of Billy and Sasha in Scrooge's household had administered a shock to his system, but all those who knew him were agreed that the shock was highly beneficial. It had jolted him out of his grumpiness and isolation, his inward-looking, bent-over, suspicious resentment of people in general. Within the space of two weeks, Scrooge's life had been changed for ever; and for the better, as he would have hastened to tell you.

Scrooge still had his moments of anger and impatience, of course. And he still clung tight to his wallet: Cratchit often remarked that it required three strong men to loosen his grip on it. But, for the most part, Scrooge had become a kinder, gentler, more relaxed and considerate person.

Within a further six weeks he was to suffer a loss which he would pain him deeply for as long as he lived – but for the moment he was happier than he had been for many years.

And there was so much to do. Scrooge's day-to-day existence hurried him along in a manner which hardly gave him a moment for reflection.

True, he had not quite forgotten that he had decided, at the turn of the year, that he must cut down his involvement in business, must cure himself of his obsession with making money, and must start to apply some of his wealth to good causes. But for the first few weeks of the new year he found such thoughts pushed to the background. Quite coincidentally, he became the subject of more business proposals than he had seen for years, and the habits of a lifetime were so deeply ingrained in him that he could not fail to give them proper attention.

Then there other calls on his time: his new companions needed advice and assistance. Billy, for instance, had to be found a tutor to teach him to read and write. And, after some enquiries, Scrooge found a retired schoolmaster living nearby who was more than willing to supplement his meagre pension by coaching Billy for three hours every morning. Scrooge negotiated a magnificently low fee, only to relent on seeing Cratchit's pained expression.

'You wouldn't exploit the kindness of an old gentleman with a paltry sum like that,' said Cratchit reproachfully. 'Would you, sir?'

Scrooge glanced at Billy and saw no support for his economies there.

'Oh, very well then,' he said with a sigh. 'Double it if you must.'

And Cratchit did.

As for Sasha – well, she was not backward in coming forward. Her brief from Mrs Bannister was that she was to soften Mr Scrooge's soul, and it was a brief which she interpreted broadly.

She involved herself in every aspect of Scrooge's existence. She put out the clothes for him to wear each day, and when she found that some of them were old and worn, or just plain dull, she ordered others. She simply charged the new items to his account.

As for the old clothes, she simply gave them away, so she did! Didn't even sell them for a few pence at Simmons and Levy's clothes exchange, as Mrs Molloy had always done. Scrooge had enjoyed grumbling about how little his old suits fetched in that quarter, but he wasn't sure that he was bold enough to criticise Sasha for just making a gift of them.

Sasha's supervision did not end with Scrooge's clothes. She made sure that he took regular meals, with a suitable balance of meat, vegetables and fruit. Scrooge came to expect to be questioned closely, on his arrival home in the evening, about what he had had to eat during the day; and Sasha was adapt at discerning when he was being less than truthful.

In the evenings, Scrooge found himself taking more hot baths than he had had in months, with mysterious oils added to the water, if you please. Even his skin was softer now.

The apartment too, was transformed. After a thorough cleaning of every room (with bought-in assistance, Scrooge noted gloomily), Sasha set about redecorating and refurnishing.

Mrs Bannister was taken on as a consultant, and each evening Scrooge came home to find that a wall which had once been a comfortable brown colour (probably for forty years), was now a pale blue. And an old chesterfield, which to Scrooge's eye had years of life in it yet (provided you avoided the odd spring), had been tossed out of the front door, awaiting the rag-and-bone man.

The boiler in the basement continued to be stoked, to the point where Scrooge positively sweated at times. But he didn't dare to criticise. If he ventured – and he did, once – to suggest that all this might perhaps be costing a lot of money, Sasha fairly tore into him, and told him he could afford it ten times over, and if he'd had any sense he'd have seen to it all himself, years earlier. And after that Scrooge thought it wise to keep mum. Ruthless, young Sasha was.

143

Absolutely ruthless.

Scrooge might have resented and resisted all this – indeed he would have fought back with words and deeds – had he had the slightest reason to suppose that he was being taken advantage of, or if he had suspected that his weakness for a beautiful face was being exploited. But he knew well enough that this was not the case. Sasha was working to orders, and the *éminence grise* behind it all was Mrs Bannister. And besides, everything that was being done was being done in his best interests; Scrooge could sense that, and feel it in his bones.

Even if he had had any resentment, or grounds for complaint, all protest would have melted away at bedtime. Scrooge was not fool enough to imagine that Sasha would have cared for him if she had been left to her own devices. But she was warm and gentle and forbearing, and also very beautiful. If she had been sent to melt his heart, Scrooge thought to himself, she had made a damn good job of it.

In the evenings, and at weekends, the young lady laid down a law that Scrooge was to go out more, meet people, and have some fun. She took him, for instance, to some of the more respectable music halls, places that Scrooge had not even glanced at for a decade or two. He attended concerts, art galleries, and even – until it was proved that he was hopeless at it – allowed himself to be led out on to the dance floor.

On one memorable occasion, Scrooge was sitting with Sasha in the bar of the Victoria Theatre, one of the more famous of its kind, enjoying a rum and peppermint during the interval. Rum and peppermint was not a drink which he normally favoured himself, but Sasha had fancied one and he ordered two. He was sitting there, idly watching the noisy crowd, when he was spotted by two young fellows from the Royal Exchange. He knew them slightly: Wilkins and Potter.

Wilkins was the first to espy Scrooge, and he could scarcely believe the evidence. He came closer.

'Why damn me,' he said. 'Mr Scrooge, as I live.'

Scrooge nodded an acknowledgement, and was dismayed to see a broad grin spread over the face of Mr Wilkins.

'Why, look at this, Potter,' said Wilkins gleefully to his companion. 'If it is not the hardest man on 'Change, out for the evening with a beautiful young lady. Who would have thought it!'

Potter indeed would *not* have thought it, had he not seen it too. He lowered his head and peered short-sightedly forward, jostled by the chattering crowd as he did so.

'Why yes,' he said. 'Stap me if it is not so!' He leaned closer to Scrooge. 'You old goat!' he said boldly. 'Who'd have guessed you had it in you?'

And off the two fellows went, fairly howling with laughter as they pushed their way to the bar.

Scrooge, who had maintained perfect dignity throughout this rather vulgar exchange, did his best not to look disconcerted. But inwardly he thought, That's torn it. I haven't heard the last of this.

Nor had he. The very next day, a veritable procession of fellows made it their business to pass by his position on 'Change and to comment on this and that. But they could hardly keep their faces straight for two minutes, and before long, if not immediately, they would say something like: 'Hear you've found yourself a young friend, Mr Scrooge! Bit of a surprise, eh what? Thought you were past all that!'

And then they would chortle wickedly, and perhaps add

145

some unrepeatable comment about still being able to do things at his age and hoping they would be able to say the same in due course.

Rather to his own surprise, Scrooge took all this in good part.

'Matter of fact,' he would say, 'the girl is me little maid-of-all-work, and I thought she deserved an evening out.'

'Of course, of course!' his colleagues would bellow, looking round to make sure that everyone within earshot was enjoying the joke. 'Done it meself, many a time!'

And off they would go, with the obvious intention of describing this merry conversation to the first ten fellows they met.

Yes, to his own surprise, Scrooge did not object to any of this at all. A reputation as a ladies' man and a debauchee was entirely new to him, but he discovered that it troubled him not in the least. And as a matter of fact, it was rather good for business.

But, in his quieter moments, Scrooge made a conscious attempt not to invest too much hope and affection in his new relationships. Yes, he was filled with pleasure at the sight and sound of Billy and Sasha. But more than three decades of business life had taught him that circumstances can change very rapidly. His beautiful Sasha, for instance, might run off with a soldier. And young Billy might be tempted to follow a circus. So, it was no good expecting things to last. Scrooge was painfully aware that it was in the nature of life that just when you thought you were happy and content, something would go badly wrong.

18

London had experienced exceptionally cold weather since well before Christmas, and from the beginning of January the situation deteriorated still further. A series of hard frosts made the streets treacherous all day and left the capital's plumbing in a state of disorder.

Then, for three more days, a heavy, smoke-filled fog settled over the city. This dense vapour might have been expected to trap any heat within it, but the reverse seemed to happen, and the cold became more intense still.

It was this type of weather which had so depressed Scrooge on Christmas Eve, and he was not pleased to see its return. At nights, only the major thoroughfares were lit by gas streetlamps, and the fog was so thick that even here the darkness was well nigh impenetrable. Such hackney-cab drivers as remained on duty were obliged to climb down and lead their horses on foot.

Even in the daytime, many a pedestrian wandered hopelessly lost along streets which were normally familiar; and Billy, whose ear for gossip and rumour was sharper than most, returned to the office after his lessons each morning with numerous tales of injuries and even deaths which had resulted from the confusion.

When the fog cleared, the wind blew from the east. Scrooge bought an atlas to demonstrate to Billy that it came all the way from Russia, with no mountains in the way to break down its bitter intensity.

The wind brought with it heavy snow, which continued,

147

with short intervals, for forty-eight hours. And for the next five weeks the temperature barely rose above freezing-point.

The result of these circumstances was that, towards the end of January, Billy was picking up excited stories about the Thames beginning to freeze over. And if it did, so the word on the street said, there would be a frost fair held on the river itself!

'Can that happen, Mr Scrooge?' enquired Billy. 'Can the Thames really freeze over, so that people can walk on it?'

'Oh yes,' Scrooge confirmed, 'it certainly can. 'It's happened several times before. Not often, mind. Perhaps once every couple of hundred years on average. But the last time it occurred was when I was a boy a little older than yourself, Billy. It was long before you were born – I remember it well.'

'They say the ice was so thick that an ox was roasted on it.'

'So it was, Billy. I saw it myself. And sheep were roasted too. The tradesmen called it Lapland mutton, and charged a shilling a slice. I refused to pay that much myself, of course, as any sensible person would, but there were many who did.'

Billy gasped. 'Wow!'

From then on, Billy's talk was of nothing but the prospect of a frost fair on the river.

At home, Sasha had assumed that the weather would not improve and had ordered several tons of coal to keep the fires well stoked. It was just as well she did, because before long supplies were exhausted. But one morning Scrooge's eyes happened to fall on the bill for these supplies of fuel, and the cost appalled him. He turned on Sasha angrily and asked him what she thought she was doing, spending his money like water.

But Sasha was no ordinary servant. Sasha would not go pale, put her hand to her mouth and suffer a tongue-lashing meekly, as most would, if only to preserve their employment. No, indeed. Sasha yelled back at him, giving as good as she got, with interest added.

'You're a stupid, mean, tight-fisted old miser!' she bawled at him. 'What's a few pounds to you? You've got more in the bank than you could spend if you live to be a hundred. Very well then, freeze to bloody death if you want to, but don't expect me and Mrs Molloy to die with you.'

And she stamped out of the room, slamming the door behind her so hard that Scrooge feared for its hinges.

He sat down with a thump on the nearest chair. He really felt quite faint. And what troubled him most, of course, was that Sasha was right.

Once again, Scrooge realised, he had made a fool of himself. He had quibbled over an amount which he would never have missed had he not chanced to see the paper. And the money was for the purchase of something which would mean the difference between life and death for some. Scrooge had no doubt that, before the winter was out, many would die from the cold – while he, on the other hand, would sit by a nice warm fire.

He held his head in his hands and wondered what on earth he was going to do with himself.

After a while he went to find Sasha, who was working in the kitchen and was not pleased to see him.

'Sasha,' he said abjectly, 'I most humbly apologise. I beg your forgiveness. I was rude and thoughtless. And, yes, you are right, I am a stupid, tight-fisted... What was it?'

'Miser, I reckon.'

'Yes, miser. Well, technically I am not a miser because I don't know how much I've got and I don't gloat over it. But in principle you are right. I am very, very sorry for shouting at you, and I humbly beg your pardon.'

Sasha couldn't help grinning. 'Changed your tune a bit, haven't you?'

'I have. Sometimes I sing the wrong tune, I know, but I look to you, Sasha, to set me straight. Now, am I forgiven?'

Sasha came to him, smiling broadly. She put her arms round his neck and kissed him. 'You are, but it'll cost you.'

Scrooge groaned. 'What is it this time?'

'Mrs Bannister is collecting for them as can't work because of the cold. All building work's stopped, for a start, so there's carpenters and brickies standing idle. And when they don't work they don't get paid, and their children starve. Then there's the watermen – they can't hardly get a boat out these days. So there's a long list of people as needs money.'

'How much?' said Scrooge, submitting to the inevitable.

'I reckon fifty quid.'

'Fifty quid?' squawked Scrooge.

'For starters.'

'But I haven't got fifty quid. Not on me.'

'That's all right,' said Sasha. 'A cheque will do.'

By the beginning of February the ice on the Thames was said to be eighteen inches thick, and not even the daily movement of the tides could disturb it. As a result, entrepreneurs of all kinds began to turn the unpleasant circumstances to their advantage.

Each morning the newspapers gave breathless accounts of the assemblage of a frost fair, just as Billy's informants on the street had predicted. And each day Billy brought back to the office a lunchtime account of the very latest developments.

By the Friday of that week there was no other topic of conversation in the office, and since business at the Royal Exchange had itself slowed somewhat on account of the inclement weather, Scrooge eventually decided that there was nothing for it – they would all have to go to see the fair for themselves. Even if it was a working day, when all responsible citizens should be at their desks.

Billy could hardly contain his excitement. 'All?' he squeaked, hopping up and down. 'We're all going to go and see it, Mr Scrooge?'

'All,' said Scrooge. 'You, me, Mr Cratchit, Sasha, and Mrs Molloy, if she wishes to come.'

Well, nothing would have kept Mrs Molloy from seeing the frost fair, short of a broken leg, and even then she would have requested that her employer should hire a Bath chair; so after a quick lunch they all set off.

The afternoon was bitterly cold, of course, though the air was mercifully still. The clouds hung low and grey, threatening more snow, but the streets were full of people, most of whom evidently had the same destination in mind.

A half-mile walk brought them to Queen Street, in Cheapside; it was from here, reportedly, that the fair covered the ice as far as Blackfriars Bridge.

As Scrooge's party approached the river, it became clear that all the streets leading down to it had been sprinkled with cinders, so that pedestrians could walk safely without the risk of skidding helplessly on the sloping ice underfoot. The enterprising gentlemen who had arranged this facility stood at the entrance to each lane or alley and demanded a fee for their work.

To Scrooge's mind, this charging of money at the

entrance to a public thoroughfare was illegal, immoral, and unenforceable, and if he had been on his own he might have argued to case at some length. But, since he was with company, all of whom were eager to venture out on to the real ice, he paid up like a gentleman and merely snarled under his breath.

Once at the riverside, there were more obstacles to be negotiated. Gangplanks which normally provided access to river boats had been hauled ashore and now provided a safe means of moving from bank to ice, but once again a small toll was involved. Scrooge smiled a suitably frosty smile and tried to think of it as money well spent.

And now, at last, they were on the ice. The frozen river Thames.

The ice was not so much white as a dirty grey. And it was far from flat, particularly at the sides and at the approach to bridges. In those parts, the movement of the tides in the early stages of the great freeze had jumbled up slabs of ice in uneven piles. At all times it was necessary, therefore, to take some care with the placing of one's feet. Mr Cratchit assisted Mrs Molloy, while Scrooge offered his arm to Sasha. Or in his case, he suspected, it might be the other way round.

Out on the ice, in the whole area below Blackfriars Bridge, a veritable village of makeshift canvas booths had been erected. Someone, a Napoleon *manqué* no doubt, had organised the village into streets which ran from bank to bank in a reasonably orderly fashion.

Most of the stalls were ornamented with flags, streamers, and signs, and one could wander for some time, eyeing the wares on offer, just as easily in the frost fair as in the streets of London proper.

And what wares there were.

152

To begin with, of course, there was food, for everyone present needed plenty inside them to maintain their energy in these curious circumstances. At present there was no ox actually being roasted, though there was talk of such an event at the coming weekend, but there were certainly many braziers providing hot meats and drinks. All the traders who normally worked the city streets seemed to have transferred their business to this site.

On sale from the various dealers in hot cooked food were eel pies, pea soup, fried fish, sheep's trotters, and potatoes. Uncooked edibles included ham sandwiches, seed-cake, plum-cake, tarts, mince pies (of which Scrooge was deeply suspicious, the insides being invisible), Chelsea buns, muffins, and crumpets. Among the shellfish, pickled whelks were particularly popular. And for the sweet of tooth there were sticks of rock and candies. Finally, there were small paper bags of nuts to put in your pocket as you walked away.

Next, drink. For the abstemious, and those who could face a cold drink, there were lemonade, ginger beer, Persian sherbet (whatever that was), and milk. Hot drinks included coffee and tea, of course. For those whose innards needed the warming effect of alcohol, numerous vendors offered beers, ales, stouts, brandy, rum, whisky, gin, hot toddies, steaming bishops, and mulled wine.

Whatever their choice, Scrooge saw to it that his friends were suitably refreshed. Billy partook of the hot eels, which were always a street boy's favourite, while the others chose a mixture of hot buttered scones and waffles, with cream and jam.

As to trinkets and mementoes to mark the occasion, why there was no end to them. To give but one example: brooches with the words 'frost fair', with the year underneath, had been already manufactured by the thousand, even though the fair had only been here for a day or two. Scrooge counted fourteen boxes behind the stall on which they were offered, and he had no doubt that they would all be sold, for the man in charge of the operation could hardly keep up with the demand.

Also doing a mighty brisk trade was a printer, who had hauled his press on to the river, and was running off little one-sheet keepsakes. These consisted of the following doggerel:

> The silver Thames was frozen o'er,
> No difference twixt the stream and shore;
> The like no man hath seen before,
> Except he lived in days of yore.

This verse was followed, at the bottom of the page, with the words: 'Printed on the River Thames for Mr J. Smith (or whoever)' and the day's date. This entire sheet of paper, with your own name on it, could be purchased for a mere shilling.

For those who wearied of shopping, there were other diversions. Skittles, for instance; the hiring of skates, for brave souls who dared to venture up-river; fortune-telling (Sasha was told that she would live to be ninety-three); and dancing reels to the sound of a fiddle (Scrooge was excused, on account, Sasha said, of having been born with two left feet).

On the southern side of the river, a stretch of ice had been flattened sufficiently to permit horse-drawn vehicles to ply to and fro. Rides could be had for a consideration. Astonishing, Scrooge, thought, that a hundred-yard ride on the ice could cost as much as a mile on a sunny street.

On the edge of the ice village, a heavy wooden stake had been fixed into the ice; a rope had been attached to the stake, and on the end of the rope was a chair. Willing victims were persuaded to sit in the chair, which was then pushed around in a circle by two brawny fellows with spikes on their boots. Young ladies who were subjected to this treatment squealed loudly in terror, but Billy, who had two goes, proudly remained silent.

As darkness fell, and after all the stalls and attractions and amusements had been visited and thoroughly explored, Scrooge and his friends unanimously concluded that it had been a day they would not soon forget. Mr Cratchit declared that he would have to come again, bringing his family this time.

They made their way slowly back to the gangplank and then up the cindered lane. There Mr Cratchit left them, to make his own way home to Camden Town.

Before he left, Cratchit shook hands with his employer, a little aside from the others, and thanked him most warmly for his generosity.

'It has been a particular pleasure of mine,' he said quietly, 'if I may make so bold, sir, to see yourself in the company of young people, and in such good spirits too, sir. I see quite a difference in you now, sir.'

'Do you think so?' said Scrooge. He was intrigued to hear what Cratchit said.

'Oh yes, sir. To my mind you've been a bit down this last year or two. Nothing wrong with you, I'm sure, but you seemed to have lost your appetite, so to speak. But since Christmas – why, you've been quite rejuvenated.'

'Oh,' said Scrooge, feeling curiously proud of himself. 'Well I'm very pleased to hear it, Cratchit. Very pleased indeed.'

19

Three days later, in the early hours of Monday morning, Scrooge was awoken by Sasha.

'You must get up,' she said, shaking him by the shoulder.

Scrooge struggled to understand what was happening. 'What?' he growled.

'You must get up. Now. Mrs Molloy is at the door, and she says that Billy is ill.'

Well, Scrooge understood that all right. He heaved the covers off himself and climbed out of bed.

Scrooge and Sasha, wrapped in dressing-gowns, slippers on their feet, made their way down the broad staircase and through the interior entrance to Mrs Molloy's apartment. There they found the lady at Billy's bedside.

By that time, Billy was already delirious with a fever of some sort. That was obvious even to Scrooge, and after a few minutes he decided that medical help was needed.

He dressed rapidly and went round to fetch Dr Medway.

As he set off, he heard the church clock strike six. The streets were still as icy as ever, and Scrooge was shaking with both cold and anguish as he reached the doctor's house.

In due course Dr Medway returned with him to Mrs Molloy's apartment. There he examined the patient, and gave instructions for his care. Warmth, plenty of liquids, a constant watch.

'Would he not be better off in a hospital?' asked Scrooge.

'No, sir. You have two ladies here who can do all that is

156

necessary, and a bit more besides, I judge. Hospital would not improve his chances.'

Chances.... That was not a word Scrooge cared for.

'If it's a question of money...' he began haltingly.

Dr Medway put his hand on Scrooge's shoulder. 'My dear sir,' he said kindly, 'if a thousand pounds would do the trick, I know full well that you would press it into my hand here and now. But money is not the answer.'

Scrooge did not loiter in Billy's sickroom. He was useless, and he knew it. Better to leave such matters in the capable hands of Mrs Molloy and Sasha.

Later that day, Mrs Bannister called, and a nursing rota was set up to see that Billy was cared for round the clock.

Scrooge had not cared to ask the doctor directly what his diagnosis was, but Mrs Bannister told him that it was pneumonia. Well, Scrooge had not spent much of his life in discussion of medical matters, but he knew what that meant.

At ten o'clock on the Wednesday night, Sasha came back to Scrooge's apartment to find him slumped in front of the fire.

'Mr Scrooge,' she said. 'I think you had better come with me.'

And twenty minutes later, with Scrooge and Sasha and Mrs Molloy beside him, Billy died.

Dr Medway said afterwards that Billy had lived for twenty-four hours longer than he had expected.

'It is no comfort to you, Mr Scrooge,' he said, 'but you must realise that half the deaths in this city are of children under ten. At least Billy lived to be twelve. And the truth is, you see, all those years of living half-starved on the street had weakened his system. He had little resistance to infection, and believe me, the city is full of it at present. Be proud, Mr Scrooge, proud that you did the best you could for him, and proud that he fought hard to live.'

For a day or two Scrooge's mind was oppressed by the what-if and the if-only. If only we had not gone to the frost fair, he would say. Perhaps he picked up the infection there. And what if we had got him into a hospital, in spite of what the doctor said.

But all of this was nonsense. Sasha told him so, and in time Scrooge came to accept it.

Some of Scrooge's longer-standing obsessions also troubled him. When the undertaker told him the price of the coffin, he protested vehemently, but found that, for once, he had met his match.

'Your reputation has preceded you, sir,' said the undertaker coldly. (He was not short of business and could afford to offend six customers that morning without losing a moment's sleep.) 'I was told that if you were offered a free ticket to heaven you would quibble about the price, sir, and it seems my informant was right. The cost of the coffin is as stated, and it is not subject to discount.'

Scrooge groaned aloud. He groaned both in despair at himself, and in despair at the horrors of the world. He bent low over the undertaker's desk, as if he had been kicked in the stomach, and wrote out a cheque without another word.

The funeral was naturally to be held in St Andrew's church, with the Reverend Mr Bannister officiating, and Scrooge had a long discussion with the Vicar about the nature of the congregation.

'There are few things more depressing,' Scrooge

declared, 'than a funeral in an empty church. And I should know, because when your predecessor buried my late partner, Jacob Marley, those present were only myself, the Vicar, the deceased, and four fellows who carried the coffin. Not a satisfactory situation, Mr Bannister, not satisfactory at all. And for this one I suggest we do something different.'

What Scrooge had in mind was that the poor and homeless of the parish should be informed that the funeral would be held at 12.00 noon, and that it would be followed by a free meal in the church hall, adjoining. The meal would, of course, be paid for by himself.

'And if you are nervous about the effect of the great unwashed upon your premises,' Scrooge added, 'I shall be pleased to pay for a thorough cleansing afterwards.'

To his credit, Mr Bannister approved this proposal, and the word was put about on the street. Hurried arrangements were made to hire chairs and tables and to arrange for caterers to provide a hot two-course meal for as many as the church hall would hold. Mrs Bannister and Cratchit were in charge of administration.

On the morning of the funeral, the weather was still bitterly cold. There were those who noted that the wind was now coming from the south-west, and said that a thaw was imminent, but for the moment winter was fighting a strong rearguard action. Not surprisingly, therefore, the poor of the parish came to the conclusion that the warmest place to be was with two hundred other people in a crowded building; the church was packed.

What was more, few of those present could ever remember having been offered a free meal before, and if the only qualification needed to get it was to spend half an hour singing hymns in memory of someone you'd barely heard of, well that was not a problem.

At the appropriate point in the service, Scrooge ascended into the pulpit to give a short address. He had assumed, at first, that the Vicar would carry out this task, but he had been told that a few words about Billy would sound much better coming from him, and so he had agreed to speak.

Scrooge paused before beginning, and surveyed the pews in front of him.

Two hundred pairs of eyes stared back at him.

They were wide staring eyes, full of hunger and longing. Men, women, and children, of all ages. Some of them looked exceptionally ragged and dirty, even by the standards of the time; and to tell the truth, when collected *en masse*, they didn't smell at all nice. However, the unsavoury aroma could be cured by leaving the church doors wide open for an hour or two afterwards. If only, Scrooge thought, all problems could be solved as easily.

One glance at the congregation was sufficient to tell him what the assembled poor were thinking. *Is he going to be long?* they were wondering. *Will the food be getting cold?* Well, he would not speak long.

But first, Scrooge decided, there was another matter to be dealt with.

'One thing I cannot abide,' he announced, 'is a runny nose. So all those who have a runny nose will now wipe it.'

Well, that was a somewhat unorthodox beginning, and there was a rumble of amusement. Perhaps fifty of those present had a runny nose, and of those fifty perhaps two had a handkerchief – or a rag which served as such. The rest used their sleeves, as they always had.

'There,' said Scrooge. 'That's better.'

And now he really had their attention, so he began the address proper.

'Ladies and gentlemen.... We have gathered together today to pay our last respects to a young friend and employee of mine, by the name of Billy. I cannot give you his last name, for I never knew it. He never told me, and I never liked to ask. And even Mrs Molloy, to whom he confided much, never knew it either.

'I think most of you will have known Billy by sight. He was young, and small, but he knew every street and alley of this parish, every shop, every cab-driver, every crossing-sweeper, costermonger, and streetgirl.

'The boy never told me much about his background, but he did confide in my housekeeper, Mrs Molloy. She has two grown-up sons of her own and knows how to deal with youngsters.

'Billy was born into a working-class family, with two children younger than himself. As is all too often the case, the father died young, leaving his widow to fend for herself. Then Billy's mother fell ill. They were evicted from their home for failing to pay the rent. And they were obliged to seek refuge with the woman's sister and her husband. But the husband did not treat Billy well. In fact, he treated him abominably. Let us say no more of it than that. And so, when his mother died too, Billy ran away, and began to scratch a living on the streets as best he could. Life for him was as the philosopher Hobbes described it in the state of nature: nasty, brutish, and short.

'That was three years ago. As for my connection with him – well, the boy came into my life on Christmas Day last, and since then I had employed him as my office boy, to run errands for me.

'I had hoped that Billy would prosper under my employment. I had hoped that he would learn to read and write fluently, so that he might find a good job in due course. A job on which he could afford a home, a wife, and a family. Or fambly, as he always referred to it. But that was not to be.

'Now this is a Christian church, and the Vicar will tell you that Billy has gone to heaven. And for those who are Christians, that thought is a great comfort. But for those who do not believe in the Christian afterlife, the loss of one such as Billy is particularly hard to bear. In the words of the great seventeenth-century physician, Sir Thomas Browne: It is the heaviest stone that melancholy can throw at a man, to tell him that there is no further state to come.

'In closing, therefore, let me quote further from that same source, Sir Thomas Browne – for these words hold true, I believe, whatever our philosophy: It cannot be long before we too lie down in darkness, and have our light in ashes.

'That being so, it surely falls to those who remain behind to use our time, such as it is, to best advantage – both for our own satisfaction, and for the sake of others.'

Billy was buried in St Andrew's churchyard. The ground being frozen solid, braziers had to be set up for twenty-four hours before six men with picks could dig the hole deep enough.

Afterwards, Scrooge caused to be erected a modest marker. It was nothing over-elaborate; just a plain piece of stone, on which were carved the following words:

Billy – a child of the street who died too young

The following week, Scrooge provided the Vicar with a sum of money sufficient to ensure that each year a Christmas feast could be provided for the poor of the parish. Oh, and with the proviso that each person attending should be presented with a gift: a brand-new linen handkerchief.

At the end of that same week, Scrooge was sitting at home one morning – yes, sitting at home, for he had not the energy to go into the office that day – when he had a caller: Mrs Bannister.

Scrooge invited the lady in, and Sasha served them coffee.

After some small talk Mrs Bannister declared that she had heard it rumoured that Scrooge was deeply depressed.

Scrooge thought about it.

'No, not exactly depressed,' he said. 'I consider it futile to rail against fate. Useless to worry about that which we cannot change. But I am weary and I am saddened.'

'By the death of your young friend.'

'By that, yes. But also by the realisation that it is not as easy to help people as I had thought.'

Mrs Bannister nodded. 'I understand,' she said. 'And I think what you need is a change of scene, Mr Scrooge. What you should do is go down to Wiltshire and stay with my sister.'

'Ah yes,' said Scrooge. 'The widow of Pewsey.'

'Indeed.'

'Would she be willing to have me?'

'She is very interested to meet you again. You have a standing invitation, sir.'

Scrooge smiled as he remembered the lady. 'Well, that's a very kind thought. Perhaps I will go one day.'

'No perhaps about it, sir,' said Mrs Bannister briskly. 'My sister and I have been in correspondence, and it is all arranged. You will go today, and she will look for you on the four o'clock train. Sasha will pack you a bag.'

It was a measure of Scrooge's fatigue that he could

163

summon no will to resist. This was clearly something that had been planned for him, several days earlier, by that all-powerful cabal: Sasha, Mrs Bannister, and her sister. As Scrooge had already learnt, and as he was to have demonstrated to him many times in subsequent years, the man who attempted to stand firm in the face of their wishes was a direct descendant of King Canute.

He simply nodded and declared that he would be pleased to take advantage of the widow's kind offer.

Sasha escorted him to the train.

'You all right, Mr Scrooge?' she asked anxiously, as she helped him into the compartment.

'Yes,' said Scrooge, 'I think I shall survive.' Though the truth was, he felt far from well. In fact, he felt horribly ill, boiling hot one minute and shivering cold the next. But he was determined not to admit it, even to himself.

'You look pale, and you're sweating a bit, despite the frost.'

'I'm all right!' snapped Scrooge.

'Very well then!' shouted Sasha in return, and she whacked the compartment door shut with a force that would have taken his fingers off had he been careless enough to leave them in the wrong place.

Sasha stamped off, but after a few moments she relented. She came back, opened the door, and tucked a warm rug around his knees.

'You get off at Pewsey,' she reminded him.

'Yes, Miss,' said Scrooge meekly.

And Sasha smiled at last.

As the train moved slowly west, Scrooge gazed miserably out of the window. Everything was grey. The sky, the snow, even the frost-encrusted trees.

Inside his head, his thoughts were in a whirl. He was thinking about the school he had visited, the hostel for the homeless men, the children's hospital, Billy, the office, Sasha, Mrs Bannister, his hostess the widow, and a thousand other things, some of them best forgotten.

And deep, deep inside, was that awful pain which would not go away. The certainty that he would never again see young Billy.

He must have fallen asleep, for when the train reached Pewsey he became aware of where he was only when the engine jerked to a halt.

Sasha had evidently told the guard to keep an eye on him, for the man came along and opened the door of the compartment, calling up a porter to carry Scrooge's case.

Scrooge stepped out on to the platform.

He must have looked very ill, even then, for he heard the porter say to him in a concerned voice, 'Are you all right, sir?'

'Oh yes, thank you,' said Scrooge.

But he wasn't all right by any means, and the platform seemed to rise up towards him.

20

It was five days before Scrooge became fully aware of his surroundings. Prior to that he drifted in and out of consciousness. He knew, of course, that he was in bed, that he was ill, and that he was being cared for, and he vaguely recognised the lady who was with him most of the time. But even when he was awake he was only half awake, and he soon fell back into a deep sleep which was close to death. And, to the extent that he was thinking at all, death didn't seem such a bad alternative.

At some point during his fifth night away from home he woke up and saw that he was in a strange room. He didn't really know where he was; but it was a nice warm place, with a big bed, and a fire in the hearth. There were no lights in the room, and no sounds within or without it, so he knew that the hour must be in the middle of the night, and that the household must be asleep. It seemed best, in the circumstances, to roll over and go back to sleep himself.

In the morning he awoke for a second time, as he thought, and saw Sasha standing beside his bed. But was she real or was she part of a dream?

'Sasha,' he said. 'Is that you?'

'It is,' she said, and smiled.

'But where am I?'

'You're at Mrs Kincaid's house.'

'Mrs Kincaid?'

'Yes. You know – the widow. Mrs Bannister's sister.'

'Ah yes,' said Scrooge. 'I think I remember.' And he did,

after a fashion. 'How long have I been ill?'

'Five days, give or take a bit.'

'I see. And how long have you been here?'

'Three days. I was sent for.'

Scrooge thought about sitting up, but decided it would be too much effort.

'You feeling better, Mr Scrooge?'

'Well, better than I was, certainly.'

'Good. You have a rest now, and I'll go and get you some soup.'

Later, after he had been helped to sit up and consume a bowl of excellent vegetable soup, Scrooge was well enough to have a sensible conversation.

'You nearly died, you know,' Sasha said cheerfully.

'Did I?'

'Oh yes. Mrs Kincaid was right worried about you. You no sooner got off the train than you dropped down at her feet in a faint. She said she hadn't realised she had that effect on people. She was all right when she got you home, but she panicked a bit in the carriage on the way here. Thought she was going to lose you, you see, and her sister would never have forgiven her.'

Sister.... Ah yes, Mrs Bannister, the Vicar's wife. 'Why so?' asked Scrooge.

'Because they've got plans for you, them two.' Sasha seemed to regard this as a huge joke, and she grinned broadly. 'You want to watch out, Mr Scrooge. A pair of plotters and schemers, they are.'

'Plotters? Schemers?' Scrooge felt vaguely alarmed. 'What plans could they possibly have for me?'

'Ooh, I dunno,' said Sasha mysteriously. 'But I reckon they have.'

The prospect seemed to cause her nothing but amusement, so Scrooge decided that his fate could not be all that terrible.

Sasha continued, addressing him as if he was his normal self. 'Do you know what they say about Mrs Kincaid in the village?'

'No, what do they say?'

'They say she's a witch.'

Scrooge had a vague recollection of having heard that said before, but he decided that he must still be asleep. Yes, that was it. This was clearly a dream. Or, if he was not asleep, was this conversation, perhaps, Sasha's idea of fun? He closed his eyes, fully intending, if he was not already sleeping, to return to that state as soon as possible. It seemed a very attractive condition.

But before going back to sleep he thought he would just go through the motions of making a reply.

'So,' he murmured, with his eyes tight shut, 'if the widow lady is a witch, is she going to turn me into a frog?'

'Nah,' said Sasha. 'You're too ugly to be a frog. You'd have to be a toad.'

Scrooge slept again.

Later that day he was visited by higher authority, in the shape of the widow herself. Sasha accompanied her.

Of course Scrooge had been visited by the widow many times before during his illness, and had been dosed regularly with her herbal potions, but this was the first occasion on which he had been fully conscious. He struggled to sit up, which was only polite, after all; but he still needed someone to help him.

When he had been raised into a sitting position, with numerous pillows propping him up, Scrooge felt it only proper to express his gratitude for the care and attention which he had obviously received.

His thanks were gracefully accepted.

'I'm afraid I've been a terrible nuisance to you,' he added.

'No more than you are when you're well,' said Sasha promptly. 'Less, actually.'

The widow smiled at this, and said tactfully that she would bring him some soup. She left the room.

Sasha sat down beside the bed again and began to work on some sewing.

After a pause, Scrooge said, 'What was that you told me about this good lady being a witch?'

'That's what they say,' said Sasha.

'Well, that's a wicked slander,' said Scrooge. 'She's a most delightful lady, and I won't have her spoken of disrespectfully.'

'Oh she's not a bad witch,' Sasha explained. 'And she's very highly respected. She's what they call a white witch, you see. She doesn't do nasty things to people. Quite the other way round – she helps them to get well.'

Scrooge still didn't understand, but he didn't pursue the matter. Although he had been brought up in the country, many decades ago, he was more used to city ways than country ways. And besides, he still wasn't thinking very clearly.

'Her husband used to be a doctor,' Sasha continued. 'He used to cater for the gentry in these parts, and she dealt with the poor. But they reckon the poor got the better part of that bargain. They got better treatment, and they got it free, too. She has a clinic every morning, and people come from miles around to see her. Herbal remedies and such. Healing hands.'

169

'Well,' said Scrooge, 'she certainly seems to have looked after me very well.'

'You would have died,' said Sasha simply. 'If you hadn't had her to look after you.'

After another week of hot soup and carefully prepared food, Scrooge was well enough to get dressed and venture downstairs. He had his first shave for some time.

The widow's house, he discovered, was located not in the town of Pewsey itself, but in a small village called Tanway, some three miles to the north-west. The village sheltered close under the escarpment which marked the northern edge of the Vale of Pewsey. Those who made the steep climb up the hill would find themselves on the Marlborough downs, with views for miles in all directions. It was said that, on a clear day, you could see the spire of Salisbury cathedral.

The village was named Tanway, so the widow informed Scrooge, because it had once been on someone's route to Tan Hill; and it was on Tan Hill that a great stock fair was held every St Anne's Day, attracting farm folk and their animals from all over Wiltshire. For that matter, horses were brought for sale from as far as Wales and Ireland. The day after the stock fair, there was always a pleasure fair. Nowadays, however, the village was on no one's way to anywhere, and was mercifully isolated and quiet. The only visitors were occasional pedlars.

The widow's home was positioned on the main street of Tanway. It was a solidly built, eighteenth-century construction, which had originally been the property of a prosperous wool merchant.

As he gradually returned to something like normal health, Scrooge was pleased to note that the weather was on the mend too. All signs of frost and snow had disappeared, to be replaced by blustery showers of rain. But there were at least occasional bursts of sunshine, offering some hope that spring would eventually arrive.

On Scrooge's first morning downstairs, Sasha read out a letter from Mr Cratchit, in which he described how the great frost fair had ended. Some of those participating had apparently been slow to accept that a thaw had set in, and as the ice on the Thames broke up a few tradesmen had been left marooned. Two men had been drowned.

Scrooge listened but said nothing. He would have preferred, on the whole, to forget about the frost fair.

Instead, he gave his attention to the widow. She was, he guessed, a year or two older than her sister, the Vicar's wife. But she now appeared to him as an even more handsome woman than he had remembered her from Christmas Day. Just the sort of woman he admired, in fact.

His attention did not go unnoticed. 'You like the widow, don't you?' said Sasha with a wicked grin when they were alone together. 'Think she's a pretty lady, Mr Scrooge?' And she laughed.

Scrooge stood on his dignity. 'I'm sure I have given you no reason to think that I am especially fond of her.'

'Oh yes you have. You go all soft when she's about.'

'Well.... The good lady did save my life, you know. And she is a lady of good breeding.'

'Unlike me. But that's nonsense, Mr Scrooge, and you know it. You're going all soppy has got nothing to do with her being a fine lady. It's just that you like 'em with a bit of meat on the bone. I've noticed that before.' And she tittered, in the manner of Mrs Molloy. 'Hee hee hee hee hee!'

Scrooge took offence. 'Hmmph!' he said, and hid himself

171

behind a newspaper.

Later, when he was alone with the widow, he thanked her for allowing Sasha into her house, and for treating the girl so generously – for Sasha seemed to be regarded as one of the family rather than as a servant.

'Oh, it's a pleasure,' said the widow cheerfully. 'You've done a good job with her, Mr Scrooge, you and my sister before you. You caught her just in time, do you see. Brought her in off the streets, I mean. If you do that with a girl, catch her early enough, you can sometimes set her straight. But once they've got established in a proper brothel, one frequented by gentlemen, and got used to eating good food and having a bit of warmth and some money, why then it's very much harder. It's an uphill task to change their ways after that.'

Scrooge swallowed hard, and felt himself go pale. 'Why yes indeed,' he mumbled.

As with the widow's sister, he had not expected to find himself discussing the mechanics of prostitution, and he hastily changed the subject.

The following morning, Sasha told him that she was going to the market in Pewsey.

'The widow lets me buy her meat,' she told Scrooge confidentially. 'Which is nice because it gives me a chance to talk to the butcher's boy. He's only a simply country lad, Mr Scrooge, but he's lovely.' She smiled happily at the memory. 'Our eyes met over a pile of giblets, soon after I got here, and I've been after him ever since.'

Scrooge was slightly taken aback at this frank confession of affection for another man, but he did his best to repress all thought of jealousy.

'Well, I'm very pleased to hear it, Sasha,' he told her. 'Of course, it's early days yet, but I'm sure you'll catch the eye of a lot of young men – it's only right and proper that you should. In due course you will no doubt want to set up a home with one of them. And when you do, I shall be very pleased to help you. I promise.'

Sasha smiled and bent to kiss him. 'Too soon to think of that yet,' she said. 'And too soon for me to come back into your bed, too. The widow says you mustn't do it for a while yet. The illness will have weakened your heart, you see. You'll be all right in a couple of weeks or so, but you have to give it time to recover.'

And off she went, with a wave and skip in her step.

Scrooge sat quite still for a moment. Had she really said what he thought she'd said? *The widow says you mustn't do it for a while yet.* Did that mean that the widow knew that he and Sasha were lovers? Had he no secrets from anyone?

While Sasha was out, the widow held her usual morning clinic. And when it was over – only eight patients that day – she took Scrooge into her pharmacy, as she called it.

The pharmacy was a spacious room at the rear of the house: a conservatory, was the term Scrooge would have used. In any event, there were large areas of glass which looked out on to the garden.

Adjoining the pharmacy was a small entrance hall with an external door which could be approached round the side of the house. It was though this door that patients gained their admission, and if necessary they could take a seat in the hallway while waiting their turn to be seen.

Once admitted to the pharmacy, they were asked to explain the nature of their problem and to answer the widow's questions. Then, depending on her diagnosis, she provided the appropriate treatment.

Sometimes, the widow explained, the treatment consisted of a standard herbal potion or an ointment of a kind which she had already mixed. On other occasions, a special brew had to be prepared, and the patient had to call back for it later. Either way, most of her medicines were based on herbs which she grew in her garden or, in some cases, acquired from other parts of the country or from abroad.

'This morning, for instance, I had a young man with a toothache. Well, I expect you could have treated him yourself, Mr Scrooge.'

'Oil of cloves?' suggested Scrooge.

'To begin with, yes. We will see how he progresses on that. Then there was a baby with diarrhoea, and an old gentleman having trouble passing his water, and so on. Common enough ailments, most of them, and all I do is use the knowledge which has been passed on to me, through the family, for a good many centuries.'

'So there is a tradition of this in your family?' asked Scrooge.

'Oh yes. On the female side. And in recent years the men have mostly practised medicine or surgery of the orthodox kind. Like my late husband.'

Scrooge did not want to dwell on her husband.

'Do you make any sort of charge?' he asked.

The widow laughed. 'Oh no. Fortunately I have a modest income from land and property. Enough to see me out. But I do get given gifts, such as vegetables or fruit, or a chicken sometimes, which I am always happy to accept.'

Scrooge summoned up his courage to ask a potentially offensive question.

'Is it true what they say about you?'

'What do they say about me?'

'That you're a witch.'

The widow laughed, and it was a genuine laugh, but she busied herself with returning bottles to the right shelves rather than look at him directly.

'I don't object to that description, if it's used in the right way. But whether I am or am not a witch depends on your definition of the term. The truth is, I practise the healing arts in a manner which has been handed down to me from generation to generation. And I add to that body of knowledge such insights as I have gained from my own experience. I hope in due course to pass that knowledge on to someone else, though I have no children, as you know. I am therefore, in a sense, the embodiment of the accumulated wisdom of the local community – at least insofar as medicine is concerned. As a result, some people call me the wise woman of the village. And they do say that witchcraft is the craft of the wise, so in that sense I am a witch, yes. I heal as best I can. Of course,' she added, turning to face him, 'we all have to die in the end. But I try not to let it happen before it has to.'

'I only wish,' said Scrooge with a choke in his voice, 'that I had had access to your skills to treat young Billy. I am sure you must know the story.'

The widow nodded. 'I do. But I did see him, you know, on Christmas Day. When he ate too much rich food and was sick, at your nephew's house, I was called downstairs to look at him. And I have to say, Mr Scrooge, that I could see at once that he was frail. It was clear to me that the merest breath of wind would soon be carrying him away.'

Scrooge gave a moan of anguish, and banged on the floor with the stick which he was using to support himself on his still-unsteady feet.

'But it is not right!' he cried. 'Not right that a man like me should survive and a boy like Billy die!' He stared into the widow's face, his eyes filled with tears. 'I am sure that you could have saved him! I am sure that you could!'

He began to sob helplessly, like a young child, and the widow put her arms around his shoulders to comfort him.

'You did your very best, Mr Scrooge. You did everything possible, and you have no cause to reproach yourself. No man can do more than that.'

But Scrooge was inconsolable.

21

On the Saturday night of that week, a barn dance was held in the village. This social occasion was open to anyone who cared to attend, and Sasha was looking forward to it.

On the day itself, she spent much of the morning consulting the widow on precisely what she would wear. It was, apparently, a most difficult matter to choose something which showed her good looks off to advantage while at the same time not causing offence to the country girls through too much ostentation.

When seven o'clock came, Sasha was called for by the young girl who acted as the widow's maid. (Like the Cook, this girl lived elsewhere in the village and came in to work on a daily basis.) And, after the house fell quiet, Scrooge and the widow sat peaceably by the fire.

Scrooge had a rug around his knees. The room was warm, the light from the lamps pleasantly golden. On all sides were ancient and well-worn pieces of furniture, old pictures, and shining items of silver.

The widow sewed. Scrooge had a book, but he didn't read; for the most part he simply stared into the fire, thinking about the past. Occasionally he dozed a little.

After perhaps an hour, the widow made them both a cup of coffee. Then, as she sat down again, she said, 'I can see that you have been thinking this evening, Mr Scrooge. And I wonder if you have ever asked yourself why it was that you fell ill at this time – and why you have survived.'

Scrooge was puzzled by this, but to give himself time to

think he said, 'Why, I am quite sure that I survived because of your excellent nursing.'

The widow smiled. 'No doubt that played a part. I would not deny it. But you survived mainly because you were determined not to die. If you had been weary of life, sickened by it, you would have died soon enough. But you are not yet ready to die, I suspect, because you know that you have unfinished business.'

Unfinished business. Scrooge thought about it. He was astute enough to know that the widow was not referring to the contracts and commitments which he had entered into via the Royal Exchange. But what other 'unfinished business' did he have?

'I wonder if I might ask,' he said, 'without in any way questioning your judgement, what is it about me that gives you the impression that I have matters still to attend to? I am not denying that you are right, please note. But I am curious as to how you came to your conclusion.'

'A fair question.... Well, when we met you on Christmas Day, Mr Scrooge, my sister and I were intrigued. We thought you a most unusual person.'

'Why so?'

'Well, to begin with, you sat alone whenever possible, towards the back of the room. You did not join in the singing and the dancing, and you did not play the silly games. True, you were not surly and difficult. You were polite and affable, up to a point. But we noted that you were a solitary person by nature, and we knew from other sources that you had a reputation as a rich man who was tight with his money. And yet you alone, of all the people there, had brought with you a boy from the streets, and had seen to it that he had a much better Christmas than he would have done without your help. You had performed an act of exceptional kindness and charity. And so there was clearly a compassionate man lurking within you some-where. A man capable of feelings even if you were not much good at expressing them. In short, we felt that you were a person wrestling with yourself – that you were in much doubt about what to do and how best to do it.'

This was such a perceptive analysis, and so much in accordance with the views which Scrooge had come to have about himself, that he felt quite disconcerted. In his own mind, he had always considered that he took great pains to disguise his hopes and fears. But now here was a lady telling him that they were writ plain, all over him, for those who chose to look.

'It is true,' he said haltingly, 'that during these last few years I have become increasingly dissatisfied with my life. Not to the point where this unhappiness has interfered with my work, or troubled my sleep. But in my quieter moments I had come to understand that my life has not been lived as best it might. And I have been thinking, it is true, about how I might best conduct myself in such years as I have left.'

He took a drink of coffee before continuing.

'At Christmas time, I am always reminded of the fate of my late partner, Jacob Marley, for he died on Christmas Eve, seven years ago. Died alone and miserable, a hard, bitter, cold-hearted man. There was not an ounce of emotion or warmth in him. Those were good qualities, one might say, for a man of business, but hopeless for a husband or father. And Marley, needless to say, was neither. He died without a wife, without children, without friends.'

Scrooge gazed into the flickering fire before continuing.

'I dreamed of Marley last Christmas Eve. I dreamed that

I saw him in death, dragging his chains behind him. And in some mysterious way his chains were made up of all the miseries and bitterness that he had accumulated during his life. And I, of course, do not wish to end my days like him.

'Furthermore,' said Scrooge with a sigh, 'as if that were not enough, I am every day reminded of my father, who was another unhappy and unfulfilled man, resentful of his condition and fate. I am reminded, I say, because whenever I look in the mirror to shave, my father's face looks back at me. And that is troubling, to say the least. For my father's habitual expression, at least in my memory, was sour, pinched, and bitter, with a perpetual sneer of contempt close at hand in ready reserve.'

The widow thought for a few moments. Then she said, 'I have been told – and I have it only third-hand, so I may be mistaken – but I have been told that you and your father fell out, while you were still a boy.'

Had it third-hand, thought Scrooge. So probably the chain of communication was nephew Fred, to his wife's aunt, Mrs Bannister, and from her to her sister, the widow.

So people had been talking about him behind his back – again. Scrooge was surprised that anyone should find him a sufficiently interesting subject for gossip. But he could hardly complain, for the talk had resulted in his invitation to this house, and if he had not ended up here he might very well not have lived – whatever the widow might say about his unfinished business.

He sighed. 'Yes, it is true that my father and I fell out. Father was not a bad man, and to be fair to him we must remember that he suffered a great blow when my mother died. He became withdrawn and depressed at first, and then almost perpetually angry. But a bereavement should not be allowed to spoil one's life for ever, and in my view he

180

allowed his loss to dominate his feelings for too long.'

'And what was the specific cause of your disagreement?

Scrooge chuckled. 'Oh! A choice of career. My father was a land agent – that is to say, he managed the estates of various landowners, some great, some small – and he wanted me to follow him into that profession.'

'And you didn't wish to?'

'No! I didn't want to be for ever at the beck and call of some aristocratic landowner – I wanted to be my own master in some way. And so, partly because I was already alienated from my father, and partly because I genuinely did not wish to spend my life in that way, I wrote him a rather rude letter. I told him that I would not accept his plan for me.'

'And how did he take it?'

'Badly. I was being educated, if that is the right term, at a boarding school at the time, and when he received my letter, my father decreed that I must be banished from home. I must stay there during the holidays as well as during the term, until I had learnt my place.'

'Oh dear.'

'Oh dear indeed. It was an unhappy state of affairs. It had one perhaps fortunate consequence, because it meant that when I was left alone during the holidays I had nothing to do but read, and so I contrived to educate myself. But in the end, after a year or two, my father's heart was softened by my sister, and I was allowed to come home at last.'

'You had only the one sister, I believe. Fred's mother.'

'That's right. And a fine woman she grew up to be. When she died, I understood for the first time something of what my father must have felt at the loss of his wife. And I have never since failed to feel pain at the fundamental injustice of life. So many good folk leave us before their time.'

They both fell silent for a while. The widow, no doubt, was thinking of her husband, and Scrooge in turn was much affected by his recollections of his sister. It upset him to think about her, even now.

After a while, the widow said, 'While I would not wish to pry, Mr Scrooge – ' (Not much, he thought) – 'I cannot help wondering why it was that you yourself never married.'

Well, he had to be careful now. A few months ago he would have spoken very sharply in response to such an approach. *Mind your own business* would have been the least of his retorts. But he recognised that he was faced with a friendly soul, one who was genuinely interested in his welfare and not just consumed with idle curiosity. He reined in his instinctive response and took a deep breath before replying.

'Well,' he said, 'after I left school I went to work for a Mr Fezziwig. And a fine fellow he was too, though I didn't always appreciate him at the time. I was an apprentice, as were a number of other young lads, and every once in a while, and particularly at Christmas, he would throw a party, or a dance of some sort, and try to see to it that we met suitable young ladies of our own age. He was a family man himself, you see, and conscious of the blessings that such an arrangement can bring.'

'And he introduced you to someone suitable?'

Ah, thought Scrooge, so she knows the story already. She just wants to hear my version of it. Well, that seemed fair enough.

'He did. Or it was through his good offices, anyway. I met a young lady – Belle by name. I found her most attractive, and in the course of time I became engaged to her. But – ' And at this juncture Scrooge again sighed heavily. 'I had by that time left Mr Fezziwig's warehouse.

He was in the cloth trade, was Fezziwig, and I handled all his finances for him. It was in that way that I came to know Marley, who provided the finance for the company. Towards the end of my apprenticeship I proposed to Marley that we should start a business together – a bold proposal, as I think now, but it seemed natural enough then. For better or for worse, Marley agreed, and so from then on I was very much taken up with the task of putting the new business on a sound footing, and securing my future. Or so I told myself.'

'You were ambitious, Mr Scrooge.'

'I was. I had the ambition to become a successful man of business, and I was less and less interested in establishing a family. Then, when my father died, I decided to use the capital which I inherited to invest further in this new enterprise. I could have used it to set up a family home, of course. But no, I decided against that.... In the course of time my fiancée came to recognise my obsession with financial affairs – an obsession which I had caught from Marley like some foul disease – and she graciously released me from my commitment. That was how she was kind enough to put it, though in reality she was weary of the shameful way I had treated her. Delaying our marriage for month after month, year after year. She had realised that, however fond I might be of her – and I have reason to suppose that she also cared for me – she would always take second place to my primary interest. And so, very wisely, she cut her losses and ran.'

'And what became of her?'

'Why, she very sensibly found another fellow. Someone far kinder and better balanced than myself, and she made a happy and successful marriage.... A good many years later, when I had come to understand what a mistake I had made,

I took the trouble to make sure that she was well and in good circumstances – just in case she needed help, you understand – and I found that she was coping very well, thank you, with a good man for a husband and fine children who were a credit to her.'

The widow rose and poured out the last of their coffee.

'Another week or two, I think, Mr Scrooge, before you can resume your nightly glass of brandy. And I trust a second cup of this will not keep you awake?'

'Not me,' laughed Scrooge. 'If the last few nights are any guide, I shall sleep ten hours with no dreams.'

The widow resumed her seat and picked up her sewing.

'So,' she said thoughtfully. 'As my brother-in-law might say, Mr Scrooge, you are not in a state of grace. You are dissatisfied with your life, and conscious of the need to change it. But the question is, what exactly are you going to do?'

Scrooge drank his coffee made a small gesture with the saucer. 'That is what I have been asking myself for some time. I have accumulated a vast fortune, and I would like to think that it could be put to use by doing good in the world. But I am damned if I know how best proceed. Do you have any ideas?'

'Even if I had,' said the widow, 'I would not suggest them to you. This is a matter which you must decide for yourself, for only in that way will you be able to live comfortably with the decision afterwards.... Why don't you take advantage of your enforced rest, here in this house, which is away from the hustle and bustle of London, and think things through at your leisure?'

'That sounds a wise proposal,' said Scrooge.

'It will be some time before you are fully recovered. And even when you are, you need feel in no hurry to leave.'

'Thank you,' said Scrooge. 'I am grateful for your hospitality.'

'There is just one small point,' said the widow pensively.

'Yes?'

'It's fairly obvious really, and I'm sure it has occurred to you already.'

'Probably not.'

'But you did say that you were weary of looking in the mirror and seeing your father's face, for that reminded you of what an embittered and disappointed man he became.'

'Yes, indeed. And in appearance I am much like him.'

'Well then,' said the widow, 'that being the case, why do you not continue what you had already half begun, while you were ill, and grow a beard?'

22

Within a week, Scrooge's beard had begun to look quite promising. His stubble had flecks of grey in it, and it still had a long way to go, of course, before it could be said to be a proper beard; but now, as he glanced in the mirror, Scrooge thought that before long he might even appear quite distinguished. Progress, as Mrs Bannister might say.

Scrooge was also making progress – and quite rapid progress at that – in terms of his decisions about how best to use his money. He sent for Cratchit, who came down by train at the end of the week. After an excellent lunch (roast beef, potatoes, parsnips, and gravy, followed by a jam tart with custard), Scrooge and his long-serving employee settled down in the now deserted dining-room and began to sort out his affairs.

'I have been having a long think,' said Scrooge, by way of opening the conversation. 'I've had a lot of time to think recently, as you well know, Cratchit, and it's done me nothing but good, I'm sure. And this is what I've decided. I've come to the conclusion that I ought to give away nine-tenths of my money.'

Cratchit was clearly stunned by this news; his mouth fell open in a manner which Scrooge judged most satisfactory. He could scarcely have made a more dramatic announcement if he had told Cratchit that he was to become Archbishop of Canterbury.

'Nine-tenths of your money,' repeated Cratchit slowly. 'Give it away, you say. Well…. That sounds an awful lot, sir.'

'Well indeed it does. And if I only had ten bob to my name it would be too much. But giving away nine-tenths of over a million will still leave me with a hundred thousand. Which ought to be enough for a fellow like me. Wouldn't you say so?'

'Well yes, sir,' said Cratchit. 'If you put it like that.'

'Money can be a great blessing,' said Scrooge, in philosophical mode. 'There's no doubt about it. But it can also be a great burden. And I have come to the conclusion that my burden is too great to be borne much longer.'

'Well,' said Cratchit, still struggling to take in the news. 'It's a very generous thought, sir. But how exactly are you going to go about it?'

'Ah, indeed. That is the question. Giving away money ain't as easy as one might imagine. For a start, a fair bit of my capital is tied up in one way or another, and it can't all be released straight away. However, what I've decided is this. I will set up a charitable trust – the lawyers can sort out the details, and I've written them a long letter for you to take back. Mr Larking at Larking and Chester, he's the best man for this sort of work. Essentially, I will sign over quite a lot of money to the trust straight away, and more as it becomes available, when my various investments are paid back.'

'This will be an irrevocable gift, will it, sir?'

'Oh yes. Has to be. And there will be trustees, of course, to manage the trust. I shall be one, and I thought perhaps the Reverend Mr Bannister and his wife might also serve. I've written a letter to them too. We might need others, in the course of time, but that will do for a start. If any one of us dies, the remaining trustees will appoint a replacement.'

'And how will the trust operate, sir?'

'Well, the money that I give to the trust will be invested,

mostly in government stock, or funds equally as secure. And the trustees will then distribute the income in the form of grants. And that's where you come in, Cratchit.'

'Me sir?'

'Yes sir, you sir. I wouldn't want you to think that you'll be out of a job if I give up my present profession. By no means. No, Cratchit, your job – if you're willing to take it, of course – will be to act as the trust administrator. We shall invite applications, from anyone and everyone you can think of who might need help to do useful things in the world. Individuals and institutions. And they will all have to fill out an application form. Very short, just one side of a sheet of paper. We don't want to be bureaucratic. And then the trustees will decide whether to approve an application. Any two out of the three trustees being sufficient to authorise a payment. The others must be able to over-rule me, you see, in case I have one of me attacks.'

'Attacks, sir?' Cratchit looked worried.

'Yes, Cratchit, one of me attacks of stinginess. You must have noticed that they come over me from time to time.'

'Oh yes, sir, I had remarked on it, now you mention the matter. Only occasionally, of course.'

'Naturally. Anyway, as I say, there seem to be plenty of people doing good work who need a bit of help, so I'm sure that the trustees will normally approve the applications. Unless we're approached by absolute rogues, and we shall look to you to spot those at an early stage.'

'Well sir,' said Cratchit, 'I'm sure I shall consider it a great honour to serve in this way.'

'You can run the trust from our present suite of offices.'

'I'm sure I could, sir.'

Cratchit paused, as if undecided whether to say what was on his mind. Scrooge noticed, and gave instructions.

'Well, spit it out, man. Don't just sit there with something on the tip of your tongue.'

'Well, sir,' said Cratchit thoughtfully, 'I was just thinking, sir, this will be a very big change from your former way of life.'

Scrooge leaned back in his chair and gave the point some thought.

'A very big change, you say.... Well, not as big as you might think, Cratchit. The way I see it, we shall be using the capital in much the same way as I do now. We shall be supporting and encouraging those with enterprise and vision. Except that in future we shall be making grants, not loans. And we shall be dealing with ventures which are by their nature not in the business of making profits. For instance, Cratchit, we can provide support for some of the charitable hospitals. And we might provide scholarships for able young men to go to university – fellows who could not afford it otherwise. And think what benefits that might bring, if only we can develop the talent that currently goes to waste.'

He paused, because the memory of Billy was still very painful.

'Take a fellow like Billy, for example. A bright lad, as I think you will agree.'

'Very bright, sir. Very quick.'

'We could have done something for him in better circumstances. And there must be thousands like him.... And we can help young women too – we mustn't forget them. Not quite sure how we could proceed in that regard, but no doubt we shall think of something. After all, in young Sasha we have a very good example of how a girl can blossom if she is given a little help.'

Scrooge lowered his voice to make sure that he was not

overheard outside the room.

'Our Sasha has quite come into her own in this house, you know, Cratchit.'

'Yes sir?'

'Oh yes. Gets on wonderfully well with the widow. Soaks up knowledge like a sponge, does Sasha. Helps in the clinic every morning. And has, I believe, found herself a young man.' Scrooge nodded knowingly. 'A butcher.'

'Well well,' said Cratchit, with an amused smile.

Scrooge and Cratchit talked through the details of Scrooge's proposals for some time, and then Cratchit prepared himself to catch the train back to London.

'You go and see the lawyers,' said Scrooge as they parted. 'See Mr Larking himself, on Monday morning, and give him my letter. He can write to me here if there are any problems. But I want everything set up so that I can sign the documents on my return to the office.'

'Any idea when that will be, sir?'

'Oh,' said Scrooge, 'I'm feeling much better than I was. But a man could get used to a life like this, you know. I'm in no hurry to move at present.'

23

A few more days passed, and it began to be possible to talk of spring. The weather was still chilly and the wind still blustery, but the sun was higher in the sky.

Scrooge was now strong enough to take short walks in the open air, and as the warmth of the sun increased, so the vitality came back into his body.

It was good for him to be out of doors, he understood that now. When in the city, he hardly bothered about the seasons. They normally had little effect on him, beyond having to decide whether to wear an overcoat or not. Even that decision was hardly worth making on most days, because it was only a short walk from his home to the office and from there to the Royal Exchange.

Out here, however, life was quite different. He had become much more conscious of the rhythm of each day – the arrival of dawn, noon, evening. He also found himself more observant of the rapid changes in the sky, and the much more gradual development of the spring season. He had, he realised, become aware of many things which had once been familiar but which he had long since neglected to notice. He remarked as such to his hostess, one Sunday afternoon.

The widow nodded. 'In the country, you would have to be a very self-centred person not to be aware of these changes. Speaking of which, have you noticed, Mr Scrooge, that in the few days' time we shall have a full moon?'

'Er, well, yes,' muttered Scrooge (who hadn't really). 'But

does that have some special significance?'

The widow laughed, and gave him a reproachful look. 'Why, Mr Scrooge, you are a city man, and no mistake. Out here we have no fancy gas lights in the street, you know, and as a result most social life in the country is clustered around the week of the full moon. Had you quite forgot?'

Well yes. Scrooge had.

All he could say, and rather lamely at that, was: 'I invested in gas for the illumination of the streets very early, you know. Did very well out of it. And you will have it here before long, I am certain of that.'

The widow smiled. 'That's as maybe. But in the coming week I am hostess to two little gatherings, and it is only right that I should give you forewarning. On Wednesday, I shall be having the usual monthly meeting of my sewing circle, here, in this house. Some of my lady friends come from as far as Pewsey, and from villages an equal distance in other directions, so we do need a clear sky if possible. We normally use the dining-room. I hope you will not think it rude of me, Mr Scrooge, but I doubt that you will much enjoy the company of a dozen or so ladies. Perhaps it would be sensible for you to retire to your room upstairs on that occasion.'

Well, Scrooge was not the most sensitive of men, but he could take a hint quick enough when struck over the head with it.

'Why of course,' he said. 'I shall take a longer walk that day, and wear myself out, to the point where an early night will be welcome.'

'Splendid. And I wonder if you have noticed the justification for the other small celebration – a little party next Saturday.'

Scrooge concentrated fiercely, anxious not to be found

wanting yet again. Birthday? Hadn't heard of one. Wedding anniversary? Hardly. Dammit, why hadn't Sasha given him a hint?

'I'm afraid,' he said eventually, 'that no specific cause for a party immediately comes to mind.'

The widow did not rub his nose in it. 'Well, it's not much of an excuse,' she said, 'but at the end of this week, the days and the nights will be exactly the same length. '

'Ah – you mean the spring equinox.'

'I do.'

Scrooge sighed in exasperation at his own failure to recognise the obvious. 'Well, I can't say that I would have guessed that. The equinox is not an event that we take much notice of in financial circles.'

'Well we note it here,' said the widow. 'And I normally give a party to mark the occasion. And now that you seem to be well recovered, I have taken the liberty of inviting a few friends and neighbours to join us, next Saturday evening.'

The widow accompanied Scrooge on most of his walks, and the following day was no exception. As they proceeded she pointed out to him some of the sights of village (there were not many, for Tanway was not a large place), and introduced him to various friends and neighbours whom they happened to meet. The widow was a friendly soul, Scrooge noticed, and she greeted the farm labourers with the same enthusiasm as the Vicar. She seemed to know everyone.

One of the principal landmarks in Tanway was the church, which was positioned at the western end of the main village street. To begin with, a walk as far as the church and back was enough exercise for one day, and on several occasions Scrooge and the widow walked slowly around the churchyard before returning home.

The chief feature of the churchyard was an ancient yew tree. It was, said the widow, probably twice as old as the church itself, which meant something in excess of a thousand years. Quite how the widow would know this, Scrooge wasn't sure, but the tree was undoubtedly venerable, because its trunk had long since split into two, leaving a space through which a man could walk.

Close to the church was the manor house, which was also old but had evidently been rebuilt and remodelled in Georgian times. It was fronted by a wall, with a handsome pair of gates.

'And who might your squire be?' Scrooge enquired, as they paused to look at the building.

'There is a vacancy,' said the widow thoughtfully. 'The family was an ancient and honourable one, but by no means fertile. Sir John, who was the last male of the line, died childless many years ago, and his widow followed him last year. She lived to be ninety, and was a good friend of mine. She was a member of my sewing circle.'

The widow turned to point back at the churchyard.

'Her grave is over there, in the far corner. The house and the estate adjoining it have been inherited by two distant cousins who live in Canada, and they have, I understand, no intention of returning. So what is to become of the property no one knows.' The widow smiled mysteriously. 'Do you fancy the life of a country squire, Mr Scrooge?'

Scrooge paused. 'Well oddly enough,' he said, 'I was born and bred in a small country town, near Newbury, but I migrated to London as soon as I left school. I have sometimes thought about returning to the country for my last years – but not yet awhile, I think.'

*

194

On the night of the sewing-circle meeting, Scrooge retired to his bedroom soon after seven, leaving the coast clear for the widow and Sasha. Both of them, together with the two ladies who came in on a daily basis to deal with the cooking and household work, had been busy all day with preparations. Sasha in particular was clearly excited by the prospect of the evening's activity.

Upstairs, Scrooge undressed and popped into bed; and he was pleased to find that it was a bed which had thoughtfully been warmed for him with a pan of hot coals. It was too early to go to sleep yet, so he read for while.

Downstairs he heard the doorbell ringing repeatedly, and the chatter of female voices as the guests arrived.

Later he heard singing. Or rather, a sort of chanting. It was not an unpleasant sound. Indeed it was really rather restful. And so, after a while, Scrooge put out his lamp, and slept.

The following morning he descended for breakfast. He was, perhaps, a trifle earlier than had been his previous habit, and he found that the dining-room was still laid out as it had been for use on the night before. The table was pushed to the rear of the room and the chairs were set in a circle.

'Perhaps we should take breakfast in the kitchen this morning,' said the widow, when she came upon him standing by the dining-room door and unsure of where to go.

'Why certainly,' said Scrooge. 'It will be very welcome wherever it is served.'

Sasha cooked for them, and Scrooge watched her affectionately as she worked. There was something about that girl, he decided. She had come on in leaps and bounds in the short time he had known her. Put on weight too, he suspected. There was a sort of glow about her – a sense of accomplishment and self-confidence which pleased him greatly. He felt a warm sense of satisfaction that a few people – Mrs Bannister, the widow, and himself – acting together, had been able to bring about a transformation which they could take pride in.

'I do hope,' said the widow after a while, 'that our meeting last night did not disturb you.'

'Oh no,' said Scrooge quite truthfully. 'Though I was somewhat surprised to hear you singing.'

The widow exchanged a glance with Sasha. 'Oh yes,' she said. 'We sang all right.'

Sasha looked back at the widow. 'And we danced too,' she said, with an obviously mischievous intent, and the two of them burst out laughing. In fact they laughed so much that Sasha had to sit down and bend her head forward over her knees.

Scrooge was so taken aback that he didn't know what to say. As soon as he reasonably could, he changed the subject.

At the weekend, as she had said she would, the widow gave another party to mark the spring equinox.

The dining-room was once again prepared for the occasion. The furniture was rearranged, and the best silver candlesticks were brought out and polished. The widow, Sasha, and the two helpers laboured all day to prepare.

Come the evening, a good pile of logs was set burning in the spacious hearth (for the nights were still cold), and Mr Scrooge was given charge of the wines. The red wines were decanted and left to breathe, and the white wines were suitably chilled.

Scrooge decided to dress up for the occasion, since the

ladies seemed determined to do so. Sasha had in fact travelled to Pewsey to buy a new dress; charged to Scrooge's account, of course.

'Dressing up' meant that Scrooge wore a dark-blue suit with a faint chalk stripe (as opposed to his customary dark grey, so dark that it was almost black); gold cufflinks (as opposed to his normal choice of small pieces of ebony set in steel); and – just to show that this was a relatively informal occasion – a white silk handkerchief tucked into his breast pocket.

His beard, he decided on looking into the mirror, was really quite presentable; in fact he had to snip off a few loose hairs to tidy it up.

About a dozen friends and neighbours, of both sexes, came in for the evening, and were served with a hot buffet meal.

When the party began, Scrooge was slightly surprised at the variety of persons present. They included, as he had expected, some of the higher levels of local society (a lawyer from Pewsey and his wife), but also some persons of much more modest status (the village blacksmith and his wife, a washerwoman). However, the mix seemed to work perfectly well, as if all present were used to such gatherings.

During the evening, the widow called upon some of her friends to provide musical entertainment. The piano was heavily used, as were the odd fiddle and a double bass brought in by guests. Several songs were performed, both solo and in chorus.

To Scrooge's astonishment, one of the solos came from Sasha.

True, he had heard her singing about the house from time to time, both here and in London, but he had not taken a great deal of notice, and it would certainly not have

197

occurred to him to invite her to sing in company.

But here she was invited, for in keeping with the catholic nature of her guests the widow had chosen to treat Sasha as one of the family and not as a servant. And Sasha sang the song beautifully.

It was not a melody that Scrooge remembered hearing before, and he could not have repeated a word of the lyric afterwards. But the sensation of having heard it – the memory of the purity of her voice, and the strange, disturbing melancholy that it induced in him – that, he knew, would stay with him for ever.

Afterwards, when all the guests had gone, Scrooge congratulated Sasha on her performance.

'I had no idea,' he said, 'that you could sing so beautifully. And that song – I wonder where you learnt it?'

As soon as he spoke, Scrooge realised that this was a question he should not have asked, because a wince of pain crossed Sasha's face. But she did answer him.

'Oh,' she said, after a moment's hesitation. 'It was a song my mother taught me.'

And then, to Scrooge's dismay, she burst into tears.

Trying his best to make good his foolish error, Scrooge took her into his arms and held her close while she sobbed.

'Oh, Sasha, Sasha, Sasha,' he said. And he stroked her head until the worst of the tears subsided.

24

After another ten days, Scrooge decided that he really had no further excuse for imposing upon the widow's generosity, and he decided to return to London, taking Sasha with him.

He half expected that Sasha would object to this decision. He thought it possible that she would apply to stay with the widow, so that she could be near the young butcher who had caught her eye. But either the affair with the butcher was less advanced than he had thought, or else Sasha had concluded that she would in any case be back in the country soon. Scrooge wasn't sure which, but either way he had the feeling that some female plotting was afoot. In any event, Sasha accompanied him without a murmur.

The two travellers reached London by lunchtime, on a Monday morning, and after a bite to eat Scrooge went into the office. There Cratchit spent the afternoon bringing him up to date on developments in his business affairs.

Scrooge listened dutifully, but he found his attention wandering. Part of him was amazed to find that he wasn't the least bit interested in business, and the other part was not at all surprised.

When Cratchit asked for decisions on what to do about certain projects, Scrooge's instinct was to say withdraw, close down, cash in. Bring it to an end. Wind it up. He proposed nothing that would harm any other participant, you understand, but as for his own involvement – why, he found that he wanted as little to do with business as possible.

How odd, he thought. A year or two ago he would not have foreseen such a change of heart.

The papers from the lawyer concerning the establishment of his charitable trust were also on his desk, awaiting his attention, but Scrooge didn't even glance at them. Later, he thought. Later.

For the moment there was a much more vital and pressing matter on his mind, a matter which kept popping back into his head even while Cratchit was explaining what had happened over the weeks of his absence. It was a matter which would have to be dealt with before the day was out – he would deal with it that very evening.

On returning to his apartment, Scrooge told Sasha to put on a smart dress, and then he took her out to dinner.

After a leisurely meal, and a stroll home, Scrooge decided that it was time to raise with her the question which had been occupying him all day. He poured a glass of brandy for himself, and a glass of port for Sasha, and sat her down in front of the warm fire in the sitting-room.

When they were both comfortable he told Sasha that he wanted to be quite sure, in his own mind, that she understood something.

'I want you to be aware,' he said carefully, 'that it is not compulsory for you to continue the arrangement which operated before I went down to the country. Before I became ill, as you will remember, we shared a bed together. And a very happy and pleasing arrangement that was. It was a privilege and a pleasure for me. But you must not feel, Sasha, that you are under any obligation to continue that practice. Especially now that you have found someone else, someone of about your own age, for whom you naturally feel some affection.'

'Ah, well now there you're wrong,' said Sasha firmly.

'Wrong about what? I thought you were attracted to this butcher lad.'

'So I am, but you're wrong about me not being under any obligation. For I am under an obligation. I have my orders, Mr Scrooge, and they come from a lady to whom I owe everything, and so I will not disobey her.'

Scrooge paused. 'I assume,' he said, 'that you mean Mrs Bannister.'

'I do. And Mrs Bannister says that you're to be made to do it every night, and no excuses. She says that it says in the Bible that a man should make love to his wife every day, and the same applies to you and me, even though we're not married.'

Scrooge could hardly believe his ears. 'A man must make love to his wife every night?' he echoed. 'I must say I am inclined to doubt that. Where in the Bible does it say any such thing?'

'Ah, that's what I said,' replied Sasha. 'And Mrs Bannister wouldn't tell me. She just said that she'd told her husband, some years ago, that that's what it said in the Bible, and he hadn't contradicted her, so she reckoned it must be right.'

Scrooge smiled. 'Oh,' he said. 'I see. Well that settles it then.'

The Vicar, Scrooge decided, must be an even more sensible fellow than he had thought.

'If you ask me,' said Sasha, 'I reckon Mrs Bannister made it all up, on account of she's desperate to have a family. But of course she never will, because they've been married for years and nothing's ever happened, and in any case she's far too old.'

'Oh yes,' said Scrooge solemnly. 'She must be all of thirty-five.' But his irony went unnoticed.

'Anyway, Mrs Bannister says that I'm to sleep with you, and to keep you at it, no slacking allowed as long as you're well, and that's what I intend to do.'

Scrooge thought about this for a moment. 'But what about your butcher boy?' he enquired.

'That's different. That's in my own time. This is work.'

Work indeed. Scrooge didn't know whether to feel insulted at being regarded as a mere job, or impressed at the girl's diligence. He was lost for any kind of response, and fell silent.

After a moment he got to his feet and poured them both another drink. Normally one glass of brandy was plenty, but tonight he felt the need of a little more. And besides, he wanted to loosen Sasha's tongue.

When they were both settled again he said: 'I never did ask young Billy about his background, Sasha. Not very much, anyway. Most of what I know about him I gleaned from Mrs Molloy. And I regret that now. I would have felt honoured if Billy had been able to tell me about where he was born, and how he came to be on the streets. So I wonder, Sasha, if you feel able to tell me something about yourself. But of course, if there are things in the past that you would rather keep confidential, then you must not feel any necessity to tell me. I would not wish to upset you. And a phrase which I have often used myself is Mind your own business, so I shan't take it amiss if you quote it at me.'

Sasha looked at him from her chair on the other side of the fireplace, and Scrooge felt his heart beat faster at the sight of her beauty.

He was not exactly in love with her – not in love in the sense that young men become hopelessly captivated by girls

– but he found her an entrancing picture. Even as he looked at her he could remember the touch of her mouth on his, and he longed to possess her physically once again.

Perhaps, he thought, perhaps he ought to be ashamed of feeling such desire for her. Perhaps it was very wicked of him. But it was surely a natural enough emotion that he felt, and he only wished that he were thirty years younger and could sensibly expect to make a life with her.

Sasha took her time about answering his question. 'What did you want to know?' she asked cautiously. 'About my background, as you call it.'

'Well, whatever you feel able to tell me.'

There was a long pause, during which Sasha stirred uneasily in her chair. Then she evidently made her mind up, and began to speak.

'I was born in Southwark, Mr Scrooge, just south of the bridge over the Thames, and my father was a carpenter. My mother took in washing, and I was the eldest of three children, the other two being a boy and a girl. We were a happy family for a while, and my mother taught me to read and write after a fashion. But our troubles began when my father died. I was eight years old at the time. After that we became poor, for my mother could earn very little with three young children to look after.

'I earned what I could for her by running errands and the like, but it wasn't very much, and when I was ten I was sent into service as a maid-of-all-work in a small trades-man's house. While I was there the mistress of the house beat me severely. She knocked me black and blue with a broom handle. I complained to my mother when she saw me, and for a while things were better, but then my mother also fell ill and died, and I had no one to stand up for me. What became of my brother and sister I do not know, for I have neither seen or heard of them since.

'With my mother gone, the mistress had nothing to restrain her in her punishment of me, and after six months I could stand it no longer and ran away. Nothing could be worse than living where I was – or so I thought.

'That first night, I had nowhere to sleep, and the girls on the streets told me of Mrs Hodge's house, which was a low lodging-house in Kent Street, and there I went because I had a penny to gain admission.

'That lodging-house was a den of wickedness beyond all description, and I was in many others like it in the years that followed. Forty and fifty young people were crammed into a small room, sleeping naked, the sexes mixed up in a jumble. Lewdness and filth ran riot. The stench was disgusting and made me sick. Boys and girls of ten and twelve years old were lying bare-skinned on dirty sheets together, and seeing no harm in it. Those that did not know how to swear and use foul language soon learnt, and most of those that were there had stolen the money to pay for their night's lodging. But sleep was almost impossible, for the noise and the yelling and fighting made it hard for anyone to rest.

'For a while I tried to keep myself apart from the filth and the crime, but I was mocked and cursed for thinking myself finer than the rest of them. Look at her for a damned modest fool, they said, and worse. And I was still only ten years old.

'A few months later I tried to make a living as a flower girl. I begged some money from fine gentlemen, for I was a pretty girl and they liked me. I bought a stock of flowers and tried to sell little bunches on the street, but some of the older girls kicked me and punched me for stealing their pitch. They left me crying on the ground and stole my stock and my money, and after that I didn't have the heart to try again. Like the rest of my kind I stole food from the street traders and begged money from strangers.

'When I was twelve I took up with a boy of fifteen and became his girl, though I didn't like him very much. He fancied me and protected me. He sent me out on to the street to go with men, and he beat me with his fists if I wouldn't. And I had often seen girls in the street who had been treated in a like manner, knocked down and kicked senseless, lying sobbing the gutter, or even unconscious, with their teeth missing and their mouths bleeding. I was afraid of that happening to me, so I did as I was told. You get frightened, and tired of the pain, and it was easier to agree. On the whole, going with strangers was no worse than going with the boy, and sometimes better.

'I walked the streets for three years, sometimes getting good money and sometimes none. I tried to get work as a maid, in a gentleman's house where they would treat me properly, but I had no character and I couldn't. No one would take me in. All the money that I had was taken from me by the boy, or spent foolishly.

'In the end I became sick of the life I was living, and I determined to change my ways before my health was quite destroyed. So I stole a piece of beef from a butcher. I let him catch me and got taken into prison. And there I met Mrs Bannister, who took me out of that place and into her home. She taught me how to work in a nice house, and how to mix with honest people. And I swear that as long as I live I shall never disobey her or let her down, for I owe her everything I have and everything I could ever hope to have.

'There, Mr Scrooge. That is my background.'

Sasha stopped speaking and Scrooge covered his face with his hands. He turned his head to one side, pressing his forehead against the wing of the chair.

Sasha stood up quite suddenly and stepped over to him. She pulled his resisting hands away from his face.

'Don't you hide your face from me!' she said vehemently. 'Don't be ashamed if you weep, for your tears show that you are a decent and honourable man. A man worthy of being respected.'

Scrooge reached out and pulled her close to him. He hugged her tight against him, rocking back and forth as if in pain.

'Oh, Sasha, Sasha, Sasha,' he said, and wept again..

And when he had regained control of himself he said: 'Sasha, if I do nothing else in this world I will see to it that you never have to go back to that way of life. I promise, I promise, I promise.'

Later, Scrooge told Sasha once again that it was only right and proper that she would one day find a man whom she wanted to marry, and that when that day came he would see to it that she was able to start her married life with a home of her own.

Then they retired to bed.

Scrooge felt exhausted. Quite apart from the effort of his journey back to London, his talk with Sasha seemed to have drained him of energy. He wanted nothing more than to crawl between the sheets and go to sleep.

But Sasha would hear none of this.

'No excuses!' she said with a grin. 'What's past is past, it can't hurt me now, and it's no use you wriggling and squirming.'

And, when she slipped out of her clothes and he saw her naked in the light of the last candle, Scrooge knew that he would, after all, be capable of making love to her.

He would have been relieved, in a sense, if he had found that his illness and general fatigue had rendered him impotent. He might have felt less guilty; less of a lecher. But that was not the case. His body gave him no escape route. Rather the reverse, in fact. He was as hungry for her as he had ever been. And, in spite of what she had said about sleeping with him being a matter of obligation, he was conscious that Sasha took pleasure from it too.

25

A week after Scrooge's return from the country, Mr Larking, of Larking and Chester, took up a suggestion which had been made to him, very discreetly, by Mr Cratchit: he called at Scrooge's office.

Mr Larking was a good deal younger than Scrooge – just a year over thirty. He was short, and slight in build, and wore spectacles which made him look like a schoolboy. His clothing, while still sober enough to indicate that he was a member of one of the older professions, displayed a certain youthful dash and style which caused eyebrows, in certain quarters, to rise.

On arrival, Mr Larking explained that he had just been passing, and had thought it sensible just to put his head in and to enquire whether all was well with the papers which he had prepared for Scrooge's signature: the papers which would, in due course, and when fully signed and witnessed, set up Scrooge's intended charitable trust; the papers which would involve Scrooge in signing over to the trust, in all, nearly nine hundred thousand pounds.

'Are there, perhaps, any paragraphs in the documents which require elucidation?' asked Mr Larking tentatively.

No, no, Scrooge assured him, everything was entirely clear.

Were there, perhaps, points which Mr Scrooge had thought of, subsequent to issuing his original instructions and which might involve amendments?

No, no, Mr Scrooge was entirely satisfied that his first

thoughts on the matter should be the basis on which to proceed.

Splendid, splendid, beamed Mr Larking. In that case, he would cease to occupy Mr Scrooge's time, because he knew full well that Mr Scrooge must be a busy man. He looked forward, he said, in a few days' time, perhaps, to receiving one copy of the papers, signed and witnessed as indicated, a copy which would enable him, as was Mr Scrooge's undoubted wish, to register the charitable trust with Her Majesty's charitable commissioners, and so to put the matter on to a proper footing – put it, as it were, in a position in which it could begin to operate, as was, no doubt, indeed Mr Larking felt quite certain of it, as was in accordance with Mr Scrooge's wishes. But if, in the meantime, anything should require explanation or amendment, why then he, Mr Larking, son of the senior partner of Larking and Chester, would be only too delighted....

Taking note of Scrooge's fingers, drumming impatiently on the desk, Mr Larking's voice dried up on him, and he departed, feeling somewhat young and foolish.

Mr Larking was much too polite (and Mr Cratchit was much too nervous) to ask Scrooge a direct question. But both men wondered why it was – if the papers were entirely in order, and entirely in accordance with Scrooge's wishes – why it was Mr Scrooge had not actually signed them. Yet. That remained a mystery both to Mr Cratchit and to Mr Larking. But perhaps, they wondered, perhaps Mr Scrooge had changed his mind. It would scarcely be surprising, they thought, if he had.

Meanwhile, even though he had not signed the papers (indeed he had hardly glanced at them), Scrooge continued to wind up his business affairs. Or rather, he tried to begin to wind them up.

The truth was, he was involved in so many damned schemes that he had almost forgotten many of them. And even in the case of the nice simple ones – the ones which were prospering and making money – bringing to an end his involvement seemed to be deucedly difficult.

As for the others – the ones which were going badly – well, pulling out of some of those would mean sending the scheme into certain insolvency, with damage to some innocent parties. And while Scrooge might once have taken such action without so much as an extra blink of his eye, he was now much more cautious.

If people asked him what he was intending to do, he told them that he planned to retire. But saying even that made him bad-tempered. He became rude and abusive, and was then obliged to apologise to people, and then he began to wonder whether he really wanted to retire, and that made him even more grumpy and short with people.... And so it went on.

Eventually, the day came when Scrooge realised that he really must give the proposed charitable trust his whole-hearted attention. So early one morning, before even Cratchit was in the office, he sat down and went through Mr Larking's legal documents line by line.

'Aha!' said Scrooge, after a time.

When Cratchit came in, he was despatched at once to ask Mr Larking if he would be kind enough to call. And when Mr Larking returned, at once, in company with Mr Cratchit, Scrooge sat him down in front of his desk and gave him the bad news.

'I have found,' he said, 'a spelling mistake.'

Mr Larking gulped. And gasped. 'A spelling mistake? In the papers which my firm prepared for you?'

'I am afraid,' said Scrooge gravely, 'so.'

Scrooge steepled his hands in the desk and gazed at the ceiling.

'One thing I will say about Mr Cratchit,' he said thoughtfully, 'is that the fellow can spell.' He lowered his eyes to look at Mr Larking. 'Cratchit is pretty much a self-taught man, you know.'

'Is he really?' Mr Larking was impressed.

'Oh yes. But very hot on spelling. Mr Cratchit knows that accommodation has two C's and a double M. He even knows that benefited has one T, which is a rare accomplishment indeed. Many respectable journals remain entirely unaware of that refinement.'

Mr Larking tutted. 'So, we have misspelt accommodation, have we? Or benefited?'

'Oh no, no,' said Scrooge. 'Neither of those. Have you any Latin, sir?'

'Er, a little,' admitted Mr Larking.

'But not enough, it appears.'

'Possibly not, Mr Scrooge, no.'

'Supersede has been spelt with a C in the middle. Whereas it should, of course, be an S.'

'Of course,' Mr Larking agreed. 'I do apologise.'

'Not at all,' said Scrooge. 'No harm done. I have altered the word, on both copies, and the correction hardly shows. I doubt whether Her Majesty's commissioners will even notice.'

Mr Larking acknowledged that this was a relief of the first order.

'But perhaps,' said Scrooge, 'in the circumstances, I should knock a guinea off your fee.'

'A very proper reaction,' said Mr Larking. And both men knew that Mr Larking would add two guineas, before submitting the bill, to make up for this reduction.

'And is there anything else which requires correction?' Mr Larking asked.

'Oh no, no, thank you. That was all. Everything else is perfectly in order.'

'I see,' said Mr Larking.

He was far too polite, as ever, to enquire as to why, in that case, he had been asked to call round. He simply remarked that, if there was nothing else he could do for Mr Scrooge, he would return to his own office; but he would be available, he assured Mr Scrooge, on request, to call again, if need be.

'If, in the meantime,' he said, 'should you wish to sign the papers, all it requires is a signature from you on each copy, and of course the signature of an independent witness below.'

'Quite,' said Scrooge with a smile.

But he made no move whatever to actually sign the papers in front of him, and so, feeling even more puzzled than ever, Mr Larking withdrew.

A few minutes later, Scrooge announced to Cratchit that he was going for a walk.

Well, this was a new one. Cratchit had often heard Scrooge declare that he was going to 'Change, or the bank, or to get his hair cut, and even, occasionally, that he was going to see a man about a dog. But never, in the entire history of their relationship, had Scrooge said that he was going to go for a walk.

Left alone, Mr Cratchit shook his head in wonder at the way the world was changing, and returned to adding up his columns of figures.

Scrooge meanwhile, made his way to the vicarage, where

he asked the maid – a new girl this time, not as pretty as Sasha – whether her mistress might be willing to see him.

Mrs Bannister, it emerged, was willing to see him, and she took him into her workroom and sat him down.

Before his arrival she had evidently been writing some letters, but she now sat in an easy chair and took up some knitting while they talked.

After various preliminaries she told him how much she admired his beard. 'Very distinguished,' she said.

'I am pleased you like it,' said Scrooge. He was very pleased with it himself. 'Beards are common enough, but not all ladies approve of them. However, Sasha seems to find it quite acceptable.'

Mrs Bannister smiled.

'Speaking of whom,' said Scrooge, 'there is something I would like to ask you about Sasha. Please forgive me if I am out of order. Overstepping the mark, or raising with you matters which should not be raised with a lady....'

'But...' said Mrs Bannister, encouraging him to proceed.

'But I have been wondering – is it true that when you sent Sasha to work for me, as your maid, is it true that you instructed her to share my bed?'

'Oh yes,' said Mrs Bannister instantly.

This was as Scrooge had expected, but it was still a surprising answer.

'But why did you do that? It seems, if I may say so, a highly improper instruction to give.'

'Oh, but Mr Scrooge, I considered that arrangement to be essential for both of you.'

Scrooge couldn't follow that at all. 'I'm sorry but I'm afraid I don't understand.'

Mrs Bannister stopped knitting for a moment. 'Well, when I first thought of sending Sasha to work for you – or rather to work for Mrs Molloy, for she was the one who was unable to cope – it was before Christmas, and I had not at that time seen very much of you. But then we met, on Christmas Day, and I was able to talk to you face to face for some time. And, both on Christmas Day and later, I heard about young Billy. And I realised at that stage that you were not as cold-hearted and mean as your reputation had painted you. But you were a cold man, with a stiff and formal manner. A man who found it hard to express any sort of affection or warmth of feeling....' She began to knit again. 'Do you know what your name means, Mr Scrooge?'

'My name?'

'Yes. Your christian name.'

'Why no, I can't say I do.'

'Ebenezer is a Hebrew word meaning stone of strength. Well, the strength part of it is all very well, but being made of stone is no help to anyone. So I came to the conclusion that you were in pressing need of someone to draw out and develop the emotional side of your nature.'

Scrooge moved uncomfortably in his chair. He hadn't realised that Mrs Bannister knew his first name; and while he recognised the accuracy of the portrait of himself which the lady had painted, he didn't much like having to look at it.

'And Sasha?' he asked, to change the focus of the discussion.

'Ah yes, Sasha. Well, Mr Scrooge, as I am certain I told you, Sasha was in her former life a prostitute. She had therefore been in the company, almost exclusively, of men who were little better than brutes – and worse, in many cases. In that life her experience of relations between men and women had mostly been in the form of one-sided transactions which occupied barely two minutes and took place up some filthy alley. So I felt it was vital for Sasha's her future health and happiness that she should come to understand that there are different and better ways of proceeding. I wanted her to spend some time as the lover of a man who would treat her with kindness and considera- tion. In that way she would come to know from first-hand experience that a man and a woman can share warmth, and affection, and laughter. There can be embraces, caresses, kisses, as between equals. There can be, and should be, concern for each other's feelings. I wanted her to experi- ence love-making as an exchange of pleasure, in a relaxed, warm, quiet, and private place, where two people can be at ease with one another. For if she never had that experience, how could she possibly look forward to being married, and to having a family of her own?'

Scrooge sighed heavily. 'And you thought,' he said haltingly, 'that I was the best man to provide all that for Sasha?'

Mrs Bannister smiled. 'Not perhaps the best man, Mr Scrooge. But the best man available at the time.'

Scrooge winced. It was a painful blow, but a fair one.

'I see,' he said. 'Well thank you for that explanation. It had been troubling me. But what if young Sasha had become pregnant?'

Mrs Bannister looked him full in the face. 'What if she had?'

'Well – would that not have been a disaster?'

'Tell me this, Mr Scrooge. If Sasha became pregnant by you, would she be better off, or worse off, than if she had become pregnant by one of her five-minute customers, twelve months ago? Would you discard her if she told you she was with child?'

'Of course not!' said Scrooge angrily.

'You would stand by her, and provide her with a home and financial support?'

'Of course I would!'

'Well then. Your question answers itself.' Mrs Bannister looked down at her knitting. 'But in any case, if you continue to observe the same sensible precautions as you have observed so far, there is no reason why should become pregnant.'

'Dear God!' said Scrooge. 'Is there anything about me which you do not know?'

'Not much,' said Mrs Bannister, and she burst into a peal of laughter so long and so unaffected that Scrooge simply had to join in.

For a while they talked of other things, but then Scrooge rose to go.

'Tell me, Mr Scrooge,' said Mrs Bannister, as she prepared to show him to the door, 'how are arrangements progressing for the establishment of your charitable trust?'

'Oh, slowly,' said Scrooge, feeling a sharp pang of guilt at his tardiness. 'Slowly. To tell you the truth, I am finding it hard to bring myself to sign the papers. It is my old problem again, I fear.'

Mrs Bannister nodded. 'Well, that is not a matter on which I can be of any help,' she said firmly. 'It will have to be your own decision, and no one else's.'

'Yes,' said Scrooge. 'I'm sure you're right.'

On the doorstep, he paused to put his hat on, tapped it into place, and prepared to set off.

'Do give my warm regards to your sister,' he said.

'I will indeed,' said Mrs Bannister. 'Though I don't expect to see her for some time. She is being courted, Mr Scrooge.'

A sudden chill of wind made Scrooge shiver. 'Courted?' he managed to say.

'Oh yes. By a baronet from Bath.'

Well. Scrooge had seldom walked so fast in his life. In fact he practically ran.

Pausing only to buy a bottle of malt whisky from a liquor merchant, he rushed back to the office, hoping against hope that Cratchit would not be at lunch.

'CRATCHIT!' he roared, as he came through the door.

'Yes sir?' Cratchit leapt up from behind a chest where he had been filing some papers.

'Fetch Mr Jarvis from next door. Give him this bottle of whisky with my compliments and tell him that I would be honoured if he would act as a witness while I sign some documents.'

'Yes sir!' cried Cratchit, who was in no doubt what documents were being referred to, and he was off and running.

When he returned, with the said Mr Jarvis (a dealer in rare books), Scrooge was sat at this desk, the papers for the charitable trust set out in front of him. His pen was poised above them.

'Watch!' cried Scrooge. 'Observe, Mr Jarvis, if you please.'

Scrooge signed. Twice.

'My word,' said Cratchit. 'That's a big bold signature, sir.'

'Well,' said Scrooge, 'it's a big bold move.'

The papers signed and witnessed, Mr Jarvis departed, thanking Mr Scrooge most warmly for his handsome fee.

'And you, Mr Cratchit, must go round to see Mr Lark-ing.'

'Yes indeed, sir. And will you be going to lunch, sir?'

Scrooge paused and thought about it.

'No, Cratchit, I think not,' he said after a moment. 'I think I fancy a breath of fresh air. To be precise, country air.'

26

Scrooge went back to his apartment and asked Sasha to pack him a bag.

'I'm off to Pewsey for a day or two,' he told her.

Sasha frowned. 'Pewsey? What you going there for?'

'Business,' said Scrooge abruptly.

'Business? Huh! You're after that widow woman, that's what you are.'

'When I say business, I mean business,' Scrooge declared. 'Now don't fret. I'm not taking you with me this time, but you'll be there again soon enough, and I'm sure your young man won't have found anyone else in the meantime.'

Sasha turned away with a twirl of her skirt. 'Can't say I'm bothered if he has,' she said with a sniff, but Scrooge was not deceived.

He took the train to Pewsey and on arrival booked himself in at the best of the town's inns: The Bear.

A question often asked in those parts was: What would Pewsey be like without The Bear? And the answer was: un-bear-able.

Well, Scrooge found it comfortable enough.

The following morning he sent a messenger to the village of Tanway (at no small expense) to deliver a note to his friend the widow, asking her if she would care to join him for dinner that evening; in which case he would send a carriage for her. The messenger brought back word that the lady was pleased to accept his invitation, and in due course

219

Scrooge and his guest met in the inn's dining-room.

During the meal, Scrooge reminded the widow that, during his time as a guest in her house, he had decided to set up a charitable trust. The widow had not forgotten. He now went on to tell her that he had, at last, and after a good deal of hesitation, signed the necessary papers. The widow said that she was pleased to hear it, and congratulated him on taking such a generous and far-reaching step.

Scrooge waved away all talk of congratulation. 'The time was right,' he said. 'I shall be much happier now it's done, so in that sense it was a selfish move.'

When the meal was over, the two of them retired to a small room known as the snug; it was a space which the landlord reserved for gentlefolk. There they took coffee and talked.

'I think I should tell you,' said Scrooge eventually, 'lest you hear it first from someone else and feel offended that I have not confided in you, that I am thinking about buying your old friend's house – Tanway Manor.'

'Are you indeed?' said the widow, with an amused smile. 'Well well.'

'You will remember,' said Scrooge, 'that one day during my convalescence we looked at it together. Just from the outside, of course.'

'I remember very well.'

'The place kind of took my eye,' said Scrooge. 'Something about it seemed to appeal to me. So after my return to London I began some correspondence with the lawyer who is acting for the present owners.'

The widow said nothing, but continued to smile. Scrooge had the uneasy feeling that none of this was news to her. So either her network of informers was even more efficient than he had thought, or she was psychic. One or the other.

Or both.

'I have made arrangements to be shown round the place in some detail. Tomorrow afternoon. And I was wondering, if it is not too much trouble, whether you would be willing to accompany me on that occasion?'

'Certainly,' said the widow. 'I should be delighted.'

'A woman's view of these things,' said Scrooge, 'is always useful.'

The following morning gave promise of a fine day, a promise which was fulfilled by a warm, sunny afternoon.

Scrooge used the same firm of carriers to transport him to Tanway as he had used to bring the widow for dinner, but this time, the weather being so pleasant, he was able to ride in an open-top landau. It was a three-mile drive, and he enjoyed the fresh air and the sunshine.

He called first at the widow's house to collect her, and then they drove together to the Manor at the western end of the village.

The gates of the Manor were this time wide open, and the carriage delivered them to the front door in good style.

They were a trifle early, by intention, and the lawyer whom he had arranged to meet had not yet arrived. Scrooge was not disturbed by that; he had wanted the opportunity to have an initial look round without supervision.

The grounds at the front of the house were a little untidy, he noticed, but that was not surprising. The previous owner, an elderly lady, had died some six months earlier, and since then the house had been empty. Presumably the staff, including any gardeners, had been dismissed.

The widow accompanied Scrooge as they walked all around the outside of the house.

'Anything known against this place?' asked Scrooge. 'Leaking roof, sinking foundations, foul smells from the drains.... Ghosts?'

'None of any of those known to me,' said the widow, and Scrooge could think of no better recommendation than that. 'My friend, Lady Brown, grew old and infirm in her last years, but we kept a close eye on her and ensured that the house was kept in good order.'

'What size of household staff would be required?'

'Well, that would depend to some extent on the style in which a man wished to live. Once upon a time, decades ago, this house was always full of people. There is ample space for entertaining, and guests used to come from all over the country – even from abroad. For that sort of thing you need a good few staff. But for a single gentleman, living a quiet sort of life, a cook and two maids would suffice.'

'And for the garden?' asked Scrooge.

'Ah well, that again would depend on how elaborate you wished to be. There is an old kitchen garden, for instance, long since abandoned, but it could be revived. I would say that, to begin with, one man and a boy could do most of what you would require.'

On their return to the front of the house, they found that the estate's lawyer, a Mr Nesbitt, had arrived.

Mr Nesbitt was from Pewsey, and was therefore a sophisticated fellow, at least by Wiltshire standards. He was about fifty years of age, bald, somewhat stout, and with a rosy complexion which suggested a fondness for port. His suit, Scrooge noted with amusement, had been chosen for its capacity to withstand contact with any number of briars and brambles.

The lawyer's basic education had been acquired at Marlborough (where he had learnt how to use his fists and, more useful still, how to kick a man in the balls); his law had been learnt at one of the less fashionable Cambridge colleges.

Today Mr Nesbitt was sweating somewhat. Scrooge suspected that this was a result of both the warm weather and the prospect of earning commission on the sale of a substantial property. A property which had, moreover, been sticking on the market.

After some preliminary discussion with Mr Nesbitt, as they stood on the steps below the front door, Scrooge and the widow were taken inside and given a tour. The house was largely empty, but in some rooms a few elderly pieces of furniture remained, presumably because they were thought to be of no value.

As in many such houses, after the owners have de-camped and most of their belongings have been removed, the Manor had a sad and depressed air about it. But Scrooge could see that it could be brought to life again.

He asked the widow if she would be kind enough to re-acquaint herself with the kitchens and assorted workrooms of the house, so that she might advise him on their condi-tion. Meanwhile, he and Mr Nesbitt began to examine the other areas.

There were two principal storeys to the building, with servants' quarters and attics higher still. On the main upper floor, at the rear of the building, there was a rather fine room which had traditionally been used as a gentleman's study. A library, adjoining it, ran all the way to the front of the house.

The great virtue of the study was that it looked out on to an avenue of beeches, which ran some two hundred yards or so before disappearing over the brow of a hill, beyond which there was woodland.

'I understand,' said Scrooge to Mr Nesbitt, 'that there is a fair bit of land which is technically part of the Manor garden.'

'Oh yes indeed. About thirty acres. And then, of course, as you know, there are seven farms which constitute part of the estate.'

'Yes,' said Scrooge. 'We will talk about them later. But where does this avenue of beeches lead?'

'Nowhere in particular. But at the end of it, just out of sight, there is an ancient circle of small stones, each of them about three or four feet high. There are twenty stones in all, and for that reason they are known as the Maidenscore. Local legend has it that when the maidens hear the church clock strike midnight, they begin to dance.'

'Do they indeed?' said Scrooge, who could remember from his childhood that stones have no ears and can therefore never hear the church clock as it strikes the hour.

With the tour of the house complete, the three visitors sat down at the dining-room table. Mr Nesbitt spread out some plans of the house and the estate, and they began to pore over them.

'What about the village?' Scrooge asked.

'No longer part of the estate, sir. It was once, in the last century, but all the houses are now in private hands.'

'And the seven farms?' said Scrooge. 'All contiguous, I see, though somewhat higgledy-piggledy in pattern. All currently occupied and in good order?'

'All but one, sir.'

'Well that is good news. You don't need me to tell you, Mr Nesbitt, that farming is going through one of its periodic depressions. Rents will have been reduced accordingly.'

'That is true,' Mr Nesbitt admitted. 'Neither agricultural

224

rents nor land prices are what they were twenty years ago. However, while the family might possibly be willing to sell the house and garden without the farms...'

'They are naturally anxious to be rid of the burden of management,' said Scrooge, completing the salesman's patter for him. 'Especially since the new owners are, I believe, resident in Canada, and would naturally prefer to convert land to cash. Very understandable.'

The discussion continued for some time. The widow gave her opinion on the present state of the domestic arrangements, and Scrooge asked detailed questions about the extent to which the farmland had been drained, whether new barns, dairies, cow-pens, and pigsties had been provided. All of these works, he knew from other contexts, would be expensive to carry out if they had not already been completed.

However, at the end of an hour, Scrooge declared himself reasonably satisfied.

'As you will understand, Mr Nesbitt,' he said, 'I have taken advice from many quarters. Since we began to correspond I have had a number of discussions with experienced parties about the pros and cons of purchasing this estate. And you will appreciate, also, that a man who has taken the trouble to inform himself could not possibly make an offer to buy at the price which your clients have named.'

Mr Nesbitt, mopping his brow, said that he was disappointed to hear that, but not altogether surprised.

'As we have been speaking,' said Scrooge, 'I have been jotting down the estimated cost of work which seems to be necessary in order to bring the farms and the house up to standard, and it amounts to a very substantial sum. Furthermore, Mr Nesbitt, with the greatest possible respect to you and your clients, I do not see any queue of potential purchasers waiting to talk to you after I have departed.'

Mr Nesbitt said with a forced and unconvincing smile that oh, that was not quite the case. He could assure Mr Scrooge that there had been an number of other enquiries. He did not add that the number was one, made three months earlier, and that nothing had been heard from the enquirer since. Nor did he admit that, given the present state of agriculture, those who were thinking of buying estates of this sort were rarely sighted.

'All things considered,' said Scrooge, ' I think I might be persuaded to make an offer at seventy per cent of the asking price.'

'Seventy per cent,' repeated Mr Nesbitt.

'That is correct. Without prospect of negotiation upwards. And, I might add, were it not for the presence here today of a lady who was a personal friend of the previous owner, and whose reproach I could not bear to countenance, I would have quoted a figure considerably lower than that.'

'Never mind, Mr Scrooge,' said the widow. 'You can afford to pay a little above the odds.'

'That,' said Scrooge grimly, 'is what I am trying to tell myself.... Well, Mr Nesbitt, I don't doubt that you have delegated authority to strike a deal, within certain limits, seeing as how your principals are so far away. What do you say?'

Mr Nesbitt rose to his feet.

'I accept,' he said. And the two men shook hands.

Scrooge was rather disappointed. It was no fun negotiating with such a complete amateur.

The business of the day completed – and a considerable

item of business it was too – Mr Nesbitt got on his horse and went home, no doubt singing to himself as he went. And the widow invited Scrooge to take tea at her house, which he was delighted to do.

'Well, Mr Scrooge,' said the widow, after they had fortified themselves with scones, cream, jam, and fruit cake (two slices each), 'that is quite a decision you have made.'

'Oh,' said Scrooge, 'I don't wish to boast, but in financial terms I have done far bigger deals than that, and signed the documents without my hand so much as trembling. You see, the Manor is a pretty good investment, all told. Of course I shall have to sit on it for a few years to perceive any rise in value, but that it will rise, in due course, I have no doubt.'

'I wasn't so much thinking of the money,' said the widow patiently, 'as of the change in your life which the purchase of the Manor involves.'

'Ah, well, there again, it seems like a natural enough progression. I began life in the country, and it seems only right to end my days there too. If I still enjoyed London life, and wanted to continue my present work, I wouldn't dream of changing. But as it is I am weary of the old ways.'

Scrooge paused and glanced at the door of the widow's sitting-room to make sure that it was closed and that they were not overheard.

'And, er, speaking of change,' he said. 'There is one further change in my circumstances, one major change, which I would be glad to bring about. But it requires the co-operation of another party.'

The widow looked at him enquiringly, but he could see that, as usual, she sensed what he was about to say.

'That change, as I believe you understand, is a change from bachelor status to that of married man. It is, of course, very late in the day for me, but I would be a foolish man indeed if I did not at least tell you that I would be greatly honoured if you would consent to become my wife.'

The widow began to pour him another cup of tea.

'Goodness me,' she said. 'Is that a proposal?'

'It surely is.'

'Well!' The widow made a half hearted attempt to look surprised. 'I will forgive you, Mr Scrooge, for not going down on one knee, for we are both mature people. But I hope that you will forgive me, Mr Scrooge, if I say that I think it would be premature to give you an answer today, or even for some time. So instead, let me make a suggestion.'

'Please do.'

'Let us pretend, for the moment, that the question has not been put. Now, over the next few months, you are going to have to do quite a lot of work on Tanway Manor before it is ready for you to move in. During that time you are very welcome to stay here as my guest, as and when you wish. Then, when your new home is ready for occupation, you can consider your position again.'

The widow laughed as she passed him his refilled cup.

'After all, we do not know each other particularly well. And it may be that after you have been under the same roof as me for some time, you will be heartily glad to be on your own again.'

Scrooge rejected this proposition forcefully, but he could not deny that the widow's suggestion was a sensible one, and he was happy to accept it.

27

Mr Nesbitt ensured that the formalities for the sale of Tanway Manor were completed rapidly. For one thing, he was nervous that Mr Scrooge might change his mind, and for another he needed his commission.

Less than two days after the signing of the necessary documents, Scrooge had found himself a retired builder in Pewsey. This gentleman, for a consideration, took up temporary residence in the village to supervise Scrooge's programme of work for the Manor.

Three more days, and Sasha had been installed in her own room in the Manor, with a new bed, to become the new housekeeper. A maid was also taken on, though a cook was not yet needed.

Scrooge, meanwhile, remained a guest of the widow.

And now began a great scrubbing and washing and papering and plastering and ordering up of curtains, carpets, tables, chairs, pots, pans, and every other sort of item which was needed to repair, redecorate and refurnish a house of substantial size.

Workmen from many miles around were persuaded (a handful of cash paid in advance usually did the trick) to postpone the task which they had in hand and to work instead for Mr Scrooge.

This process did not make Scrooge the most popular man in the county (other than with the tradesmen and craftsmen, of course). However, as he pointed out to anyone who complained, if the work was all done in one go, and quickly, then everyone could return to their old ways; the jobs which had been postponed and held up would, he was sure, be completed in record time thereafter. Continued grumbling was assuaged by the gift of a few bottles of champagne and a personal letter, which usually charmed even the surliest temperament.

Sasha was happier than Scrooge had ever seen her, at least after he had put her mind at rest on one point. She had, in the first instance, been concerned about the domestic arrangements in the Manor.

'If I am sleeping here, Mr Scrooge,' she said, 'and you are sleeping at the widow's, how am I to be true to my promise to Mrs Bannister?'

'I think,' said Scrooge carefully, 'you should regard your commitment to Mrs Bannister as having been discharged, Sasha. And if you have any doubt about the matter, please feel free to consult her. My understanding is that Mrs Bannister gave you her instructions so that we should both, you and I, have an experience which would stand us in good stead for the future. It was never intended that the arrangement should be permanent – only that it should prepare us to go on and form relationships with others.'

Scrooge paused and saw that Sasha was still frowning.

'Now I am flattered,' he continued, 'that you should not seize hold of the first excuse you can find to vacate my bed for ever.'

Sasha smiled at him shyly, a little embarrassed.

'And I for my part have come to love you, and will always love you, in an avuncular sort of way. But you are a young and beautiful girl, Sasha, and it would be selfish and wrong if I were not to release you at this point. And besides,' he added, 'I do have hopes of finding a substitute.'

At which Sasha laughed out loud. 'So I was right then,

was I? You do fancy that widow lady.'

'Ask no questions,' said Scrooge amiably, 'and you'll be told no lies.'

Scrooge's conversation with Sasha reminded him of something that he had been trying hard to forget; something which he knew he ought to do, but had been putting off.

He had decided some time earlier that he really ought to make sure that the widow understood the nature of his relationship with Sasha. In view of the fact that Sasha and the widow were as thick as thieves, he suspected that the widow already knew all she needed to know. On the other hand, you could never be quite sure unless you asked, and for his own devious purposes Scrooge wished the matter to be understood now, rather than have it emerge at a later date.

Choosing his moment carefully, when the widow was engrossed in an evidently tricky bit of embroidery, he coughed to announce that he had something to say.

'Er, there is just one point which I would like to clarify with you,' he began.

'Yes, Mr Scrooge?'

'It is something which I should, in fact, have made clear to you even before I took the liberty of proposing marriage. And for that I apologise. But I, er, I thought that, even if it is a little late in the day, I ought to clarify for you the nature of my feelings for young Sasha.'

'Sasha?' said the widow, looking up absent-mindedly from her embroidery. 'Oh yes, I can see that you are very fond of her.'

Scrooge coughed again. 'Yes, well, fond certainly. But since you have also been kind enough to help her in various ways, perhaps I should confess that my fondness, and interest, have been expressed in ways which you may not approve of. In short, I have – ' At this point Scrooge coughed again, several times. 'I have, er, in the past – not now, of course – but in the past, I have been in the habit of inviting her to share my bed.'

'Really, Mr Scrooge?' The widow affected, for the moment, to be surprised.

'Yes. Now I realise,' he continued hastily, 'that this is in some ways reprehensible. Not quite the way in which a responsible and upright fellow would carry on. But I must ask you to believe that there were unusual circumstances.'

'Oh yes.'

Scrooge paused. 'What do you mean, oh yes?'

'Well, what I mean, Mr Scrooge, is that I understand the circumstances very well. In fact, if it will put your mind at rest, and I see that you are somewhat exercised about it, let me say that the suggestion that Sasha should be put to work to warm your chilly soul was originally made by me.'

'By you?'

'Yes. On Christmas Day. At your nephew's house. What that man needs, I said to my sister, is a good woman to warm his bed. Ah, said my sister, I believe a have a candidate. And that, Mr Scrooge, was that.'

'Oh,' said Scrooge in a small voice. 'I see.'

While the work on the Manor was continuing, Scrooge fell into a routine.

In the mornings he would work on business relating to his charitable trust. Once a week Cratchit would come down from London, bringing with him the correspondence and other paperwork – of which there was a great deal – and every morning Scrooge would sit at the dining-room table and plough through it.

Once the trust had been formally established, Scrooge had instructed Cratchit to write hundreds of letters to organisations and individuals who might be interested in the prospect of financial assistance. Two extra clerks had had to be employed (on a temporary basis, Scrooge hoped) to keep up the pace which he demanded.

Letters had gone, for instance, to the headmasters of many schools, pointing out that young men of promise and ability who could not afford to go university might seek a grant from Scrooge's trust. Hospitals had been asked whether they were in need of funds for new buildings or staff. Refuges for the homeless had been invited to state how they would use a donation. The vicars of all the churches in the London, and in Wiltshire, had been approached and informed that a source of help was available in their work with the poor. And so on.

As a result of these letters, application forms for assistance were already beginning to arrive. Scrooge found them fascinating reading. In each case he made a recommendation – yes, no, and if yes, how much – and passed the forms on to his fellow trustees for further review and decision. To his great satisfaction, both Mr and Mrs Bannister had agreed to help him in this work.

On the whole, Scrooge preferred to help those who were obviously prepared to help themselves. He favoured applicants who said that they had collected so much, but needed a little more to meet the full cost of a project. He liked young men who told him that they had borrowed part of the cost from Uncle George, but were still a few pounds short. And ladies who told him that they had arranged for the elderly and infirm in their parish to be fed once a day, but perhaps it was not too much to hope that another meal

233

might occasionally be provided.

So passed the mornings.

In the afternoons Scrooge went to view the work in progress on Tanway Manor. He also began to make a tour of the farms on his estate, and to get to know the tenants.

There was a great deal to do, and at the end of each day Scrooge found himself feeling tired. All this country air was doing him good, he was sure, but he was conscious that he was much more physically active than he had been in the city.

One Sunday afternoon, at the end of a pleasant stroll in the spring sunshine, Scrooge called in at the Manor. He was not there entirely by chance, and, as he had expected, he found Sasha giving tea to her butcher friend from Pewsey: his name was Bradley Bowman. The young man had walked the three miles to see Sasha and would shortly walk back.

Bradley was twenty, a bigger man than most, with broad shoulders and strong arms. Today he was naturally wearing his best suit, but he was at ease in it, not letting the stiffness of his collar be reflected in his manner. He was dark-haired, with skin which tanned easily, despite his mostly indoor work. And, perhaps the key to his attraction for Sasha, he had a dazzling smile, which came readily enough when he spoke.

Scrooge had made it his business to find out something about Bradley. The widow had, of course, been his principal informant, but he had tapped a few other sources as well, for he was not about to let Sasha fall in with a wrong 'un.

He had discovered that Bradley was well thought of and well liked. His worst vice was a fondness for skittles. Interestingly enough he had been born in Tanway, the second son of a farm labourer. He had learnt to read and write in the small school run by the late Lady Brown, in Tanway Manor itself, but was not a book man and never would be. At fourteen he had been apprenticed to a butcher in Pewsey, and he had lived in a room over the shop ever since. His parents were now dead.

After a few minutes Scrooge decided that he liked the young man. What he liked most was his calm confidence and self-possession. There was none of the clumsiness and awkwardness both of speech and movement which country people so often seemed to display in the presence of their betters. Bradley had a country accent, of course, and it was sometimes hard to follow, for Wiltshire had a vocabulary all of its own; but he was articulate and thoughtful, and had a gentle sense of humour.

Well, thought Scrooge afterwards, why should he have expected anything different? He should have known that Sasha would not have admired a fool.

The following day, when he saw Sasha on her own, Scrooge took her aside and said that, if and when she decided that Bradley was the man she wanted to spend the rest of her life with, he would see to it that they were established in their own business.

Sasha smiled and kissed him on the cheek. 'You're a good man, Mr Scrooge,' she said.

'No I'm not. But I might be, one day, if I work at it.'

'Anyway, don't be in such a hurry to marry me off.'

'Why, doesn't the lad want to marry you? He'd be a fool if he didn't.'

'We'll see. Maybe he does and maybe he doesn't. But I haven't told him about myself as yet – about my life before I met Mrs Bannister, I mean. And then I have to tell him about you. And when he's heard all that he may drop me.'

'I doubt it,' said Scrooge. 'He'd be a complete bloody fool

235

if he did.'

Sasha shrugged. 'Well, perhaps. But even if he still wants me I'm going to make him wait a while. Do him good.'

In the middle of May, the time came for the monthly meeting of the sewing circle, and Scrooge tactfully announced that he was going back to London for a couple of nights. He had decided that he would keep his city apartment open for the foreseeable future, with Mrs Molloy in charge.

On his return he asked how the meeting had gone.

'Oh, very well, thank you,' said the widow.

She thought for a moment, and then said: 'But perhaps, come to think about it, there is something you should know about my little group.'

'Yes?' said Scrooge.

'Yes. You did, after all, take the trouble to make sure that I understood about you and Sasha. So I, for my part, should be equally frank and tell you that the, er, the sewing circle is not quite a sewing circle in the ordinary way.'

'Ah.'

'We are, in fact, a group of ladies who choose to celebrate the rites of the old religion.'

'Ah,' said Scrooge again. 'Old as in pre-Reformation?'

The widow laughed. 'No, Mr Scrooge. Far older than that. And I think, before I try to explain any further, you and I should take a trip to Avebury.'

28

Some two weeks later, choosing a fine, warm day, the widow acted upon her suggestion: she took Scrooge to see the sights of Avebury.

To carry them to Avebury, she borrowed a neighbour's dogcart. (A dogcart was a small horse-drawn carriage. Originally such vehicles had been designed to carry dogs when going shooting, but in country they were used as a general means of transport.)

The widow and Scrooge travelled west at first, to the village of Alton Barnes, and then they took the steep road north, at a gentle pace. On their left, they passed a huge hill topped by an ancient burial mound known as Adam's Grave; on their right was Knap Hill, where there were also traces of an old settlement.

Everywhere they went the hedges were thick with May blossom, the woods and fields greener than Scrooge could ever remember them. Spring, when it had come at last, seemed to have decided to celebrate its victory over the harshest winter for decades.

They covered some fifteen miles in all, and the journey took most of the morning. But, as they approached Avebury, Scrooge could begin to see why the widow had brought him.

On his left, running parallel with the road, he saw a mile-long avenue of upright stones, rising up a gentle slope. These stones had obviously been placed in position by human effort, rather than left there by nature; each stone was taller than a man, and would have required a score of labourers to raise it on to its end. Scrooge was impressed.

As they came over the brow of the hill, however, he was quite stunned. For what he saw then was a massive, long bank of earth, thirty or forty feet high. On the other side of the bank was a deep ditch, thirty to forty feet deep, and beyond that a wide flattened area extending for some distance. These man-made structures of bank and ditch were curved and formed a huge circle, about a quarter of a mile in diameter.

Forming another circle, just inside the ditch, were yet more standing stones, of enormous size and weight, standing about ten yards apart. Once there had evidently been a full set of them, all around the perimeter of the circle, but now there were some gaps in the sequence.

It was clear at a glance that this whole area had been created by very early inhabitants of Wiltshire. Probably, Scrooge thought, the work had been carried out before the arrival of the Romans, for there was a primitive and rough aspect to it all which suggested a less civilised and polished form of civilisation.

Furthermore, Scrooge was in no doubt that landscape had been planned and laid out for a purpose. But what that purpose was he could only guess.

As the widow brought the dogcart to a halt, he turned to her for illumination. 'Can you explain?' he said simply.

The widow smiled at his puzzlement. 'Well, Mr Scrooge, the ancient stones at Avebury obviously have religious origins, and once had religious purposes. They constitute an open-air temple of some sort, as I'm sure you can see. The main circle, through which the road now runs, is approached by the avenue of stones that we have just passed. Both of these features must have taken hundreds of

238

people, and many years, to construct. Such an undertaking would not have been contemplated, much less built, unless the local community regarded it as a vital part of their lives. So they must surely have used this temple to worship whatever gods they believed in.'

The widow turned to look at him.

'Beyond that, Mr Scrooge, we cannot say very much. The truth is, you see, there are no written records, and not even any folk memories to give us a hint. All we can be sure of is that the stones certainly pre-date Christianity in this land, and that when the Christians came they did their best to wipe out all earlier forms of religion. But, in the case of Avebury, and of course Stonehenge, the structures were so enormous and so solidly built that some of them have resisted all forms of attack.'

After a further brief survey of the scene, the widow decided that lunch was called for, and they moved on to the village of Avebury itself.

The village was located more or less at the centre of the great circle, but the area enclosed by the ditch and the ring of stones was so large that the houses seemed quite isolated within it. Fortunately there was an inn, and there both the travellers and their horse found refreshment.

After lunch they went for a walk along the top of the great bank. Scrooge estimated that the earthwork was a good three-quarters of a mile in circumference. And from this vantage point, he could see that, within the main circle, there were the remains of two smaller rings of stones.

He pointed to them out to the widow and asked what she thought was the purpose of them.

'No one knows for sure, Mr Scrooge. But I surmise that the main circle was used to mark the major astronomical events of the year – the longest day, the shortest day, the death and rebirth of the sun at the season we call Christmas – and so forth. Such ceremonies were probably attended by thousands of people from the surrounding area, and even from further away. Pilgrims, in other words. And the priests or elders probably performed ceremonies which were designed to ensure the fertility of the land. They may have offered sacrifices, either animal or human. As for the smaller circles – well, this is just another guess – but they might perhaps have been used for ceremonies for particular occasions. Such as weddings and funerals.'

'I see,' said Scrooge. 'Well it is certainly an impressive arena, there is no doubt about that. But now, if I am not being too tactless, may I ask how this place relates to the practices and beliefs of your own circle – the sewing circle of Tanway? For you have already told me that, in your own way, you celebrate the rites of the old religion.'

The widow laughed. 'You may certainly ask that question, Mr Scrooge, and I will give you as honest an answer as I can. But the truth is, once again, we do not know what the connection is between Avebury and my circle of friends. I can only tell you that my circle's practices and beliefs, to use your terminology, have been handed down through the female line of my family for many generations. I have written records going back some two hundred years, but there were undoubtedly oral traditions before that.'

'And your group consists solely of women?'

'It does, though I know of other groups and other traditions which involve men. In my case I have a book in which is recorded everything that was passed down to me, together with such wisdom and knowledge as I have been able to accumulate in my own lifetime. Every witch has one,

240

copied from her predecessors. It is known as the book of shadows, perhaps because what we know as the truth is elusive, and as hard to pin down as a shadow. Furthermore, it has a habit of shifting and changing with time.'

'And you keep your ceremonies secret, I understand.'

'We do. Not because there is anything disgraceful or wicked about them, but because we could, in theory, be prosecuted under the witchcraft act of 1736. The penalty for conviction is one year in prison, and most of us can think of better ways of spending a year.'

'And what, if it is not impertinent to ask, what exactly do you worship?'

The widow frowned. 'Worship is not a word that I like, Mr Scrooge. And to set your mind at rest, let me say that we certainly have nothing to do with the worship of the devil. The devil is a creature in whom I do not believe. He was invented by the early Christians as a means of damaging the reputation of the old religion. But if we worship at all, we do so by acknowledging the existence of an intelligence behind nature – some ultimate creative force.'

'And is that force a god?'

'Some would say so. Some would personify it in that way. But the old religion, at any rate as handed down to me, does not believe in one god, or even in the trinity of father, son and holy ghost. We speak instead of the goddess, a female creative force. And the goddess, being female, has three aspects. Virgin, mother, and crone. Birth, mother-hood, death, if you will. And the goddess, in her triple form, was spoken of and worshipped in these parts long before the Christians came. Some believe that she will still be here when the new religion has faded and died.'

'And do you believe in this goddess?' Scrooge was nervous about asking this question, but fortunately it seemed to amuse his companion.

'I am inclined to think that there are many gods, in the sense that many places have their own spirit or atmosphere.'

Scrooge walked on for a while, seeking to absorb what he was hearing and trying to relate it to what he saw around him. Then he continued.

'On that night when you held a meeting of your circle, and I was upstairs in my bedroom, I heard you singing and chanting. Was that – and I may not be using the right words here – but were you practising magic?'

The widow pondered. 'Hmm. Well, magic is a fair word for it, I suppose. In any event, it is the equivalent of Christian prayer. We meet once a month, usually on the night of the full moon, and we perform rituals which are very ancient in form, and which have survived because they have been proved to be efficacious. They are designed to draw down power, and we seek to use that power for the good of others.'

'And can you tell me, without breaking confidences, something of what you do to draw down that power? It sounds very intriguing.'

The widow smiled again. 'Men always want to know our secrets! But there isn't much to tell. We may dance in a circle, perhaps, and in the summer we would do it out of doors, around a fire. And as we dance, we chant. We use a form of words which attempts to mobilise and focus the goodwill of all those present to bring about some beneficial ends. For instance, since we are very much an agricultural community, we seek to preserve and enhance the fertility of the land – for without that we all perish and die. More specifically, we try to make the sick well, and to make the weak stronger. We worked hard, when you were ill, for you to get well again. And we do this in addition, of course, to using more mundane methods such as good nursing and the right choice of medicine.'

'Well it certainly seemed to work in my case,' said Scrooge. 'Without your care and attention, and the efforts of your friends, I think I would probably have died.'

'I think you would too. And that is the point. What we do is not so much worship a goddess, Mr Scrooge, as undertake work of a practical nature. We try to mobilise and apply our collective will-power. Which is, I believe, witchcraft in the sense of it being the craft of the wise.'

'But you are, nevertheless, pagans,' Scrooge suggested.

'Are we?'

'I think so. If memory serves, pagus in Latin means the countryside. So a pagan is one from a country area, is it not?'

'Yes, I suppose so.'

'And does that definition disturb you?'

'Not in the slightest,' said the widow good-humouredly.

Scrooge paused in his questions while they approached a stile and climbed over it.

'And yet despite your beliefs,' he continued, 'you still go to church on Sunday?'

'Occasionally. A great deal more often than you, I notice.'

'Oh well,' said Scrooge, 'I think I am one of nature's sceptics. A doubter. But in your case, if I follow you correctly, you see no incompatibility between what you have been brought up to believe, and attendance at church?'

'None whatever. Even within the Christian church there are many strands of belief, and there is no need for them to fight unless they are determined to do so. We all grope

243

towards the light as best we can.'

The widow came to a halt and indicated the great circle of Avebury.

'Look around you, Mr Scrooge. What you see here is a ruined cathedral, perhaps three or four thousand years old. And the churches which you now find in villages such as Tanway are simply the latest version of the circles and henges of the past. Each of the churches that we have today is the focus of life in a village community. It is the place where the rhythms of life – birth, marriage, death – and marked with due ceremonial. The ceremonies inevitably change over the centuries, but the circumstances of human life do not.'

Scrooge felt quite privileged and honoured that the widow had spoken to him so frankly, and towards the end of the day, as they were heading for home, he thanked her handsomely for her kindness.

'And what of that small ring of stones in my grounds?' he asked. 'The Maidenscore, I believe it's called. It's a decidedly modest construction, when compared with the great stones of Avebury, but I would guess that it was built at much the same time, by much the same people. And with much the same intent. Has your group ever made use of it?'

'Indeed we have. Only in the summer, of course. But the previous owner of the Manor, Lady Brown, was for many years the leader of our circle. I only took over from her when she became infirm.'

'I see,' said Scrooge. 'Well perhaps, if it is of any help or interest, perhaps I might say here and now that you may feel free to use the circle in my grounds whenever you wish.'

The widow, who had the horse's reins in her hands, took

her eyes off the road for a moment and looked at him.

'Why thank you, Mr Scrooge,' she said. And then she leaned over and kissed him on the cheek.

Scrooge experienced a sudden surge of excitement at the mere touch of her mouth on his face. His heart beat faster and he felt as if he were a young man again.

Hmm, he thought. I wouldn't mind a bit more of that.

29

During the summer, while work on the Manor was continuing, Scrooge again went to London whenever a meeting of the sewing circle was scheduled. The widow insisted that this was not necessary, but Scrooge told her that he was obliged to go to London from time to time in any case.

One reason why it was not necessary for him to be absent was, of course, that in the summer the sewing circle held its meetings out of doors, rather than in the widow's house. And, since the new owner of the Manor had proved co-operative, the summer meetings were held in the stone circle known as the Maidenscore.

No one told Scrooge formally, but he could tell that Sasha had now been admitted as a full member of the widow's circle. He could tell because there was a distinct change in her attitude.

During all the time Scrooge had known her, Sasha had never been lacking in confidence, but because of her background she had clearly considered herself a second-class citizen. A second-class citizen who could stand up for herself, poke you in the eye and call you a bastard and worse, but second-class none the less. She had considered herself inferior, and in some ways, Scrooge suspected, she had despised herself. She had considered herself weak and foolish.

Now, however, there was something different about her. Scrooge wasn't sure that he could put into words quite what it was. But somewhere along the line Sasha had been made to understand that she was as good as anyone; that she had every reason to be proud of herself; and that she could determine for herself the direction of her future life.

One afternoon in early June, Scrooge unexpectedly came upon Sasha in the widow's kitchen. She was sitting at the table, writing in a leather-bound notebook. In front of her, propped up against a jar of flour, was a similar but older and much-handled volume. And Scrooge didn't need to be told what that was.

Sasha was concentrating hard, for reading and writing did not come easily to her. Her tongue, poked out of one corner of her mouth, made her almost a caricature of the earnest student, and she was so bound up in what she was doing that she didn't notice Scrooge at first.

Scrooge paused only long enough to take in the scene, and then he withdrew immediately, with an apology. But as he walked away he found himself curiously moved. If he had done nothing else in life, he thought, he could take satisfaction from the fact that he had brought Sasha to a place where she was loved and trusted and cherished; a place where she could build a future for herself.

When Scrooge returned from London he enquired, politely, whether all had gone well at the recent meeting of the circle.

'Very well, thank you,' said the widow.

'The stones have not been damaged in any way by the change of ownership?'

'Not in the slightest.'

'Good. And who have you bent to your will this time?'

'None of your business, Mr Scrooge.'

'Probably not,' he admitted. 'However, although it may

247

be coincidence, I must say that on my return to Tanway I have found myself possessed of an overpowering urge to ask you once again – would you do me the great honour of consenting to become my wife?'

The widow was flattered, he could see that, but she raised her eyebrow in a mild reproof.

'Mr Scrooge, I thought we had agreed that you would wait until you had been living in your new house for a while before you raised that matter again.'

'Well yes, we did sort of say that. But it will be another month at least before the Manor is ready, and a fellow can't help feeling frisky you know.'

'Frisky indeed.' The widow almost snorted. 'A little self-control would not go amiss. But since you have brought the subject up, Mr Scrooge, perhaps I should point out that we have no knowledge of each other physically. And while I cannot testify as to what the current practice is in London, I can tell you that out here in the country the normal arrangement is for a man and woman to make love together on a number of occasions before they decide whether or not they should marry.'

'Well, I have no objection to that,' said Scrooge.

'Possibly not, but today is not the day for it.... Perhaps,' said the widow, moving away to attend to some business elsewhere, 'perhaps we might consider it before long.'

Midsummer's Eve fell a few days later, when the moon was still bright, and it so happened that late in the evening Scrooge came upon the widow as she looked out of a window into the gathering dusk.

She seemed so extraordinarily beautiful, in that soft half-light, that he put his arm around her waist and kissed her cheek. It was not by any means a chaste kiss, but the

248

lady did not resist. She turned to face him, a smile on her face.

'Why Mr Scrooge, I sense that you are feeling frisky again.'

'Yes, somewhat, I must confess.'

'Well, if that is the way you feel, there is only one place to be on a night such as this.'

Scrooge's pulse-rate began to increase. 'You mean... upstairs?'

The widow laughed. 'No! Outside, of course. And some distance from here, at that. Are you game?'

'Game for anything,' replied Scrooge.

They set off, the widow leading the way.

It was a warm, close evening; the air was still and heavy, and the darkness was already beginning to close about them. But the widow told Scrooge not to worry. Even if the moon disappeared entirely, she said, she could still find the way.

After they had been walking for a while, Scrooge posed a question: 'May I ask where, exactly, we are going?'

'About a mile, all told. You have, I believe, visited Home Farm?'

'Several times. Third biggest of my farms, with Mr Marlby in charge.'

'Yes indeed. And did you notice, on the bottom field, in the valley, a single standing stone?'

'Er, no,' said Scrooge. 'Can't say I was shown that.'

'Well, it's there. It's a single stone, rather like those we saw at Avebury, perhaps twice as tall as a man.'

'And that's where we're headed?'

'It is.'

'And it's, er, worth a visit is it?'

'Oh, very much so, Mr Scrooge. Very much so.'

After perhaps half an hour they came to a stile, and there the widow paused.

'Look,' she said.

Scrooge looked, and there, a hundred yards ahead of him, he saw the stone he had been told about. In the moonlight it seemed to give off a curious glow, as if it were luminous.

'My word,' he murmured.

'Oh yes,' said the widow. 'It is at its most powerful tonight.'

'Why tonight?'

'Midsummer's Eve, sir!'

'Oh, yes. And powerful, you say?'

'Very.'

'In what respect?'

'The stone, Mr Scrooge, is known as Adam's Pillar, or sometimes by a more vulgar name.'

'Well yes,' said Scrooge. 'It has a sort of...'

'Phallic appearance.'

'Quite.'

'And it is said by local people that men who make love to a woman who is standing with her back to that stone will find themselves possessed of a stamina and power which they have not hitherto experienced. But both parties have to be naked, of course.'

'Of course,' said Scrooge. 'Of course.'

And when they reached the stone he was in such a hurry to comply with this last condition that he popped two buttons off his shirt.

Later, when Scrooge found himself with his forehead

pressed hard against the cold stone of Adam's Pillar, and his cheek side by side with the widow's, he moved himself gently and luxuriously within her. He pressed her harder against the rock.

'My word,' he said. 'I do believe this works.'

'Of course it works, you old fool,' murmured the widow. 'It's witchcraft.'

30

The work on the Manor house took longer to complete than Scrooge had hoped. But then, building work always does take longer to complete than was originally hoped; it is an immutable law of the universe. In the end, however, by late July, the house was sufficiently repaired, renovated, and refurnished for Scrooge to be able to move in.

Long before that, for he was an impatient fellow, he had asked the widow, for a third time, to marry him. And at last she had agreed.

The wedding was held in late September, at about the time of the autumn equinox. Scrooge often became depressed and bad-tempered in the autumn, when he noticed the days perceptibly shortening, but this year, because of the change in his circumstances, he was in fine form.

Among all the obvious wedding guests were a significant number of Scrooge's business acquaintances. They could hardly be called friends, for in financial circles Scrooge had not gone in for friends. Some of them freely admitted that they had come only because, had they not witnessed the ceremony with their own eyes, they would never have believed that old Scrooge had got wed.

These businessmen were naturally anxious to see what sort of a withered old maid would have him; and when, in due course, they discovered what a fine figure of a woman the future Mrs Scrooge was, their astonishment was redoubled. Indeed there was, regrettably, a good deal of ribald comment as to what it was, precisely, that the lady saw in him.

The bride and groom took a short honeymoon in Torquay, where the weather was still mild. And on their return they took up residence together in Tanway Manor.

Thereafter, as was only proper, the widow acquired a new name: Mrs Scrooge. To Mr Scrooge she was Charlotte, and to her he was Ebenezer.

Of the baronet from Bath, who had allegedly been courting the widow and might reasonably have been expected to be a serious rival to Mr Scrooge, nothing was ever heard. For his part, Scrooge had a strong suspicion that the titled gentleman had been nothing more than a figment of Mrs Bannister's imagination. But he didn't really mind.

By Christmas, Mr and Mrs Scrooge had just about succeeded in organising their affairs as they wanted them, and they were therefore able to celebrate that season in the style for which they later became famous throughout the district.

Each year at this time, in Charlotte's mythology, the goddess had to become the great mother, and give birth to the sun once again. This was an event which called for great festivity, for if the light faded and was not reborn, all life would die with it.

That first Christmas, as in all subsequent years, pretty well everyone who was known to the couple was offered hospitality at about the turn of the year. 'Everyone' therefore included all Scrooge's London friends: Mr Cratchit and family (quite a lot of them); Mr and Mrs Bannister; Mrs Molloy; Scrooge's nephew Fred and his wife; Fred's wife's sisters; Mr Larking; and even Mr Topper, who was before long to be married to the plumper of Fred's sisters-in-law.

Local guests included Sasha's beau, young Bradley; all seven of the tenant farmers and their families; the Vicar of Tanway (who seemed either oblivious of, or complaisant with, all ancient and pagan customs); Mr Nesbitt and his simpering wife; various luminaries from Pewsey; and the whole of the sewing circle, together with their assorted husbands, children, mothers, aunts, cousins and companions. In other words, very nearly the whole village.

Tanway Manor was a big house, but even so not all of these people could be accommodated at one time. There were therefore a number of parties and celebrations: on Christmas Eve, Christmas Day, New Year's Eve, and Twelfth Night, in particular. Almost throughout the twelve days of Christmas the house was filled with music, laughter, and light. All levels of society, rich and poor, young and old, the well-bred and the cottage-dweller, all were mixed together in a (mostly) joyful jumble.

The main room in which the festivities took place was the Hall, a high-ceilinged and generously proportioned space which lent itself well to entertaining large numbers. Here there was a huge hearth, in which there was always a log fire. And, naturally enough, it was here that the yule log was lit from a fragment of the previous year's. The new log was kept burning for twelve hours, to ensure good luck in the coming year. The half-consumed remains were then stored, to guard the house against fire and lightning, to be brought out again at the following Christmas and so to repeat the cycle. The word yule, Scrooge discovered, was derived from the Norse term for a wheel; and thus turns the wheel of the year.

To one side of the great hearth was a large Christmas tree, appropriately decorated; it was always of particular interest to children. That first year, and in all later years, it was fifteen feet high, and was covered with glass baubles, small pictures, lollipops, and barley-sugar whistles. Tiny, rosy-cheeked dolls peeped out from behind the greenery. If you looked carefully, you might find a real watch hanging there. Little girls, who had dolls' houses at home, might here furnish them with a miniature French-polished table, or chairs, bedsteads and wardrobes. Small boys could infuriate their elders by banging on the drums and tambourines which they had unearthed from dark corners. There were books, work-boxes, paint-boxes, humming-tops, needle-cases, bags of sweets, real fruit made artificially dazzling with gold leaf and red paper; and there were imitation fruits, made of papier-mâché, which would open to reveal all kinds of small surprises.

The walls of the Hall were, as you would expect, hung with holly, ivy, and mistletoe, taken from the woods on Scrooge's land. The mistletoe, at Charlotte's insistence, was cut with a golden knife, and it was never allowed to touch the earth, or it would lose its power. Its chief power, of course, was its capacity to persuade young ladies to be kissed. Scrooge was not above claiming a kiss himself, when the opportunity arose, but when he did he was scrupulous in removing a berry from the mistletoe. When all the berries were gone the kissing would have to stop, but he noticed that some of the young men, disgracefully, took half a dozen kisses under the white berries without so much as thinking of nipping one off.

On Christmas Eve, the health of all present was drunk from a special wassail cup, made of silver. And later that night, as on all the nights of the celebration, foolish games were played. Riddles were posed. Blind man's buff caused uproar, especially as Scrooge had seen to it that there were

255

wide curtains and shadowy places where young couples might steal a kiss, or even a little more. And there was dancing; always dancing, to a piano and fiddle. Even Scrooge hopped a step or two, after he had taken wine at dinner.

After it was all over, that very first year, Mr and Mrs Scrooge considered that it had all been thoroughly successful; they determined to do the same, in every year that was left to them.

To Scrooge, in particular, the events of the Christmas season had been a vivid reminder to him of how much his life had changed in twelve months. He might have ended his days as crabbed, bent, bad-tempered and lonely old man. But as things had turned out, he was happily married, living in the country, and surrounded by good friends.

There was, however, one memory which particularly hurt and subdued him, and that circumstance did not, of course, go unnoticed.

As they were clearing away the last of the great tree, and packing up the decorations for another year, Charlotte asked her husband what it was that was troubling him.

Scrooge paused as he lowered a tin drum into a box.

'Well,' he said sadly, 'when I contemplate the events of this season – the food and the drink, and the dancing and singing and silly games – I cannot prevent myself thinking how much young Billy would have enjoyed it.'

Part Four

31

Scrooge had lived in the city for a long time. While there, he had seen the seasons come and go, after a fashion, but he had seldom paid them much attention. Now, however, he experienced each nuance of nature at first hand.

Every morning he worked on the papers relating to his charitable trust, with Mr Cratchit continuing to come down once a week. In the afternoons, Scrooge went for a walk, usually alone.

He no longer dressed as a city man, but as a country gentleman, and one who was not afraid to get his boots dirty.

Occasionally he went fishing, just as he had as a boy. It was coarse fishing in the river and the tributary streams which ran through Scrooge's land, and the fish were mostly roach, bream, chub and pike. They were nearly all inedible, and Scrooge normally put them back.

In the evenings, he read, just as he had always read, and in the course of time he accumulated a substantial library, wide-ranging in its subject matter.

The rhythm of this daily activity was soon entered into; it suited him, and remained with him for the rest of his life.

In the course of time, Scrooge came to understand his role in the village of Tanway.

Whether he liked it or not, he was the squire, with the formal title of Lord of the Manor. He was gentry, and stood at the top of the social tree. Below him were his tenant farmers, with the local tradesmen, and other farmers nearby, also on the second tier; below them were the working population, mostly of farm labourers.

Although it was a relatively small village, with agriculture its main activity, Tanway also boasted residents who worked in a variety of other useful occupations. There was a dressmaker; a cobbler; a baker; a saddler; a blacksmith and a wheelwright; a carter who sold coal; several bricklayers and carpenters; a labourer who doubled as a barber; and an inn-keeper who ran a general dealership in his back parlour.

Scrooge was universally recognised as the head of this social unit. It was his job to know all the villagers by sight and preferably by name, and to greet them cheerfully. It was not his business to go into their houses – that was his wife's right and duty. And very welcome she was too, especially in winter, when she provided support for the elderly, the sick, and the poverty-stricken, with gifts of blankets, soup, and the occasional rabbit.

It was certainly not Mr Scrooge's job to undertake any actual work; and definitely not physical work. Once, when Scrooge was rash enough to start digging his own rose garden, he was watched for a few minutes by his head gardener, until eventually the man could stand this display of incompetence no longer. He seized the spade from Scrooge's hand, with an exasperated cry of: 'Let I do it, Mr Scrooge! Let I do it!'

After that, Scrooge learnt his lesson.

Charlotte Scrooge, as the widow now was, also had a rhythm to her life. Each weekday morning she ran her clinic, and these days it was held in a spare room at the side of the Manor. The local sick and injured continued to flock to her door with an unending series of broken bones, twisted ankles, fevers, coughs, colds, wheezy chests, sore throats, rheumaticky joints, gouty toes, swollen thumbs, and a funny feeling in me stomick, missus. All were treated with patience, kindness, and a combination of herbal remedies and healing hands which proved surprisingly effective.

Pregnancy and childbirth in the village were dealt with jointly by Charlotte and the local midwife, Mrs Redknapp; the latter was, needless to say, a member of the sewing circle.

The sewing circle had, of course, its own rhythm of meetings. Scrooge was never invited to participate in the meetings as such – and he never had any wish to be – but he considered himself privileged in that his wife occasionally read to him from her book of shadows. In this way she educated him in the ways of the old religion.

Scrooge and Charlotte had already agreed that, in his new role as Lord of the Manor, and hers as his consort, they should bring about a revival of some of the old traditions and celebrations which had their origin in the religion of the distant past. Some of these points in the year, such as Christmas, were too well known to require explanation or further elaboration, but some had been half forgotten or neglected, at least in Tanway. Now, the Scrooges agreed, was an appropriate time to inject some new life into them. The object would be not to produce converts for the old religion – Charlotte averred that she did not care tuppence whether people believed in it or not, so long as they behaved themselves – but to provide social events in which all members of the village could participate, and so to strengthen the sense of community.

Early in the new year, Charlotte suggested that she

should have a word with Scrooge about Imbolc.

'Imbolc, my dear?'

'Yes, Ebenezer. February Eve.'

He was none the wiser, so that evening Charlotte explained.

'In the old religion, Ebenezer, there are eight festivals in the calendar year. They are known as sabbats, and all are related to the movement of the sun and the fertility of the land. The first of these sabbats is Imbolc, which is an old Irish word which means something like 'in the belly'. In any event, the feast of Imbolc, which some call February Eve or Candlemas, is to celebrate the returning light. It has its origins as a ceremony in honour of the Irish goddess Brigid, who is the Celtic goddess of fire. Brigid is a virgin, and her threefold nature rules smithcraft, poetry and healing. Hence my own interest in her.'

'Candlemas,' said Scrooge thoughtfully. 'Now I seem to have heard of that. Though I never took much notice.'

'Few people do. But many centuries ago the church took over the pagan festival of Imbolc, as it took over all others, and in the Roman church the second of February is the feast of the purification of the Virgin Mary. It is the day on which all the candles which are to be used during the year are consecrated. In the old religion, the candles were lit to hasten the warming of the earth, and the revival of life. And ideally, Ebenezer, there should be a wedding.'

'Ah!' said Scrooge. 'Now I begin to see.'

Both Scrooge and Charlotte knew that, in the previous autumn, Sasha had taken her courage in both hands and had explained to her admirer Bradley Bowman exactly how she had lived in London; she had also told him about her liaison with Mr Scrooge.

Bradley had listened carefully, and thought for a while.

262

Then he had said that it was as well that one of them should have some knowledge of the wickedness of the world, for he knew nothing of it. He had once known a man who stole a loaf of bread, and the fellow had felt bad about it ever since; and he had heard of a market-woman in Devizes who short-changed a customer and dropped dead immediately thereafter. But apart from that he knew nothing of vice and sin.

As for Mr Scrooge, said Bradley, why he was a hard gentleman on the surface, but he had clearly treated Sasha with great consideration and generosity; so there was no harm in that.

So, Sasha had said, trembling violently, Bradley would not be too dismayed if she asked him to take tea with her again next Sunday?

By no means, said Bradley. And, having had said tea, and having had time to think about what she had told him, he had promptly asked her to marry him. No doubt he had been inspired by Mr Scrooge's example.

'Aha!' said Scrooge again, his eye gleaming. 'So Imbolc is the time for a wedding, eh?'

'It is.'

'And have you consulted our young friends?'

'I have.'

'And they are content?'

'They are.'

'Hooray!' said Scrooge. 'Then a wedding there will be.'

Three weeks later, Sasha and Bradley were married in Tanway church. The wedding breakfast was held in the Hall of the Manor.

The tables were decked with snowdrops; the woods that year were full of them.

In a rash moment, Scrooge had promised a feast of a thousand candles. In the end, of course, there were far less than that, but there were still a great many. Every sort and kind of candlestick was pressed into use: brass, silver, and iron, they were begged, borrowed, and temporarily purloined from every house in the village. Saucers, jars and fragments of broken pot were also pressed into use, and the Hall fairly blazed with light. None of these candles, of course, was located near anything flammable, and all were carefully watched.

With the Hall crammed full of guests, the bride and groom entered last. The bride wore a tiara and a white veil, and she looked so beautiful that Scrooge, who had given her away, wept copiously.

Her husband lifted the veil and kissed her, to great applause.

Their health was drunk in rum.

The candles remained lit until sunrise, and with the coming of the sun they were then allowed to go out.

Later that year, Scrooge took great pleasure in handing over to Bradley the keys to his own butcher's shop in Pewsey. (The retirement of Bradley's employer, encouraged by a generous offer from Scrooge, facilitated this arrangement.)

'Thank you very much, sir,' said Bradley, his face beaming and rosy with pride.

'Not at all,' said Scrooge. 'I can afford it. And in any case, I shall expect to be paid back.'

Bradley looked alarmed. 'Paid back, sir?'

'Oh yes. With the birth of a child. And before long, I hope.'

Bradley relaxed. 'Oh, yes, sir. I shall do my best.'

'If it is a boy,' said Sasha, 'we have agreed that we shall

call him Ben, after you, Mr Scrooge.'

'And if it is a girl, will she be the new Sasha?'

'Oh no!' Sasha shook her head. 'No, she will be Sarah. For that, of course, is my real name.'

32

'**The old folk name** for the spring equinox,' said Charlotte, 'is Lady Day – which some take to be a reference to
the Christian feast of the annunciation of the Virgin Mary.
But in the older tradition the lady concerned is Ostara –
called Esotre by the Venerable Bede – and she is the
Germanic goddess of the dawn.'

'And it is after her, I take it, that Easter is named?' asked
Scrooge.

'So it would seem. In any event, the time when night and
day stand equal is a time for new beginnings. The Easter
egg is a powerful symbol for the emergence of life from
apparent death. And it is a time for you and me, Ebenezer,
to review our lives and plan new projects.'

In Mr and Mrs Scrooge's second year in occupation of
Tanway Manor, there was a new beginning which provided
much pleasure to them both: Sasha gave birth to a baby
girl. The child was named, as expected, Sarah.

The new baby was not, of course, old enough to participate in games, but, for the village children who were of an
age for such activities, a treasure hunt was organised. Eggs
of all kinds were hidden in the Manor garden, and rewards
were provided for those who found the most, or found
those which contained treats.

As for new projects, Scrooge made it a habit at this time
of year to discuss with Mr Cratchit such initiatives as had
crossed his mind or been suggested to him.

Most of the work with the charitable trust was reactive; that is to say, applications for funding were made, and the trustees decided whether to approve them or not. But in the spring Scrooge always made a point of initiating one or two projects himself.

In one year, for instance, he set up a special fund for children at boarding schools who, for one reason or another, were obliged to stay at the school during the holidays. Having been in that position himself, he knew how miserable an experience it was, and he arranged funding so that those children who were not able to go home were made welcome somewhere else.

In another year he advertised for a medical man who would be willing to undertake research into pneumonia, the disease which had carried away young Billy. He set up a prize to encourage good design; he established libraries and reading-rooms for the working man, particularly in the north of England; he provided grants for able students to travel abroad.

For all of these schemes, Scrooge became adept at persuading other charities and philanthropists to match him pound for pound; in that way his money was able to go much further.

Perhaps, however, the project which gave Scrooge the most satisfaction, in that second year at Tanway, was one which he dreamed up over Christmas, when thoughts of his late partner came to him once again.

Scrooge advertised for a young entrepreneur who had some experience of running music halls. He found one: a lively fellow in the midlands. This impresario-to-be had already bought and run successfully a music hall in Birmingham; and he had concluded that there was ample scope for more of the same. Scrooge now proposed that he,

Scrooge, should back the young man in establishing a small chain of such establishments.

Of course, this was a proposal which was in some ways scarcely eligible for charitable funding; it was more of a business proposition. However, Scrooge had been clear from the start that he wanted to be able to provide pump-priming funding for business ventures if he wished, and the terms of the trust provided for that. So, with his fellow trustees' consent, he decided to make a grant to this particular applicant, to assist him in developing and expanding his business.

There was to be one condition. The proposed string of theatres must be known, henceforth and for ever, as Marley's Music Halls.

Cratchit, who was fundamentally a serious man, was very dubious about the whole enterprise. 'Can't see how this kind of thing does much good,' he complained.

'But my dear fellow,' Scrooge argued, 'just think of all the fun and laughter that such a place generates. The audience is presented with music, dance, colour, humour, skill. What could be more worthwhile than to cheer up and entertain, at the end of a long hard day, those who have been working in commerce and industry?'

Cratchit was unconvinced. 'Dens of vice, those places are, Mr Scrooge. Rude songs, carryings-on in the gallery, loose ladies in the bar, and pick-pockets waiting for you when you come out of the door.'

'All true,' said Scrooge. 'But if those who frequent the music halls were not watching the show, they would only be in the pub. I prefer the former arrangement. So we will make a grant.'

'And what about the name?' said Cratchit. 'What's Mr Marley got to do with it?'

'Why, he was the sourest, bitterest, most po-faced and humourless man that ever lived,' said Scrooge. 'What better joke could there be than to name music halls after him?'

Cratchit grumbled on. 'In any case, the young gentleman may not agree to that condition. He may want his own name over the door.'

'Oh, he will agree all right,' said Scrooge. 'Just wave the cheque book under his nose, Cratchit. That will do the trick.'

In the course of time, Scrooge's grant to that young man proved to be one of his most spectacular successes. The entrepreneur flourished, his empire expanded, and substantial profits were made.

Although the original funding had been in the form of a grant, which did not call for repayment, the grateful owner of the company soon paid it back in full, with additional sums in later years, saying that if Scrooge could use the money as wisely as he had in the first instance, he was welcome to more of the same.

Before long, to Scrooge's everlasting amusement, the name of Marley became synonymous throughout England with a good time on a Saturday night.

33

According to Charlotte, May Day was called Beltane in the old religion, and was so named after the Celtic god of light, Bel. The first of May was also, Scrooge pointed out, the midpoint of the five-day Roman festival in honour of Flora, the goddess of flowers.

All of which set Scrooge thinking. After five years as Lord of the Manor of Tanway, and husband of the lady in charge of the sewing circle, he had realised that customs and traditions were perfectly capable of being changed and developed; of being bent, if the fancy took one, to conform with one's own ideas of what constituted fun or a worthwhile activity. So it was that, in his fifth year at Tanway, Scrooge decided to organise May Day to suit himself.

He began (after discussing the matter with his wife, of course) by approaching the Vicar of Tanway, the Reverend Mr Green.

The Vicar had been in Tanway for ten years now, but he was still a relatively young man: no more than thirty-five, Scrooge guessed. To Scrooge, the Vicar was Mr Green in more ways than one, for he seemed to live in a dream world of his own, pottering round the place with a vacant smile on his face. He was the youngest son, by a long way, of a well-connected family, but had no money and no prospects of any.

For a while Scrooge wondered whether drink was a cause of the Vicar's amiable vagueness ; or possibly an even more exotic substance, such as opium. But no. Everyone assured him that Mr Green was a perfectly respectable gentleman, with no vices whatever. He was interested, almost exclusively, in the study of nature. Flowers, insects, and birds were his passion, and he spent his days observing them with evident pleasure and satisfaction, making copious notes on their comings and goings.

The Vicar knew, of course, the Latin names of every conceivable plant and creature. Human beings, on the other hand, he found hard to identify. Church services he also found difficult to remember, and sermons were inclined to be short, and recycled. But no one really minded, for he was the kindest and most considerate person you could hope to meet. Just a bit forgetful, that was all.

Eventually, Scrooge concluded that the Bishop had deposited Mr Green in Tanway because it was an obscure, out-of-the-way spot where he could do no harm to anyone.

Scrooge began then, with Mr Green.

'My dear sir,' he said, having served the gentleman with tea and a slice of cake, 'you will have observed, I am sure, that my wife and I have made it our habit, wherever possible, to preserve and continue the old country customs.'

'Indeed,' nodded the Vicar. 'I have observed that, with much pleasure and interest, Mr... er....'

'Quite,' said Scrooge. 'And we hope – in fact we try very hard to ensure – that nothing we do, or encourage, or support, should find itself in conflict with the teachings or practices of the church. For it would be unfortunate, in so small a community, if we were to sponsor or approve of anything which might cause embarrassment or dismay to yourself.'

'Very considerate,' murmured the Vicar, whose eye was

momentarily distracted by a jackdaw outside the widow. 'And much appreciated.'

'That being the case,' said Scrooge, 'I would like to explain to you what I have in mind for a little May Day celebration.'

Which he proceeded to do. He then asked for comments.

The Vicar put down his cup of tea, 'Have you ever heard of a gentleman called George Herbert?' he asked.

'No, I can't say I have,' said Scrooge.

'Herbert was a Wiltshire man. Rector of a parish down Salisbury way. He wrote a helpful little book which was, in essence, a guide to country parsons. In it, he argued that a country parson should be a lover of old customs, provided they are good and harmless. If they are not good, he should pare the apple, so to speak, leaving his flock with the parts that are wholesome. And what you have described, Mr... er..., sounds wholesome enough to me.'

'Splendid,' said Scrooge.

So it was that May Day of that year, and for many years to come in Tanway, was celebrated as a public holiday, at least in the afternoon. And it began with the May Queen riding on a horse through the village.

The first Queen of the May was a cheerful sixteen-year-old girl called Nancy, the baker's daughter; she had been chosen from a short list of three. Applications had been invited, and Scrooge had been rather surprised by the number of volunteers. However, it was more tactful, he felt, for the choosing to be done by Charlotte rather than himself, for the Queen of the May was, of course, to ride naked. For Scrooge to have been involved might have been thought prurient. And perhaps, that first year, the fact that young Nancy had a mass of long golden hair was also a

272

factor in her selection. For the hair provided, to begin with at least, a modest covering for her bosom if not for the lower parts.

Wearing no more than a head-dress of flowers, the Queen paraded on horseback (and she did not ride side-saddle) along the length of the village street; she arrived at last at the Manor, where she came through the gates to loud cheers.

In the Manor garden, where the maypole was erected, she remained on the horse and declared the May Fair open; as she did so she threw her arms sideways, in a gesture which both symbolised the act of opening and, simultaneously, gave the spectators a glimpse of charms which had previously remained hidden. Even louder cheers resulted.

The May Queen then slid down from the bare back of her horse and was promptly provided with a white cloak, on which were embroidered golden flowers. Cries of 'Shame!' were heard.

The Queen's arrival was followed by a carefully re-hearsed dance by the village children. The dance took place, of course, around the maypole, each child holding a ribbon which was fixed to the top of it. The dancers proceeded both clockwise – that is to say, moving as the sun moves, or deosil – and anticlockwise, or widdershins.

To those who asked, and even to those who did not, Scrooge explained that this dance symbolised the inter-weaving of life and death. The maypole itself was a symbol of fertility, and in an agricultural community there was nothing more natural than that.

Later in the afternoon, a team of six men from the village performed an ancient ceremony known as the reindeer dance. It was so called because, during it, each man held a set of antlers above his head. Whether these antlers actually came from reindeer Scrooge very much doubted, but they had been found lying in a barn, neglected for decades, and only the very oldest members of the community had any memory of their being used in the past.

Much earnest debate had ensued about exactly how the reindeer dance had been performed, and Scrooge had had to buy many a pint before memories could dredge up even a semblance of the routine.

There was general agreement that the dance, by six men, had been preceded by a tour of the neighbouring farms, but the steps of the dance were the subject of fierce argument. Eventually, however, a format was devised which satisfied all; and the ritual, having once been revived, was performed each year on May Day for as long as Scrooge lived. (And for many years thereafter.)

The May Fair offered all the usual attractions of a small country gathering: a coconut shy; pony rides; a fortune teller (Mrs Redknapp, the midwife, disguised as a gypsy, with an upturned goldfish bowl for a crystal ball); a game called boule (French, it was alleged); and several stalls where you could buy such things as a belt or ribbons or a brooch at special prices.

Refreshments were available, generously provided free by Mr and Mrs Scrooge. Those who became bored, and some of the younger folk did, were free to wander off into the woods and collect May blossom; or occupy themselves in other ways.

In the evening, young men lit bonfires on the village green, and a few cattle were driven between them for good luck. Some of the bolder youths leapt over the top of the fires, for the same reason, with no more harm done than an occasional singe.

As for young Nancy – that first May Queen – she caught

the eye of a young nobleman from Devizes. Word of Scrooge's intention of having the May Queen parade sans her clothes had spread some distance, it seems, and the gentleman had ridden three hours to see what he could see. What he had seen evidently met with his approval, for he was married to Nancy within three months, and she gave birth to his heir nine months later.

After that, there was never any shortage of candidates for the office of Queen of the May. The guinea which Scrooge traditionally gave the young lady for her trouble was considered irrelevant, when compared with the other opportunities which the post provided.

Young Nancy was not the only one who benefited maritally from that first of Scrooge's May Days. The Vicar, Mr Green, was also wed soon after.

It came about in this way. Mr Green, it was noticed, did not avert his eyes from young Nancy's charms. Indeed he remarked to Charlotte Scrooge, more than once, upon how beautiful the May Queen was. 'It makes me realise,' he said sadly, and without any guile whatever, 'how much I am missing by remaining a bachelor. But then,' he added, 'of course no one would ever have me.'

The sewing circle considered the matter, and decided that marriage would do the Vicar nothing but good. A search was therefore instituted, and before long word was received of a Miss Haines, of Calne.

Miss Haines was in her late twenties, and of a good family, but she remained single as a result of what was, by common consent, the plainest face in the county and a pronounced lack of income. Somewhere along the way – accounts differed – her father had contrived to lose such wealth as he had inherited, and until recently she had lived a sheltered life with her elderly mother. Now the mother was dead, and Miss Haines occupied her time with charitable works.

This single lady was a good-hearted soul and she had many hidden virtues which the local gentlemen had overlooked. The chief of these, according to her dress-maker, was that she had a splendidly voluptuous figure which was capable of providing much satisfaction to a considerate husband; said figure was currently, and criminally, going to waste.

The sewing circle set to work, the couple were brought together, and before long a proposal was made and accepted. Only one task remained.

It was widely believed that Mr Green, though expert in botany and the like, was hopelessly ignorant of human physiology. Miss Haines, likewise, had led a very sheltered life. Since it was the sewing circle's view that, on a wedding night, it is useful if at least one party has some idea as to what goes where, Mrs Redknapp was deputed to give Miss Haines instruction. 'Think of it,' Miss Haines was advised, 'as a sort of confirmation class.'

Miss Haines proved to be an apt pupil, though astonished by what she was told, and on return from her honeymoon declared that the whole experience had been a revelation, both to her and her husband.

Before long, the vicarage required a room to be converted to a nursery.

34

On Midsummer's Eve, Charlotte always cut and stored five plants. These, her book of shadows told her, would on that night have special powers. The five plants were rue, roses, St John's wort, vervain, and trefoil.

In the eighth year of her marriage, Charlotte was assisted in this task by a young friend called Sarah, who was Sasha's daughter. Sarah had two brothers and a sister but those three were, as yet, too young to help. Besides, Sarah was slightly special. Charlotte could see that she had the mark upon her.

At the end of that same week, the Manor was the site of a cultural celebration, of sorts. Scrooge was not much interested in music, but each year at this time he hosted a concert, or perhaps a performance of Shakespeare. The house was open to anyone who wished to attend, but usually the audience consisted mostly of gentry. This year the entertainment was provided by a choir from Bath, who sang a series of songs through which Scrooge dozed peacefully and quietly.

At the interval, he was prodded awake, and he realised that he had had an interesting dream. Later that night he told Charlotte all about it.

'You remember the white horse at Westbury,' he said.

'I certainly do.'

'And you have heard of, if not seen with your own eyes, the Cerne Abbas Giant.'

'I have indeed.'

'Well it suddenly occurred to me, in my dream, that what we need is something of that sort at Tanway. What we need, my dear, is a wise woman.'

Charlotte gave him a look of amusement. 'Is that so, Ebenezer?'

'Well that's what I think anyway. How would your goddess feel about it?'

'Flattered, I should think.'

'There is no prohibition about graven images and the like?'

'None.'

'Very well then. We will put Tanway on the map. We will carve into the hillside an image of the goddess, and we will call her the wise woman of Tanway.'

On the hills which rise from the Vale of Pewsey, and elsewhere in the south of England, solid chalk lies close under the thin surface soil. Uproot the grass, scrape away a few inches of dirt, and you have a bright white material staring you in the face. This circumstance has permitted the creation of a number of pictures or images, carved into the side of hills. A line cut into the chalk, perhaps two or three feet wide, can be seen for miles from the plain below.

Most of the hillside images have traditionally been horses, but occasionally human figures are seen. The Cerne Abbas Giant, to which Scrooge had referred, was famous for being in possession of a large, erect phallus.

Scrooge now set about designing his female figure. He recruited an artist from Bath, who after several iterations came up with a simple but bold outline. The artist, a rather shy and retiring type, needed several attempts before he could bring himself to outline a bosom of sufficient generosity to satisfy his sponsor. Allowance then had to be made for the fact that the hillside sloped, and this would have a foreshortening effect when the figure was seen from the plain below. Eventually, however, Scrooge had a suitable design.

Next, a team of men, women, and children was recruited to carry out the work on a succession of Sunday afternoons. A free lunch was provided, and a party atmosphere reigned, the general cheerfulness of the participants being enhanced by the thought of being paid for their labour at the end of the day.

The hillside which Scrooge had chosen was on his own property, half a mile north of the village, where the escarpment rose steeply. The land there was far too steep to plough and all that would be lost was a few square yards of grazing.

Scrooge and the artist marked out the design with a hundred or two coloured flags, and both men supervised the digging. Occasionally Scrooge would descend to the plain below, view the work from there, and bellow up comments through a megaphone.

In a month, the figure was carved. And a fine figure of a woman it was, one hundred and thirty-one feet from head to toe. It was no more than an outline of a human being, of course, with no subtlety of detail, but it was female in every respect, just as its counterpart in Cerne Abbas was male.

Scrooge was delighted. 'Life,' he said, 'is fleeting. Nothing endures for ever. The light which is so strong at Midsummer will fade before long. But it is for each man to leave some sort of a mark on the world if he can, and this one, at least, will outlive me.'

Not everyone, however, shared Scrooge's enthusiasm.

Three years after she was created, the wise woman of

Tanway attracted a stream of criticism from a clergyman who visited the Vale while on holiday. He was a man in his fifties, short of stature, and suffering from gout which made him remarkably bad-tempered.

On hearing that the hill figure was of recent origin, that it lay on Scrooge's land, and that it had been created at Scrooge's command, the clergyman called on that gentleman and roundly abused him for his creation.

'This figure,' the clergyman fairly howled, 'is an incitement to immorality, sir! It is wickedness incarnate, and it should be erased from the hillside immediately! Why, I have seen with my own eyes, young people climbing upon it and frolicking!'

'Frolicking, sir?' enquired Scrooge mildly.

'Yes, sir, frolicking!'

'Oh, I do hope so,' murmured Scrooge.

The clergyman, quickly recognising that he would get nowhere at the Manor, stamped off the to vicarage to seek support from a fellow churchman.

But the Reverend Mr Green was no help to him either. He said that the figure reminded him so much of his own dear wife that he really couldn't take exception to it.

Mrs Green just smiled happily.

The visiting clergyman, reluctantly accepting defeat, returned to his parish in East Anglia. On arrival there, he went down on his knees and thanked the Lord for making sure that the land there was perfectly flat.

The clergyman's attack was so ferocious that it caused Scrooge to wonder why his figure was so feared. He enquired of his wife as to whether she thought it possible that the wise woman might have some restorative or stimulative properties, as was the case with Adam's Pillar. Charlotte said that she wasn't sure. The lady was a bit new to have accumulated any powers as yet, but perhaps they should ask her and see.

So it was that, on the next Midsummer's Eve, near midnight, Mr and Mrs Scrooge stood at the feet of the wise woman, removed their clothes, and paused to see what effect she might have on them.

'Fancy a frolic, my dear?' asked Scrooge.

'You'll have to catch me first,' said Charlotte, and she set off up the hill.

Now, it may have been the influence of the wise woman, or it may have been the fact that Charlotte ran out of puff. But either way, Scrooge caught up with her somewhere around the wise woman's navel and proceeded to frolic with her at some length.

'My word,' he said when they had finished. 'That wasn't bad for a man who is over sixty. I think there may be something in this.'

His wife reached out and took his hand. 'Trust not these modern heresies, Ebenezer,' she said. 'When it comes to practical results, the old religion is best.'

35

Charlotte and the members of the sewing circle often spoke of Lughnasadh, by which they meant the harvest time, named after the god Lugh. And who was Lugh? Apparently he was another Celtic fire and light god. His weapon was the spear, and he was a harpist, poet, healer, and magician.

Scrooge did not care for the word Lughnasadh. He preferred Lammas, which had a more Anglo-Saxon ring to it. Lammas meant loaf-mass, which was the Saxon feast of bread, when the first of the year's grain harvest was made into new loaves.

Whatever it was called, harvest time denoted, in a sense, the end of summer and the beginning of autumn.

Each year, Scrooge went to watch the last of the harvest being gathered in. He usually went to Home Farm, which was run by Mr Marlby. It was the nearest of the seven farms which Scrooge owned, and traditionally had the closest ties with the Manor.

It was there, one hot August afternoon in his fifteenth year in Tanway, that Scrooge came upon Sasha and her four children. As the harvesters cut more and more of the corn, the rabbits and other animals moved ever inwards, taking shelter in the centre of the field. But at last there was nowhere else for them to go, and they ran for their lives, out in the open, while men, women, children, and dogs all did their best to capture a free supper.

Scrooge stood on the edge of the field with Sarah, who at thirteen was the eldest of Sasha's four children. Sarah was a big girl, tall for her age, and with her mother's colouring. Her ambition was to be Queen of the May, and Scrooge felt sure that she would be, before long.

Sarah and Scrooge stood quite alone, everyone else being involved in the hunt. Together they watched as the rabbits scattered and the hunters pounced, more often missing their prey than catching it.

'I like it when the rabbits escape,' said Sarah quietly.

Scrooge laughed. 'So do I,' he said. 'But in due course all creatures come to the end of their time, Sarah.'

As the shouting and laughter continued, Sarah turned and gave Scrooge a very direct look. 'Is it true that you and my Mummy were lovers?' she asked.

Scrooge blinked, but knew that he had to give an honest answer.

'Yes,' he said, 'we were. Long before she met your father, of course. But why do you ask, Sarah?'

'Because she always speaks of you with great affection.'

Scrooge caught his breath. 'Well,' he managed to say after a moment, 'I am very fond of her too. In that sense we are still lovers. You see, Sarah, I never had any children of my own, and I regret that. There was a boy once whom I would have liked to treat as my son, but that was not to be. The gods decided against it, so to speak. So in a way I think of you and your sister and your brothers as my family.' He looked at her. 'Do you mind?'

Sarah smiled. 'No of course not.'

And then she kissed him and ran to join the others.

That night, as in previous years, Scrooge held a feast for all the labourers who worked on his farms. Hiring and firing was left to the tenants, but at this time of year Scrooge always saw to it that the men had a modest reward for their work. Home Farm was usually the location.

At teatime, bread, butter, and jam were provided, together with copious amounts of beer. In the evening, there was rabbit stew and more beer.

Charlotte's book of shadows stated that the harvest time was also sacred to Artemis, the Greek goddess of the moon and the hunt. And so, when the moon was full, the sewing circle had their own little party for her. It took place in the stone circle, at the end of the avenue of beeches, and there Charlotte and her friends danced naked in the moonlight, just as their ancestors had, thousands of years earlier.

Meanwhile, after their feast in the Home Farm fields, the men brought out a broken and worn-out wagon wheel, five feet in diameter. Its hub was of seasoned elm, the spokes from oak to give it strength, the rim sections made of ash.

The wheel was taken to the top of a nearby hill, covered in tar, and set alight. Then it was pushed forward, so that it began to roll down into the valley. It moved slowly at first, but then gathered pace, running faster and faster and faster, bouncing and spinning, leaping over humps and mounds, until at last it crashed to a halt.

It seemed to Scrooge, as he stood and watched the wheel go tumbling down the hill, that its progress was much like that of his own life. Running faster and ever faster now, but soon to come to an end.

Late that night, when everyone had gone home, Charlotte and Scrooge sat together in the quiet of his study.

'This is the time,' Charlotte reminded him, 'for letting the past go its own way, Ebenezer. And what are you going to do about that?'

Scrooge thought for a moment. 'I am going to sell my old apartment building in London,' he said. 'I shan't go back to London again, not if I can help it.'

'So – you are severing your last link with the city?'

'Yes.'

'It's taken you a long time, Ebenezer. Fifteen years. But now you are a countryman at last.'

'Well,' said Scrooge with a sigh, 'you always did say that you would make a pagan out of me one day.'

36

At about the time of the autumn equinox, when night and day stood hand in hand as equals once again, it was Charlotte's long-standing practice to invite Sasha's children to the Manor to carry out a number of old customs.

Each year a corn man was created. Sarah was always in charge of this operation, and it was a brave sibling who dared to disobey her instructions. Once made, the corn man was burnt at sunset, demonstrating through fire the death of vegetation and the rebirth yet to come.

Each autumn, too, the last sheaf of the harvest at Home Farm was collected and stored in the Manor's outhouse. In the new year it would be given to the birds in the Manor garden, as a gift to the winter.

But unfortunately, although Scrooge enjoyed watching the children undertaking these tasks, the autumn was a time when he tended to become depressed.

'How old am I now?' he asked Charlotte plaintively, one day in late September.

'You are a hundred and six, Ebenezer.'

'A hundred and six? How can I be a hundred and six?'

'Because you were born aged thirty-nine,' said Charlotte briskly, and went about her business.

Scrooge did the sum in his head. So he was sixty-seven. Hmm.

There was, however, one event in the autumn which Scrooge always did enjoy, and that was the Michaelmas dinner.

The rents for Scrooge's farms were paid twice a year, six months in arrears, and the second payment came at the end of September. On that occasion Scrooge always gave a dinner for his tenant farmers and their families, and a splendid occasion it was too. The main course was always goose.

Every year, Scrooge chose a guest of honour. After he had closed down his apartment building in London, for instance, he brought Mrs Molloy down to live in the village. She was now eighty years old, and in that year he made her his principal guest.

In his seventeenth year at Tanway, Scrooge chose to honour his wife. There was no particular reason for this choice. He had just decided that he was getting on in years himself, and it was time he demonstrated to the world how much she meant to him.

At the end of a splendid feast, Scrooge stood up and made a short speech. In it, he acknowledged that at this point in the calendar he often became grumpy and difficult to live with.

'Even more grumpy and even more difficult,' said Mrs Molloy, *sotto voce* to Mr Marlby, seated next to her.

'It is a time,' said Scrooge, 'when the god of light is defeated by his twin, the god of darkness, and a sort of gloom settles upon me. And how best can we combat darkness? Why, with new light, of course. Hence the log fire in the hearth, and the numerous candles which surround us tonight.

'It was at this time of year that my wife and I were married, and it was with the thought of light in my mind that I made a visit to Bath recently, in order to choose an anniversary present for her. Dear Charlotte has consented to be my very special guest of honour tonight, and I would like now to present her with a gift. It is a gift which, in a very inadequate way, demonstrates how much I owe to her, and it attempts, in so far as any gift can, to thank her for her love and support over the years.

'I was once told, by Mrs Molloy no less, that if I worked hard I might one day become halfway human. I would like to think, Mrs Molloy, ladies and gentlemen, that through my wife's wisdom and guidance I have managed to become almost wholly human.'

Whereupon Scrooge opened a velvet-covered box on the table in front of him and took out a diamond necklace. The gems sparkled and shone in the candlelight, and there was a spontaneous round of applause.

Later, when all the guests had gone, Charlotte gave her husband a special and private kiss.

'This must have been very, very expensive,' she said, as she stood in front of a mirror and looked at the necklace. 'So it must be true what they say – there's no fool like an old fool.'

Scrooge demurred. 'I think you might allow me one act of reckless extravagance in a life of careful thrift,' he suggested. 'And I can always take it back if you like.'

'Oh no,' said Charlotte. 'I wouldn't want you to do that.'

37

To Scrooge's mind, Halloween was always a curious mishmash of customs and practices, pagan, Christian, and who-knows-what.

The name of the festival clearly derived from the fact that it was the night before All Hallows Day; which was, in so far as Scrooge could understand it, the day on which the Christian church honoured the hallowed. And the hallowed, apparently, were the blessed dead, or saints.

Charlotte's view was that in the Celtic calendar the thirty-first of October had been the last day of the year, and Scrooge certainly had no doubt that the basic nature and date of Halloween had been lifted wholesale by the Christians from some earlier pagan rite.

In any event, Charlotte and Scrooge always began Halloween by arranging a party for the children of the village. Apart from the usual provision of a large tea, with lemonade, piles of sandwiches, cakes, trifles, and sweets, there were also games.

Bobbing for apples, when a child had to try to lift an apple out of a barrel of water by using teeth and no hands, was always messy but fun, and appealed to the noisy and extrovert. A variant of this game was trying to take a bite out of apples which were hanging on a string.

Making a jack-o'-lantern out of a pumpkin was an occupation for the quieter ones, with nimble fingers. Holes were carved in the pumpkin to make facial features, and a candle was placed inside. The result might have the pleasing effect of terrifying a younger brother or sister.

Those children who were of a thoughtful nature could cut the skin off an apple in one piece and throw the peel over their shoulder. It was said, by some, that when the peel fell on the ground it would reveal the initial of one's lover to come.

After the food and games, the children would go out into the garden and have a bonfire of dead leaves and wood. Sausages would be cooked over it, and there would be shouting and laughter and squeals.

Later still, the house would go suddenly quiet, and Scrooge and Charlotte would take dinner alone.

Charlotte regarded Halloween as the festival of the dead, and in Scrooge's nineteenth year at Tanway she reminded him of this.

'I want you to remember, Ebenezer,' she said, 'that Halloween is the time when the veil between the worlds of life and death stands open, and the dead can return, if they wish, to meet with their family.'

'But my dear,' said Scrooge gently, 'you know that I don't believe that the dead are anywhere. They are gone from us for ever, dissolved back into the ashes and dust from whence they came.'

'And yet,' said Charlotte, 'on this very night, each year, you always have an extra place laid at dinner. For young Billy.'

Scrooge glanced at the empty chair, and the unused knives and forks. For a moment, the silver seemed to blur in his vision.

'Ah yes,' he said. 'But that is just a little conceit of mine. A sop to my sentimental nature.'

Charlotte smiled. 'Which rather proves my point. If they are nowhere else, Ebenezer, the dead are inside your head.

They live on in your memory.'

She rose from the table and prepared to leave. Later the sewing circle would be meeting, and she had things to do. She came round and kissed Scrooge on his cheek.

'I want you to remember tonight that it will not be long now before you and I join all those who have gone before. And you will live longer, and easier in your mind, if you have made your peace with the past. Let go all ancient hurts and wrongs, real or imaginary. Let them shrivel and crumble like the leaves in the fire.'

When Charlotte had gone out, Scrooge went up to his study. From here he could look out over the avenue of beeches. Tonight, of course, the night was dark, but if he stood close to the window he could just see the outlines of the trees, running away into the distance.

He sat down at this desk and thought about what Charlotte had said. He thought about his father and mother, and his sister; he thought about Marley, and Billy; and many others.

Then he picked up his pen and began to write a letter to his father. He set out all the wrongs which he felt his father had done him, and he listed all those slights and insults and thoughtless troubles which he had given to his father. He weighed them up and balanced them out, and decided that the score was about even. It was, he suggested, time to regard all those matters as closed; finished and done with – best forgotten and cast out into the darkness.

When he had finished the letter, Scrooge read it through.

Yes, he thought, that will do.

Then he placed the letter in an envelope, and took it over to the fire. He placed it on top of a crackling log and held it in place with a poker.

He watched as the paper blackened and twisted. It burnt with a yellow flame, consuming itself, and with it went all Scrooge's anger about the past.

A little later, he went down into the cellars and prepared a dozen lanterns. Then he loaded them into a wheelbarrow and set off into the darkness.

He pushed the barrow up the avenue of beeches, and beside each tree, left and right, he placed a lantern. There was one for his father, one for his mother, one for his sister, one for Marley, and one for Billy. There were others.

The lanterns in place, he went back inside to his study. There, with a screen in front of the fire to hide its light, he placed a chair before the window.

Now, when he looked out on to the avenue, he could see a remembrance of all those he had known and loved.

Scrooge poured himself a large brandy and sat by the window for a long time. Sometimes the lights below became blurred with his tears, and sometimes they flickered in the wind and struggled to stay alight.

Eventually, they all went out.

38

In the November of that same year, a curious thing happened to Scrooge: he was invited to preach a sermon.

It came about in this way. In Pewsey there was a certain Mr Fiddling, a haberdasher by trade, and a lay preacher by inclination. Mr Fiddling was famous in Pewsey chiefly for having been a keen cricketer in his youth. He was not a very good cricketer, but he was always chosen to play in the Pewsey XI, because his participation enabled the visiting team to say, on occasion, that one of their players had been caught Fiddling behind the wicket. It was a simple joke, but one which provided harmless amusement for several years.

Now a mature, smartly dressed man of about fifty, Mr Fiddling had given up cricket, but he was a keen member of a local chapel. The chapel had once, Scrooge understood, been affiliated to the Methodist church, but there had been some sort of disagreement and schism; the minister had departed, and nowadays services seemed to be conducted mainly by Mr Fiddling.

All this Scrooge knew because he had had dealings with Mr Fiddling through the charitable trust. Mr Fiddling had applied for funds to repair the chapel roof, and Scrooge had seen no reason to deny him.

The day came, however, during one of their discussions about progress on the roof (dry rot had been discovered, leading to additional expense), when Mr Fiddling asked Scrooge a question.

'I wonder, sir,' he began, as they drank tea together,

'whether you have ever preached a sermon.'

'Can't say I have,' said Scrooge. 'I spoke at a funeral once, many years ago. But I'm not a church-going man, Mr Fiddling. Don't listen to many sermons, never mind give 'em.'

'Hmm,' said Mr Fiddling pensively. 'Because I was wondering, do you see, whether you would like to preach a sermon to my little flock.'

Scrooge was surprised. So much so that he didn't quite know what to say. 'Well.... I'm not much of a speaker.'

'Oh come now, sir, you are too modest. I have heard you lecture about that ancient stone structure – the so-called Devil's Den at Fyfield. And I heard you give a talk about the Roman remains in the Manor garden.'

'Well, yes,' Scrooge admitted. 'I do occasionally pass on little bits of knowledge that I've picked up over the years. But you do need to understand, Mr Fiddling, that I wouldn't claim to be a practising Christian.'

'The Roman Catholics don't think I'm one either,' said Mr Fiddling. 'And the Church of England people have their doubts. No, Mr Scrooge, the point is this. My little flock is interested in hearing different points of view. We have had a series of sermons this year about many aspects of life. We had a talk from a university man about the Roman and Greek gods, for instance. Very scholarly it was. And I'm sure we should find your views on life most enlightening.'

Scrooge was sufficiently interested not to reject the idea out of hand. 'But what would you want me to talk about?' he enquired.

'Choose your own subject, sir. You are a well-read and thoughtful man. You have been kind enough to show me your library, and I doubt that it has an equal outside the great houses of the nobility. I am content to leave the choice of the subject matter to your discretion. But perhaps, since you have told me that you are not a Christian, perhaps you should tell us what your religious views actually are.'

After some thought, and a discussion with Charlotte, Scrooge accepted Mr Fiddling's invitation.

So it was that, on a Sunday in late November, he found himself in the congregation of the Canal Road chapel, taking part in the lusty singing of a well-known hymn.

Shortly afterwards Scrooge climbed the steps to the pulpit, and looked down on a modest assembly of perhaps sixty people. He knew most of them by sight: they were artisans, shopkeepers, and servants; the middle and lower ranks of society; solid, respectable folk, sober and reliable in their habits. They looked up at him expectantly.

'My friends,' Scrooge began. 'Your pastor has invited me to speak to you. It is mighty brave of him, for he has no idea what I might say. But he did suggest that, since I do not consider myself a Christian, I might speak to you about my own views on life and death.

'I have in my library a copy of an essay by Sir Thomas Browne, the seventeenth-century physician. Now Sir Thomas definitely was a Christian. He believed in the life everlasting, though not, interestingly enough, in the resurrection of the body. And in his essay, about the burial of the dead, Sir Thomas says this: Diuturnity is a dream and folly of expectation.

'And what does he mean by that, you may wonder. As I do myself. What I think he means is that you cannot expect to live for ever. It will not be long, as he says elsewhere in his essay, before we too lie down in darkness and have our light in ashes.

'That being the case, and since death may visit us at any time, it is useful – at least in my opinion – to have a set of principles upon which to live, and upon which, in due course, to die.

'I have now almost completed my threescore years and ten, and I am not likely to learn much more about these matters than I know now, and so Mr Fiddling is right this is not a bad time to pass on to you such opinions as I have formed. Let me begin then with some thoughts about how to live.

'I can only speak from a personal point of view. I am not a professional philosopher, and barely an amateur one, but for my own selfish reasons I had to think hard, some twenty years ago, about how to conduct the rest of my life. I think I succeeded fairly well in that I have lived happily and contentedly since that time, and I hope and believe that I have done a bit of good in the world.

'But it was not always so. I have to say that the first fifty years of my life were not very satisfactory. True, I was in good health, and I did well financially. But it was a cold, empty, dissatisfying life.

'I had the chance to marry when I was young, and foolishly gave it up. Fortunately, the lady did much better for herself, and is happy with children and grandchildren. I myself, however, had no family and few friends. I had a business partner who was an even more solitary man than I, and when he died I was largely alone. Nobody cared for me. I was shunned. Even the very dogs in the street avoided me, as if I had bent down to pick up a stone. In business dealings I was almost feared.

'I had my reasons, and what I thought of as justifications, for living as I did, but that way of living led me to isolation and loneliness. I had become bitter, and angry, and sour. All these feelings were made far worse by the time of year which now approaches – Christmas. It was a season which most regard as a time of goodwill, but it filled me with rage and fury. All those collecting boxes being rattled under my nose! Why should I give money, I asked myself, to the undeserving poor? Let them stew in their own juice.

'I might have gone on in this way, and might have died without changing my life, as my business partner did. But I could sense the unhappiness and the miserable old age which lay ahead of me. And as I approached my fiftieth year I began to be aware that if I was to have any useful or rewarding times in the future I must make an effort to adopt a different attitude.

'The turning-point came when, by pure chance, I met two young people. A boy and a girl. Both were homeless and poor. Both had been scratching a living on the streets. Prior to meeting these two young people, I had closed my eyes to the poor. If I thought about them at all, I considered that their fate was their own fault. They had made their bed, and they must lie in it. But when I got to know these two young folk better, I realised that what had happened to them was not because of their own mistakes or actions. And I realised too that things could be done, with money, to help those who were experiencing similarly hard times.

'Fortunately, I had by that time a considerable fortune at my disposal. And when I began to think about how that money could be put to good use I had the guidance of two fine people to help me. You will not be surprised to learn that I refer to the Vicar of my local church in London, and his wife. It was through them that I came to meet the lady who has since become my own wife. And it is she who has kept me more or less sane and sensible ever since. I owe her a great debt, ladies and gentlemen, one that I am pleased to acknowledge publicly.

'So it was that at the age of fifty I changed my life considerably, and for the better. I stopped trying to earn more and more money, and I began to think how my resources could be used to good purpose.

'I left the city and moved to the country. I had been born in the country, but I had forgotten its ways. I had lost touch with the rhythm of the seasons. I had ignored the fact that we depend wholly on nature for our survival, for in the city men think that milk comes out of taps, and that bread is manufactured in factories.

'Such then are my credentials – very thin – for advising you on how to live. My sole claim to wisdom derives from the fact that, with the aid of others, I transformed my life and attitudes. I became, I think a better person – certainly a happier one.

'Do not misunderstand me. I do not believe in selling all you have and giving it to the poor. In my view that would be unproductive. But you should be generous with what you have, without being gullible and foolish.

'Be thoughtful and kind if you can – and if you can't, apologise afterwards.

'I advise you to live among others – to be a part of the community. Take pleasure from the natural world, for the works of man are ephemeral. Note the movement of the seasons. Celebrate the turning-points of the year.

'Mark the great occasions: births, marriages, and deaths. For it is in this way that we give our lives structure and such meaning as it is possible to find.'

Scrooge paused and took a sip of water.

'And now, since diuturnity is indeed a folly of expectation, let me turn to the question of how to die.

'The answer to that question rather depends of course, on what you believe about life after death. Sir Thomas Browne, who was a learned man, tells us that many of the ancients believed in reincarnation. He also pointed out that a belief in immortality occurs at all times and in all places, and is therefore natural. Not to have any hope of a future life would be, he argues, a bitter blow.

'It seems to me, however, that the truth about our future existence, if we have one, is beyond our grasp.

'We appear to be living on a globe which floats in space. We cannot go far into the earth, or far above it. We do not know how this world began, or how it will end.

'Human understanding, in this respect, can be compared with human strength. Most of us can walk a mile in twenty minutes or so. A fit young man can run a mile in five minutes. Similarly, some of us, the fast intellectual runners so to speak, have a glimmer of the meaning and purpose of human life – some shadowy glimpse of the truth about who made us, who we are, how we came to be here, and where we are going. But to understand all aspects of the mystery of creation we need to be able to run a mile in the single tick of a clock. And that we cannot do.

'All we can do, then, in the absence of certainty about such mysteries, is form our own conclusions.

'For my part, I see no reason to personify the forces of creation into sentient beings, or gods, who listen when we pray to them or pay attention when we make sacrifices.

'As to the afterlife, I again see no evidence for the belief that there is one. True, the thought of eventually being reunited with those we have loved provides great comfort, but that is scarcely a sufficient reason for believing that it is likely to happen. My own view is that we come from nothing and nowhere, and we return to nothing and nowhere.

'Our memorials may last a very long time, and the burial mounds of Wiltshire are testimony to that. But in the end they are ploughed flat by the forces of time. All is vanity, feeding the wind, and folly.

'But wait, you may say. If there is no judgement after death, no heaven, and no hell, does it matter how you live? And my answer is, All the more so. If life here on earth is miserable, painful, and lonely, then what to the Christians might be a simple cause for regret, to be remedied in the hereafter, becomes to one like me an intolerable loss, one which all good men and women must strive to overcome.

'Ladies and gentlemen, since you have been good enough to invite me to address you this morning, let me now summarise my views.

'I recommend, as a rule of thumb for deciding how to conduct yourselves, the Christian sentiment that you should do unto others as you would have them do unto you. It is not, incidentally, an exclusively Christian precept. You will find it, I believe, embodied somewhere in all the major religions of the world – and it is there for the simple reason that it is a practical philosophy which generates, on the whole, satisfactory results.

'I believe also in the threefold principle of the pagans. That is to say, I believe that whatever you do in this life, good or bad, returns to you three times over. This is a salutary thought to hold in one's mind when considering a course of action.

'As for death – why, you should die with as much dignity as you can muster. Preferably at the end of a long life, surrounded by one's wife and children if that is possible, and by one's friends if it is not. If I were a praying man, that is the sort of end I would pray for.'

Scrooge looked down at the faces in front of him. He saw interest and attention in all of them. Except the fat boy in the third row, who had fallen asleep. It was, he decided, time to conclude, before any others of the congregation followed suit.

'Ladies and gentlemen – I think I have spoken long enough. And I thank you for the compliment you have paid me in inviting me here today.'

39

In the summer of his twentieth year at Tanway, Scrooge celebrated his seventieth birthday; and he was in fine form for it. But as the autumn rolled on, he became conscious that he was no longer as young as he had been. His daily walk seemed to become more arduous, and he paused for breath more often than he had in the past.

He remarked one day to Charlotte that he thought he was slowing down a little. 'But you were never very quick to begin with,' she told him. However, he noticed that she took a little more care of him thereafter; she began to dose him with a syrup prepared from the dried leaves of foxgloves; and once, when the weather had turned cold and he was late returning from a walk, she came out to meet him.

So Scrooge came to his last Christmas. He had thought for some time that he might not see another, but he was not distressed. He had done what he needed to do.

He had disposed of all his money except that which was required to provide a comfortable life in the country for himself and his wife. He had lived for threescore years and ten.

Throughout England, and for that matter abroad, there were young men in posts which they would never have obtained if Scrooge's trust had not funded their education. There were women too, who as girls had lived like Sasha but had had their lives changed through Scrooge's funds, and were now living in good homes, as proud wives and mothers.

Every night of the year, Marley's music halls provided harmless entertainment and laughter.

In the hospitals, patients and doctors benefited from new wards and the best facilities.

Elsewhere in the big cities, the homeless could find shelter for the night.

Churches had been repaired, schools had been built, libraries had been stocked with books.

Yes, Scrooge thought, it had been better to use the money in these and similar ways than to store it in some dreary bank.

His one last concession to his old life had been to provide backing for a business in Pewsey which printed cards for people to send to each other at Christmas. Scrooge had the notion that this new-fangled custom (a German idea, some said) was going to become more and more popular. And so far the cards were selling very well.

Christmas Day of that final year arrived, and with it came guests. It was a smaller gathering than in many years, but Scrooge didn't mind that. The Cratchits, for instance, were spending the day with their youngest son, Tim, and his wife; they were planning to come down to Tanway a day or two later.

At lunch, Scrooge had Sasha sit next to him.

Sasha was a mature woman now: powerful, well-built, and capable. The mark of the goddess, as Scrooge had long since learnt to call it, was strong upon her. Scrooge knew, without being told, that she had taken over from Charlotte as leader of the sewing circle, and he had no doubt that she carried out her duties with grace and authority. Her beauty dazzled his eyes.

This year, as if to make the point that life continues,

Sasha's daughter Sarah had produced her first child, and in the morning Scrooge had been allowed to watch her being fed.

The Reverend Mr Green and his wife, with their three children, were also present.

Scrooge ate sparingly at lunch, sat quietly afterwards, and let all the activity revolve around him. He knew that this would be his last such celebration, and he tried to take particular note of who was there and what was happening; but in the afternoon he dozed a good deal.

On Boxing Day morning, at about eleven o'clock, he was conscious of a great pain in his chest, and when he awoke, in bed, they told him that he had collapsed while trying to climb the stairs.

Scrooge himself doubted that he would see the new year in, but he managed it – just. And in those final few days everyone came to see him to say their farewells.

'I saw death in the cards,' said Mrs Molloy. 'Just before Christmas. I thought he was coming for me, of course, but your wife told me I was wrong. I didn't believe her, though – I thought she was being kind.'

Scrooge smiled. 'You should know by now that my wife is never wrong.'

The last to see him was Sasha. She came every day, but on the first of January they both knew that this would be the end.

'There's to be no blubbing, Sasha,' whispered Scrooge.

She smiled. 'No. I promise.'

'Mr Cratchit blubbed.'

'Yes, so I heard. Let the side down something shocking.'

Sasha kissed him and squeezed his hand, and then she left.

*

Shortly afterwards, Charlotte came into the room.

When she was sure that nothing further could be done to make him comfortable, she sat down beside the bed. She took hold of his hand, just as Sasha had done.

'I am going to sit with you a while, Ebenezer. For soon you will fall asleep. And as you sleep, you will dream. It will be a special dream – one which is my last and best gift to you. In this dream you will meet once again a particular friend from the past.'

'Do you think so?' said Scrooge wonderingly.

'Oh yes. I am sure of it.'

Scrooge did sleep, and when he awoke he was astonished to find himself in London. On Queen Street, in Cheapside, to be precise, at the top of one of the lanes which led down to the Thames.

Scrooge gazed around him, and took in the scene. It was late afternoon, almost dark, and midwinter too, for there was snow on the ground. The weather was bitter and cold, and his breath was white on the air. The snow that had been trodden flat underfoot was now polished ice, and it had been scattered with ashes to provide a footing.

There were gas lamps in all the shops, casting a yellow light and long shadows as the people passed by. And what people there were! The streets were full of shoppers and sightseers, wearing long, dark, winter coats and boots, scarves around their necks, hats pulled well down over their ears, and with heavy bags in their hands.

Scrooge stood for a moment, taking it all in.

Then a voice from behind was raised in greeting. A thin, piping voice. A boy's voice.

'What cheer, Mr Scrooge!'

Scrooge turned round to see who was addressing him.

305

'Why, Billy!' Scrooge was astonished. 'I thought you were dead!'

'So I am!' cried Billy. 'And so will you be soon! But first we must go to the frost fair.'

'The frost fair?' said Scrooge. 'Is it still open?'

'Never closes!' cried Billy. He seized Scrooge's hand and began to pull him down the lane. 'Come on! Get a move on!'

Scrooge followed as Billy led the way down the slippery, treacherous path to the river. They passed groups of young and noisy revellers, making their way home, and overtook slower and more cautious citizens who were still picking their way towards the lights and the noise.

The reached the watermen's gangplank which led out on to the ice, and here Scrooge had to pay a toll for both himself and Billy. He groped in his pocket.

'Hurry up, Mr Scrooge!' chided Billy. 'It's only a penny!'

'Only a penny!' Scrooge answered. 'Why, that was a lot of money when I was a lad.'

Despite his words, he reached into his pocket and took out a guinea.

'Here, old fellow,' he said to the elderly man who was guarding the way. 'Here's the toll for two of us, and you may keep the change.'

The toll paid, Scrooge and Billy negotiated the gangplank on to the ice. Meanwhile the gatekeeper looked closely at the coin he had been given. 'May the great goddess bless you, sir!' he called.

And now they could see the full extent of the frost fair. It seemed to stretch as far as the eye could see, upriver and down, from one bank to the other, stalls and barrows and carts and tents all laid out in lines. There were flickering torches and glowing lamps, the whole scene lit by the efforts of man and by the stars in the clear sky above.

Billy led, and Scrooge followed. Past the booths decked with streamers they went, not even pausing at the eel-pie stall or the seller of fried fish. They ignored the vendors of steaming bishop and mulled wine, though Scrooge was tempted because of the cutting cold. They passed the skittle alley and the donkey rides, and did not even pause to watch the dancers who whirled to the fiddler's tune.

On and on they went, moving westwards through the bustling, noisy crowds, proceeding ever upriver. They walked until the stalls began to thin out, and the noise began to fade. And then they saw, all on his own, one man standing out on the ice.

He wore a black, full-length cloak, this man. His head was covered with a cowl, and he stood very still, as if he could stand there all day and never taste the winter.

'Here he is, Mr Scrooge,' said Billy, as they came up to the man. 'This is the feller what hires the skates.'

'Skates?' queried Scrooge. 'Do you mean we're going to skate?'

'We certainly are. Pay him the fee, Mr Scrooge.'

Scrooge hesitated. He did so not so much because of the money, but because of the disturbing stillness of the figure in front of him. But then the man turned, and under the hood Scrooge could recognise the features.

'Why, I know you,' said Scrooge. 'You're Charon, the boatman.'

'Used to be,' said Charon. His face was almost hidden under the hood. 'But you can't use boats in this weather. So I'm hiring skates now.... Come on then, give us your money.'

'How much?'

'Shilling each.'

'A shilling! Outrageous.'

Charon shrugged. 'Please yourself. It's a shilling or walk.'

Billy nudged Scrooge. 'Come on, Mr Scrooge. We've got to go upriver. And you can afford it.'

Billy was right, of course. 'Yes indeed, I can afford it,' said Scrooge. 'I apologise.' He reached into his pocket and took out all his change. 'Here. Take it. Take it all, Charon. It is no use to me now.'

Moving quickly and nimbly, Billy selected two sets of skates from the pile at Charon's feet, and in a trice he had laced them up on the pair of them.

'Now – give 'em a try.'

Scrooge pushed tentatively forward, and he found that he could skate just as easily as he could walk. Easier, in fact. His feet glided over the ice with no effort whatsoever; it was as if he were being transported on the smoothest and quietest set of wheels imaginable. He twirled and circled and came a halt.

'Ready then?' cried Billy. His cheeks were red and his eyes were bright and his face his seemed to shine with good health and vitality. How marvellous, thought Scrooge, to see the boy so happy and well.

'Yes, Billy,' he said. 'I'm ready.'

'Last one there's a cissy!' cried Billy. And he set off at a cracking pace.

Billy led, and he skated right in the centre of the river, flashing effortlessly over the ice like a swallow swooping through the air. Faster and faster he went, but Scrooge had no trouble in keeping up, just a few yards behind.

And as they sped along, Scrooge could feel the bitter wind on his face. The ice beneath his feet crackled and sparkled as the steel of the skates cut into it. Bright flashes of light came from the boots of Billy, in front.

Before long, they got into the rhythm of things. They

adopted a long-distance pace, skating easily and smoothly. Left, right, left, right. Long, even strokes, carving and slashing the ice.

At first, to both sides of them, there were silhouettes of buildings, and bright, twinkling lights. But before long those lights faded and the shores became invisible.

The stars, too, gradually faded and vanished. The night closed in around them.

Scrooge concentrated hard on the blades on Billy's boots. Even in the thickening gloom he could still see a flicker of silver with each movement of the feet.

Left, right, left, right. Ever onwards, into the darkness.

The dark became thicker and deeper. The sound and sight of the skates ahead disappeared. The air lost its cutting bite.

Left, right.... Left, right.

Now all that remained was a dark tunnel, the outline faintly visible, and it was all fading to grey.

Left, right, thought Scrooge.

Fading, fading, fading. And he skated to the beat of his heart.

Left, right.

Left....

Right....

Left....

Left....

Left.

Other books from Kingsfield Publications:

Topp Family Secrets by Anne Moore

A family saga from a practised hand.

Not many members of the family know the story of Grace Topp's two sons – not even the boys themselves....

On 1 January 1940, in conditions of great secrecy, Grace Topp gives birth to two babies: both boys. There is something very unusual about them.

One of these boys, christened Peter, is brought up by the well-to-do Ernest Marshwood and his wife as their own son. The other boy, Eddie, is cared for by Grace's working-class parents.

As they grow up, in the same town, the two boys come to know each other – but they are certainly not friends.

In their teenage years, Eddie's girlfriend is Myrtle, the daughter of a cleaning-lady; Peter's choice is Jennifer, daughter of a solicitor. But each girl finds herself involved with her boyfriend's rival.

Neither Eddie nor Peter, Myrtle nor Jennifer, knows the truth about the birth of Grace's boys. But, in the background, there are some who do.

ISBN: 1 903988 00 4

Passionate Affairs by Anne Moore

A fascinating new novel about two obsessive and reckless love affairs.

In 1960, Daphne Bannister is a respectable married woman; her husband is a housemaster in a leading public school. Daphne understands well enough that having an affair with one of the boys in her husband's care is likely to lead to social and professional disaster; but she is still not deterred.

Robert Duval, another boy in the school, is only fourteen when he becomes equally besotted with a young French girl.

For Daphne and Robert, in their different ways, falling in love is like becoming afflicted by a kind of madness. In each case, love takes the form of an obsession which distorts their judgement and makes them willing to take appalling risks.

In *Passionate Affairs* Anne Moore has written a stunning account of two pairs of lovers who willingly risk scandal and disgrace in order to consummate their overwhelming desire.

ISBN: 1 903988 02 0

Beautiful Lady by Patrick Read

A wartime thriller to rival the novels of Robert Harris and Len Deighton.

In late December 1940, the British people are fighting for survival in the war against Germany. The Earl of Westrow, a Fascist supporter, puts into effect a plot which has been conceived by the Germans. He kidnaps the fourteen-year-old Princess Elizabeth.

Westrow and the shadowy figures behind him believe that by threatening the Princess's life they can force King George VI to sign a peace treaty with Germany.

Jane Padget, daughter of the King's Legal Secretary, and Seymour Jensen, son of a US Embassy official, are witnesses to Princess Elizabeth's capture. With time running out, these two young people embark on their own mission to resolve the crisis.

Joseph P. Kennedy, Wallis Simpson, and Joachim von Ribbentrop all feature in this story of a plot to change the course of the war.

ISBN: 1 903988 01 2

The Suppression of Vice by Patrick Read

A dazzling new crime novel: blackmail, murder, and sin in Victorian London.

London, 1867: Algernon Swinburne is a famous and successful poet. When one of his old school chums is stabbed to death, Algernon is determined to bring the murderer to justice.

Algernon's investigation involves him with both the Society for the Suppression of Vice and a member of the royal family: an unhappy mixture. His investigation also lays bare a record of blackmail, murder and sin in high places.

Patrick Read's new novel finds a master of crime fiction in top form: he shows us the reality which lay behind the respectable veneer of Victorian England.

ISBN: 1 903988 04 7
Available from January 2003